"I could always . . . help you out." I'm proud of my voice—deep and melodious, soothing yet exciting. Or, well, I hope that's how it sounds to her.

She blinks at me, but even as I watch, her pupils get huge. Oh, yeah—at least part of her wants this. Wants me. Wants to feel good. I scoot a little closer and put one hand on her knee.

"What are you doing?" she whispers. Half-scared, half-curious —the anger is suddenly gone. Progress.

"Seeing if you'll let me touch you," I reply evenly, massaging the muscles just above her joint. "I'd really like to show you what you're missing," I continue, unable to resist a smirk. "I bet you'll like it, too."

Visit

Bella Books

at

BellaBooks.com

or call our toll-free number

1-800-729-4992

Wild Nights

(Mostly)
True Stories of
Women Loving Women

Edited by
Therese Szymanski

Bella
BOOKS

2006

Bella Books, Inc.
P.O. Box 10543
Tallahassee, FL 32302

Printed in the United States of America on acid-free paper
First Edition

Editor: Therese Szymanski
Cover designer: Stephanie Solomon-Lopez

ISBN 1-59493-069-4
ISBN 13: 978-1-59493-069-0

For all of the many beautiful lesbians around the world, all living and having their own (mostly) true adventures every day.

Acknowledgments

Once again, I would like to thank all my friends who helped me with this endeavor, most especially Barbara Johnson and Joy Parks, as well as those who came through with after-deadline stories I begged for when I took over this project, most particularly, Victoria A. Brownworth, Karin Kallmaker, Joy Parks and Radclyffe. (As someone said, I ought to acknowledge as many femmes as possible.)

I would also like to thank Bella's incredible staff and its talented proofreaders, Ruth Stanley and Pam Berard, without whom I'd not have the confidence to think I could actually edit.

Contents

True Fiction:
Where Reality Meets Fantasy

When I sat down to edit this book, I started by thinking about the ever-increasing number of true-story anthologies published in the past several years. Why the interest in such books? Why so many of the same type of books and stories? And, finally, what sets "true" anthologies apart from collections of tales on other topics?

The answer I kept coming up with was simple: Voyeurism. People get a thrill out of living vicariously through others. They like to have the adventures without the risk. They also like to see how the other side lives—and with true stories, they feel as if they might have a chance at doing the same things. In fact, such stories might even give them ideas as to what they might want to, or might actually, try themselves. Or with a partner.

I've read a few true-story anthologies myself and always assumed that most stories were not, in fact, true. In editing this book and e-mailing with the various contributors, I've been surprised to discover just how many of these tales are indeed true. Or at least mostly true. (I can only guess that many authors in this collection heated up the sex just a touch—including yours truly.)

What I realized, however, in reading through the hundreds of stories submitted to this book was that a great many of the very finest and most delightful tales of heated and exciting lesbian sex were told in a particular voice (first-person POV, for those who are curious). I reckon this sort of telling excites the reader more than a detached third-person narrative, and is also much more intimate and believable. I found such tales to be especially compelling, interesting, and heated—so I decided to include only first-person stories in this book.

After all, if you were telling a true story, wouldn't you use the "I" word and say it in your own voice about yourself?

I did, however, decide to break one of my own primary rules and include two stories by the same author in this book so that I have the final word (finally) in one of my anthologies: The final story is told in a decidedly... different... voice than any other in this book. I've included this tale because it gets right to the heart of the voyeuristic matter while, perhaps, poking a teasing finger at it.

But don't take any of this the wrong way: This book is meant to turn you on. That is its single purpose. That is what it's meant for—its sole reason for being.

I hope it serves its purpose well and that you enjoy it. And I'll be even happier if it drives you to appreciate some aspects of life a little more. This is a book that shows how reality can live up to your wildest expectations—even if it's just through your imagination, with perhaps a little help from some others . . .

Reese Szymanski

Backstage
Karin Kallmaker

She's looking at me again. I can feel it.

She should be using her eyes for her job. It irritates me that I can feel her gaze running across my bare shoulders the same way it did when I met with her before the evening began. It's distracting and I don't need some damned butch boy looking at me like this.

I tuck my cell phone back into my miniscule evening bag as I give my assistant the bad news. Our keynote speaker is going to be forty-five minutes late. She hurries off to tell the stage manager while I make my way toward my boss. Four months of careful planning of the evening's agenda have been undone by airport fog. He'll have to deal with it.

All the while I know she's looking at me. What's her game, anyway? I pause for a moment to shower more thanks on one of our VIPs. I'm caught between the magic of being a lowly meeting planner who gets to talk to a two-time Oscar winner and the sickening dread in my stomach that there is still enough time left in the evening for things to go wrong. I don't need a security guard's smoky gaze burning the back of my neck.

I steal another look at her.

I only look because I want to let her know that I don't appreciate the cheap come on. But on the way to her face I linger on the broad shoulders so effectively framed by her suit jacket. I study them too long. When my gaze meets hers she is mocking me, knowing I was looking.

Then that hot look drops to my gown, making me acutely aware of the thin silk and tight bodice. It pales next to those of the invited guests. Our guests include women of vast personal wealth, actresses, lobbyists, entertainers, prime-time journalists and sports stars. My gown might be Vera Wang, but it's the only one here that was bought off the rack.

The tennis bracelet I dropped a month's salary on wouldn't pay for a half an earring on most of these women. It doesn't take a fashion consultant to discern that I must be hired help. She's looking at me like I'm an hors d'oeuvre. I can't let her get to me. She doesn't know anything about me and she shouldn't be looking at me as if she does.

But my eyes are drinking in the way she moves.

My conversation with my boss is short, the number of tasks I must see to grows. Raising money is an art form and my job is preparing the canvas where the artists persuade the donors to get out their checkbooks. I need to keep an eye on the champagne and buffet tables, watch the circulating waiters, let the orchestra know they're playing for another thirty minutes, tell the hotel manager to get his people set on removing abandoned glasses and plates, find the other two speakers who will now go ahead of the keynoter, notify the Development Director about the change in plans, and all in the next twelve seconds. I remind myself to smile and always appear to be In Control.

I do not need . . . my nerves are at their limit. I don't want her gaze tracing lines across my body. I'm abruptly too aware of how tight and low the strapless bodice of my gown is.

She started it.

It was a brief conversation, just a quick review of the contract for the security crew and a confirmation of the placements I'd mapped out with the head of the firm. I had a million details to see to in less than thirty minutes, and I hadn't really looked at the person who would be the main floor security supervisor for the night. I gave my spiel and started to leave when she murmured in a voice of velvet, "I'll keep you safe and sound, don't worry."

That's when I realized the slender short-haired figure belonged to a woman. Startled, I'd looked right into her eyes just as her fingertip brushed the crook of my elbow, leaving me with the breathless sensation of being naked. I don't have time for her. Not now, I had thought, as I stalked off to my next task.

She says something into the radio strapped to her wrist, then heads in my direction. Damn her. I'm just overkeyed. I've worked on this night for the last six months, to the exclusion of everything. Everything.

God, she walks toward me like she owns me. The closer she gets the more she doesn't look at me. Her gaze scans the crowd. She wouldn't be part of the detail the security firm supplied if she wasn't good at her job. No hint of mockery remains. She's humorless and remote as she reminds me the detail has hit the two-hour mark and they'll begin short break rotations. People who have to pee don't focus very well.

I nod. I can be distant, too. Her eyes are almost black. I feel the room still for a moment as she shifts her shoulders. Her arms curve slightly and I can't breathe. It makes no sense. It's—not going to happen. It can't. Not tonight. I don't need this, her. I open my mouth to ask her to stop and realize I can't tell her what she's doing to me. The orchestra has segued to the theme from "Laura" and though she hasn't moved, her eyes say she wants to dance with me. Her eyes say she wants more than dancing. I—I have work to tend to. Damn her. I want to say, "Later, go away, I don't know."

I'd have to kiss her to know for sure.

I hurry away and I can tell she is watching me walk. What am I thinking? It's just nerves, all the planning. An agenda shake-up is a pain, but a minor problem. I'll get to keep my job if that's the only blip of the evening. I forget about her, almost, but I feel her watching me. I catch her at it a couple of times. Those eyes.

The keynote speaker shows up and speeches are over without a hitch. The orchestra leaves, the rock band turns up the volume, the guests seem eager to stay. The ballroom sparkles with jewels and laughter. My boss looks calm but pleased. Checkbooks have opened.

Midnight. The party starts to wind down and I can't stop thinking about how her arms might feel around me.

I'm half-drunk. I haven't eaten since lunch and two glasses of champagne—one with my boss, one with my own staff—have left me giddy. By one a.m., the big names have left and those who remain are dancing to the band to the exclusion of all other activity. The honorary event committee chairwoman is complimenting my work as I stand at the edge of the dance floor.

Someone stops near me, at a discreet distance. I am suffused with heat.

The chairwoman takes her leave and I turn away. The high of the evening is waning, and part of me doesn't want it to end. I'm already thinking about the next fundraiser, the guest list, who we might be able to bag for it.

Her voice is like velvet. "My shift is over."

"Lucky you." She doesn't look at all tired from hours of standing on alert. She could run a marathon, I'll bet. Meanwhile, I know my shoulders are drooping and my expression weary.

"You don't even get to dance?"

I shake my head. "I could, I suppose." Some of my staff have been on the floor for thirty minutes. I feel funny about joining them, of letting go after being In Control for so long.

I finally realize she is holding out her hand. She isn't asking.

I don't know how to dance to rock and roll in a floor-length Vera Wang gown. If I take her hand, dance with her, it might lead to . . . I have a suite upstairs, compliments of the hotel, all to myself . . . I can't do this in front of my boss, in front of my staff.

God, that voice. "Have mercy on me."

Her hands are on my hips as she draws me onto the dance floor. I put my hands on top of hers, thinking I'm going to remove them, I'm going to escape. Her gaze burns its way down my body and my dress feels two sizes too small. My irritation from earlier in the evening comes back. I'm not an appetizer to be devoured in public. There's no mercy in me.

I roll my shoulders forward to give her a good long look down my dress. When her gaze finally climbs back up to my face she meets my defiant eyes.

I haven't disconcerted her in the least, that much is plain.

"That dress was made to torment me." Her hands are moving my hips. I don't know the song. I let her lead me, feeling dizzy, my hands still on top of hers.

She spins me in place and when I'm facing her again my crotch is against hers and her hands have moved from my hips to the small of my back.

She wants to kiss me. If she kisses me, I'll know for sure.

Her leg is between mine and I catch myself before I grind down on her thigh. I won't give in to the usual butch move. We sway for a few minutes. I can feel her breath on my shoulder. Her hands pull my hips into her and I realize I am exhausted and very, very wet.

She can't kiss me here. I don't want my colleagues, my boss—I don't want anyone to see what this beautiful butch is doing to my composure. I can't take her up to my room. I haven't even kissed her.

Her fingertips run up my back as if she is learning how the dress will come off of me. I can't remember my room number. I'd have to get out the card the hotel gave me. Everyone would see. I need to kiss her now. I don't know what to do.

Her voice can burn me. "Meet me backstage."

I watch her go, my head feeling so hot I wonder if I'm sick. She walks like she has an assignment, disappearing past the band and into the darkness behind the staging area.

I get two gin and tonics from the bar, tucking one into the folds of my skirt while I sip from the other. Is everyone watching me follow in her wake? Another sip, then I am in the semi-darkness, working my way past the band's empty amp cases and the strewn leftover decorations. The dark figure turns to me as I join her.

"I brought us drinks." My voice sounds unnaturally calm. I can hardly hear myself over the pounding of blood in my ears.

She reaches for the glass I offer, but doesn't drink. She takes the other glass, too, and sets both on the floor. She unstraps the radio from her wrist and pulls off the earpiece. Off duty. I'm not off duty. Anyone could be looking for me. The party is only a few feet away, at the edge of the darkness that hides us.

In a rush that takes my breath away, she pushes me onto the case behind me. My toes are barely on the floor. Her hands are gripping my waist as she leans into me.

She's going to kiss me. She's going to have me.

The sounds of the party are all around me. Someone laughs. Footsteps fade as they cross the stage.

I wait for her to take the kiss, her lips inches from mine. But she doesn't. I have to ask.

I'm moaning and I can't stop.

"What do you want?"

"Kiss me." I need her lips against my mouth.

Her hands sweep over my shoulders to twine around my neck. Her kiss is ferocious, possessive. Her thigh is between my legs as her tongue makes my mouth hers. I can't breathe, I don't need to breathe. I cup the back of her neck and return her kiss. It's yes. It has to be yes with a kiss like this.

"If you wait in my room I could join you in an hour," I murmur when she releases my mouth. I don't know how much time has passed, but the kisses were long as she learned my responses.

I am pleased she is slightly out of breath. "That seems like a good idea."

I should go back to the party now but my hands are pulling up my skirt. Her lips come to mine in a fever, her thigh churning against the soaked crotch of my panty hose. My wet is going to smear all over her pants. Everyone will know she had me.

I can't wait for another hour.

Nearby, two voices shout over the music about directions to an after-hours club. My skirt is around my waist and her fingers have found the zipper in the back of the dress. She pulls it down part way and the bodice loosens enough for her to free my breasts.

Her teeth find my hardening nipples as her hand plunges between my legs, pressing the fabric of my panty hose hard against my clit. I have to open my legs wider for her. Not here, I'm thinking, this is dangerous, and I squirm to push down my panty hose, to get rid of the barrier between her fingers and my hungry, eager cunt.

She puts her hands on my knees, pushing them even farther apart. I feel like a river.

"Take what you want," I tell her, feeling disbelief deep down in my mind at the degree of my surrender.

She's on her knees in front of me. I have my hands in her hair. I'm on tiptoe, trying to hold still, but at the touch of her tongue between my legs I move against her mouth, giving myself to her. It feels so good to have her know that I am soaked for her. I hold my scream in my throat, shivering with the effort.

The music almost drowns out her words. Damn her, she knows what I am, what I can be when I let go.

"We both know what you have to have now."

My nails are in her scalp as I feel one finger slide into me only to slowly withdraw and be replaced by another. She tells me how wet I am. Her tongue goes back to flicking over my clit, a steady pulse that leaves my shoulders shaking.

One finger becomes two. I don't know where this will stop. The band is saying goodnight. I want to scream. I want her to fuck me. I hold my dress up with one hand while the other reaches between my legs to cup her cheek while she feasts on me.

Shuddering, I realize two fingers have become three, and as quickly become four.

Yes.

I want to scream it. I want this, right now, this beautiful butch playing me this way, consuming me.

When her fist goes into me it lifts me off my feet for a moment. She's hard and deep and her tongue is sending shivers up my body to my nipples. I can't spread my legs any wider. My hands leave their grip on her to grapple for leverage behind me so I can fuck her back.

I am taking it . . .

Taking it . . .

Taking it . . .

Taking it . . .

Taking her fist . . .

Fucking back.

The music's ending. The party's over. Someone will turn on the houselights so the cleanup crew can start. I don't want it to end. Fuck, I want her to fuck me like this forever, I don't care who sees us. I am completely filled as she rides me hard. I'm not going to come yet, I don't want to.

Her free hand finds my bare, heaving breasts and she takes hold of one nipple, tugging downward, pinching, making me ache, fuck. I have to come now. I can't hold it back. I'm going to make a mess of her jacket sleeve, her face.

"Give it up to me."

Every muscle in my body has tensed. My legs convulse around her shoulders. She releases my nipple to grip my waist and I climax against her mouth, her fist hard in my most receptive depths.

Please, let that be only the beginning.

She rezips me and pulls down my dress, then holds me tight in her arms. After a minute or two I hear her say something to one of the musicians.

The houselights come on.

It is a dizzying effort to raise my head from her shoulder, which is wet from my cunt. Her face is covered with my scent.

I tell her my room number and slip the key into her pocket. Her smirk is back, but fades as my eyes tell her she hasn't satisfied me yet.

She started it.

Upstairs I'm going to finish it.

Popcorn, Sodas and Sex
Radclyffe

I scanned the skimpy half-page entertainment section, looking for something to occupy my time until I could outlast the stifling heat and maybe fall asleep—at least long enough to catch a few hours rest before I had to get up and look interested in the prospect of buying 500 acres of sand and scrub pine out in the middle of nowhere. Being the point "man" for a land development company wasn't all it was cracked up to be. I spent as much time in backwater counties talking to eager farmers as I did wheeling and dealing with real estate entrepreneurs in slick offices in LA or Fort Lauderdale. This was definitely one of those "up-country" excursions.

I scanned the movie listings in the nearest city, which was a 40-minute drive away on twisting roads with which I wasn't particularly familiar. I didn't really want to see the last episode in the Star Wars saga all that badly, especially considering it had been released on DVD a year earlier.

Then I saw something I hadn't seen in years. An honest to God drive-in theater listing. I hadn't been to one since I was in college and all I could remember was the cramped front seat of my car, stale popcorn, flat soda and hot sweaty sex. I smiled. Not bad for a few bucks and a couple of gallons of gas. I looked at the playbill.

Seed of Chucky, Starsky and Hutch, The In-Laws . . . things weren't looking so good. And then, a glimmer of hope. Bound. So what if I'd seen it more than a few times and it was a solid decade old. Some women you never tire of looking at. Jennifer Tilly as sexy Violet was one of them. I grabbed my keys and my county road map and headed out the door. The sun slanted into my eyes, a hazy yellow filtered through the dust kicked up in the unpaved parking lot by the most recent arrival. A dirty black Mercedes coupe was just pulling in next to my rental car. It wasn't the typical vehicle for this part of the country. I squinted as the driver stepped out and blinked hard when I saw Jennifer Tilly. Shining shoulder-length black hair, lustrous red lips, lush body and a lazy smile that made my clit quiver as if she'd flicked it with a ruby red nail.

"Hello," Jennifer said.

I stared, looking foolish, I'm sure.

"It's just too hot out on the Interstate, even with the air-conditioning on in the car."

She walked around and opened her trunk and started wrestling with an oversized suitcase. I finally got my brain to connect with the rest of my body and leapt to her side.

"Here, let me get that for you."

"Thanks, I appreciate it."

She smiled at me, her eyes doing a slow crawl down my body and back up to my face. Since I hadn't planned on running into a movie star, I was wearing shapeless navy blue cotton shorts with no belt, a sleeveless gray T-shirt—clean but faded to the point that the lettering was indecipherable—and boat shoes without socks. Oh so very much not my suave best. She, on the other hand, somehow managed to look wrinkle-free in a sleeveless white linen blouse and charcoal slacks.

When I'd yanked the monster out of the car and onto the

ground, trying to look as if lifting the thing hadn't nearly given me a hernia, she held out her hand. "I'm Sheila. Sheila Tyler."

By this time of course, I'd figured out that she wasn't really Jennifer Tilly. She was better. I shook her hand and told her my name.

"I don't suppose you have any idea what there is to do around here?" Sheila asked, turning in a circle and surveying the landscape. "It's beautiful country, but I hadn't really planned on stopping tonight. I don't even have a book with me." She shook her head as if surprised. "I had this sudden urge to stop driving and I just pulled off the highway and here I am." She blushed. "I'm not usually impulsive."

"Well, the sign says the rooms have cable but mine doesn't. There's no pool, so a swim is out. The air conditioning is, well . . ." I shrugged and hefted her suitcase, aware that the weight made the muscles in my arms and shoulders tighten. I caught her glance lingering on my chest and knew that the same jolt that had stiffened my clit had made my nipples tighten into small hard knots. She looked into my eyes.

"So how were you planning to spend the evening?"

"I was just about to go to the drive-in movies."

She threw her head back and laughed, a dark-chocolate smooth and rich laugh. "You're kidding."

I laughed too. "Nope."

"You'll roast."

"I'll open the windows." We headed toward the motel office. "Besides, the sun's almost down, and it will cool off a little bit after dark." Somehow I managed to open the door for her and not knock her over with her suitcase. "You're welcome to join me."

She stopped just inside the door and studied me with a tiny smile. "I'd have to change."

"I can wait."

"What are we seeing?"

"Seed of Chucky." Her eyes widened and I grinned. "How about Bound? Ever seen it?"

"As a matter of fact, no," she said contemplatively. "But I'd like to."

I nodded toward the reception desk where a thin, balding man appeared to be dozing behind the counter. "I'll get some sodas from the machine outside while you get settled. Coke okay?"

"Perfect."

I leaned against the fender of my rental car, wishing it was a '57 Bel Air convertible, and drained one can of soda while I waited for Sheila to change. She came out wearing khaki shorts and a tank top and looking as fresh as if she'd never been kissed. Maybe she hadn't. Not by someone like me.

"Is everything all right?" she asked, regarding me curiously.

I jumped and spun around the car to open her door. "Everything is just fine."

She slid in and didn't ask me anything else, and I was glad. How could I tell her that the hot summer night and the fresh, simple way she looked and the buzz of anticipation in my belly made me feel as if I was sixteen again and about to go on the date I'd always wanted, but never had.

While I fiddled with the radio, she navigated, searching out the small blue road signs that marked the county roads. We missed a few turns and had to backtrack a time or two, but it really didn't matter if we were late or not. The journey was proving to be every bit as enjoyable as I hoped the destination to be. We didn't talk about our jobs or where we lived or where we were going. We talked about the last books we'd read and the music we liked and laughed when I had to stop for a flock of chickens in the middle of the road that appeared wholly unconcerned by our presence. Sheila leaned out the window and made shooing motions while I inched the car forward, praying that I wouldn't feel a bump at any moment.

Finally we saw the giant movie screen looking obscenely out of place amongst the rolling hills and valleys, and I turned onto the macadam road that sprouted clumps of scraggly grass through cracks in its uneven surface. I hitched up one hip to pull my wallet from my back pocket but Sheila stopped me with her hand on my arm.

"You buy the popcorn, I'll get the tickets."

Her fingers were cool and firm. She leaned across me to extend a $20 bill out the window and her breasts pressed against my bare upper arm. I jammed my foot down hard on the brake to keep my hips from jumping, but it didn't do anything to stop the wetness I felt pooling between my thighs. I stared straight ahead and hoped to God she didn't recognize the sex seeping from my pores.

When she settled back into the passenger seat, I inched the car forward over the rough ground. A half dozen cars were scattered over a lot the size of a fairground.

"Where to?" I asked in a strangely gravelly voice. I tried to swallow around the desire in my throat and started to cough.

"Here," Sheila said, offering the can of soda she had been sipping from on the drive. "Let's park in the back. The angle is always better that way."

I nodded and drank, aware that as my lips touched the can they were exactly where hers had been only moments before. I wondered if that counted as some sort of phantom kiss. I jockeyed us into a space that actually had a speaker attached. At least half of the places within sight had only wires dangling from bent poles.

"This place is in pretty rough shape," I commented.

"It's good we came when we did then," Sheila said pensively. She reached down beside her seat and worked the controls for a few seconds before turning to me. "Can you pull the car forward a little bit so that we can see the screen from the back seat? I can never get comfortable with my legs under the dashboard." Then, without waiting for me to answer, she opened the door, hopped out, and just as swiftly got back in the rear. She rolled down the windows on both sides, then leaned over my seat, one hand on my shoulder, her breath warm in my ear. "Go ahead. I'll tell you when it's just right."

I turned the key in the ignition so hard I was surprised it didn't snap off. With one quick glance at her out of the corner of my eye, I drove us forward until she said, "There. Stop."

"Is that good then?" I asked inanely. All I could think about was her hand on my shoulder. Her fingertips rested just beyond the edge of my T-shirt collar, against my neck. I wanted to rip my shirt off and scream, "Oh please touch me." My nipples ached from the constant contraction, and I knew that only her fingers rolling and tugging them could soothe the hurt.

She brushed her hand lower over my chest, then drew away. "After you go get us some popcorn and come back here with me, everything will be perfect."

I was out of the car so fast it must have looked like the seat was on fire. As I hurried off toward the low, square building that housed the concession stand and the restrooms, I heard her laughing. On the enormous screen behind me, the credits started to roll.

Ten minutes later I was back, my arms filled with popcorn and fresh sodas. The cardboard containers of Coke were sweating and the insides of my arms were wet from condensation. I stopped next to the car and leaned down to look in the open window. Somehow she'd managed to push the front seats forward and she was stretched out with her legs propped on the console between them, her head tipped back. She turned lazily when she saw me and smiled.

"Oh good. I missed you."

My knees got wobbly but I managed to stay standing. She held out her arms and I passed the drinks and popcorn in to her. Then I followed. The movie was already in progress, but I wasn't watching the screen. I angled in the seat so I could see her profile while I pretended to watch Jennifer Tilly. I couldn't remember now why I'd thought Jennifer was so hot. My whole body was wet and it had nothing to do with the heat.

I couldn't get comfortable. My stomach hurt from tamping down the arousal that sluiced through my cunt like a raging river cutting canyons in age-old rock. I shifted, trying to find a place where my muscles didn't cramp and my clit didn't ache.

"Stretch your legs out next to mine," Sheila said, leaning forward to set her drink and popcorn in the front seat. When I eased my legs onto the console next to hers, she settled back, one thigh half on top of mine, and put her hand in the bag of popcorn I held in my lap. "Do you think she's sexy?"

"Who?"

Laughing, Sheila gave me a look. "Are you watching this?"

"Seen it." My insides tightened into a hard knot. What the hell. "You're much sexier."

Her breath caught and she took my soda from where I held it balanced on my knee. She sipped through my straw. "Are you flirting?"

"Do you want me to be?"

"Have you ever made love at the drive-in?"

I groaned and my thighs jumped with a life of their own. She must have felt it. "Not exactly."

"Meaning?"

Her voice had gotten low and soft.

"Meaning I rolled around a little in the back seat when I was a teenager, but I'd hardly call it making love."

"Mmm," she said musingly, dipping into my popcorn again. "There's something to be said for taking your time with the good parts."

"Sheila," I started to say, not sure what I was going to say next. I'm so hot I could burst into flames; I'm aching to touch you; Do you even want me to touch you . . . but the words died in my throat when she dropped a handful of popcorn in my lap.

"Oh, sorry," she murmured, delicately reaching between my legs to collect the fluffy white blobs. The backs of her fingers brushed my crotch.

My hips jolted so hard, my body levitated and my breath whooshed out like I'd been punched.

"Sorry."

She didn't sound sorry. More amused. And when I looked

down, her hand was still there, her fingertips resting gently on the seam of my shorts right over my clit. She pushed in, slow and steady, and I crushed the paper bag of popcorn in my fist. A mushroom cloud of kernels erupted all over us both.

"Uh," I muttered.

"Don't worry. I was done." Sheila leaned over me, her hand squeezing down on my crotch, and kissed me lightly on the mouth. "With that."

Then she took the soda from my other hand, poured the contents out the window, and dropped the container on the floor. While I looked on in a haze of confused lust, she calmly braced her arm on the seat next to my head and levered herself over me until she straddled my waist, her knees on either side of my hips. My body finally caught up, and I tugged her blouse from her shorts as gently as I could.

She made a little humming noise when I slid my palms up to her breasts. Her bra was tissue-paper thin, her nipples small and hard. Before I could, she reached one hand down the front of her blouse and unhooked the clasp between the cups. Her full firm breast came spilling out and I squeezed, not so gently now.

"Oh yes," she sighed, moving her hands from the seat to grasp fistfuls of my hair. "Play with them. Just like that."

While she kissed me thoroughly, her tongue starting at my lips and exploring every dip and hollow deeper inside, I circled her nipples with my fingers, closed down around them, and thumbed the tips. She drew back and caught her lip in her teeth, watching my hands move under her blouse while she rocked in my lap.

"Take your blouse off," I whispered hoarsely. There was no one nearby, and the movie flickering on the edges of my vision afforded me enough light to see her. And I wanted to see all of her. I kept up the nipple play while she bared her upper body. The instant her breasts appeared I covered one nipple with my mouth. I licked and strummed it with my tongue and she crooned with pleasure. I was so lost in the sound and the sweet taste of her I didn't realize she'd put her hand down the front of my shorts until I felt a vise-like grip my clit. I groaned with the sudden stab of pleasure and almost came. "Easy."

"You know," Sheila panted unevenly, "I always wanted to do this."

"What?" I asked, kissing my way back and forth from one nipple to the other.

"Make love in a car at the drive-in."

"Why didn't y . . ." I choked when she twisted and tugged on my clit and my vision went red. "You're going to get me off doing that."

"Keep pulling my nipples," Sheila ordered, jerking me off more gently. "I want to come with you sucking them." She slid one finger down between my lips and dragged hot, slick come back up over the head of my clit. "Lick me while I make you come. I want to feel you come in my hand."

I sucked and bit and squeezed and she rubbed and pinched and stroked.

"Oh yes I'm coming soon," she whispered, her mouth against my ear. "You're making my clit tingle so . . . nice. Oh. Are you . . . coming? Come soon. Come . . . oh."

She writhed on my lap, rubbing herself against her own arm where it disappeared down my pants. I didn't care about coming— I just wanted to watch the pleasure shimmer across her face. Her breasts got hot and heavy in my hands. She shook and shuddered and moaned and while she came I unzipped her shorts.

"Oh nice," she finally sighed, sagging against me.

"Yeah," I said and skimmed my fingers over her hard clit. She twitched and gasped. "You're not done."

She laughed. "Not hardly." She sucked on the skin just above my collarbone. "You didn't come."

"I got distracted." She still had her hand in my pants and slid half off me so that her head was on my shoulder and her body curled along mine. Her fingers skittered over the stiff length of me and I groaned. Now I felt how close she'd gotten me with all the clit play.

"Who's not done, huh?" she teased.

"Ten seconds," I said through gritted teeth. I was lying. It took three seconds and two long strokes down my cleft and back up again to send me shooting off like a cannon. I must have done something to her clit while I was bucking and shooting because I heard her cry out in surprise and then she was pushing my fingers inside her and coming all over them.

"What a great movie," she murmured some time later.

"Uh-huh." My hand was still inside her and my arm was cramped from the angle but I didn't care if it fell off from lack of blood flow. Not as long as I could feel her pulsing and quivering all around me the way she was still doing.

"You know when I first saw you outside the motel," Sheila said lazily, "I thought you looked just like Gina Gershon."

"I thought you'd never seen this movie before," I said with a laugh.

"Mmm, well, not at the drive-in." She kissed me and ran her finger lightly back and forth over my clit, making me shiver. "And you may not have noticed, but Gina's got nothing on you."

I pressed my palm down on my shorts over her hand. "You'll get me wired up again."

"Well, I like reruns." She tightened inside around my fingers. "And there's still plenty of popcorn."

A Night at the Opera

for LBK: RIP

Victoria A. Brownworth

The new millennium may have more bling and more elegance, but the Eighties were flashier and sexier. Ripped fishnets were *de rigeur* and leather, leatherette and pleather were simply everywhere. Hair was big, bigger, biggest and so were heels. Lips were the bruised, lush red-purple of aroused pussy and eyes were outlined in liner so thick and black it looked like it was applied with a Sharpie.

I was an s/m queen in the Eighties, a dominatrix femme top with a retinue of suitors and another of toys. My hair was high, my stilettos higher. My lips were full and painted very dark to emphasize the whiteness of my skin. My stockings were held up by a lacy black garter belt, my breasts pushed up by black lace bras. Sometimes I wore panties and sometimes I didn't, but if I did they were the sort that could be torn off easily. Torn, not slipped off

girl. Soon our games moved outside the bedroom. We liked to pass. Her voice was deep and taxi drivers would ask her what she thought about this or that sports team while I sat with my hand in her lap. Just a cute couple out on the town. Pretty soon she was The Boy and I was the highest high femme in town.

Then we went took our show to the opera.

It may seem discordant with Eighties punk rock and in-your-face politico-sex, but opera was the perfect s/m backdrop for us. It's all high drama—love at first sight, love and sex, sex and love, dying for love—all over the top, just like we were. L had never heard opera before she met me and then she couldn't get enough. The first time I played "Un Bel Di" from Puccini's *Madame Butterfly* for her, she became as hot for opera as she was for me. That afternoon I saw the frisson pass through her as Maria Callas sang of what would happen when her lover returned. But it was *La Boheme* that became L's favorite. L was an artist and I a writer—just like Mimi and Rudolfo.

My long-time mentor, M, watched our affair. A bit of a sexual outlaw himself, like most straight men he liked the image of two women together. I'm not sure what he had in mind when he gave me tickets to the Met for my birthday, but I knew it would be a night to remember.

L was a bartender at a chi-chi restaurant and I was a newspaper reporter. We didn't have a lot of money, but we pooled our cash for the trip. I borrowed a friend's studio apartment in Chelsea for a couple of days and we hopped the train to New York.

But no trip like this—our first time at the Met—would be complete without a little sexual tension, so I worked it: I borrowed an evening gown and a fur coat from another friend and L rented a tux.

Then we headed to New York.

Our night at the opera was going to be another chapter in our ongoing sexual adventure, a game to end all games. How would we top this? It was *the Met*. We'd played dress-up all over our own town, but we knew the territory. We'd never been to the Met.

Would we pass or be called out—and tossed out—exposed as sexual outlaws? The risk made it all the sexier.

We got to New York, changed clothes and took a cab to the Met. There I was, my blonde hair softly elegant instead of high, my gown a decollete silk, the requisite pearls at my neck and ear-lobes and the ubiquitous garter-belt hidden transgressively underneath it all, with the fur over everything, grazing my bare white shoulders. L was supremely handsome in her tux, cummerbund and tie, her hair slicked back like the day I first saw her at the LFW. Before we left my friend's apartment I pressed my hand against the zipper of her trousers, feeling her dick hard and ready for later, after the opera. We kissed quickly and went off to *La Boheme*, eager to be on time.

It's hard to explain the rush of two poor kids in their twenties who loved opera going to the Met on a Friday night in full (if borrowed) evening dress, one of them passing for a boy, the other passing for a rich girl.

It was romantic and sexy and risky all at once. We were turned on all evening.

We *were* the opera: Mimi and Rudolfo at the Met. We passed alright; the only rough moment came when L brazenly headed for the men's room at intermission. She entered and exited and I breathed a sigh of relief. We were who we appeared to be. I leaned forward against the balustrade and pulled her to me by the lapels and kissed her in the middle of the second tier of the Met. People glanced, smiled, and looked away. We were two lovers at an opera about two lovers.

The opera was stunning and so were we. After it ended we headed out to a restaurant—an attractive young couple in New York for a late dinner after the show. We were so into the game, we were so who we had made ourselves up to be, that we were holding hands across the table in our high-toned, straighter-than-straight restaurant. I had slipped my foot out of my stiletto and slid it into her lap, massaging her stiff dick and watching her want me. The sexual tension was mounting between us. Our waiter smiled—either because he was queer and was onto us or because we were what we appeared to be, just another straight couple in love out on the town.

Back at the flat L undressed me slowly, unzipping my dress and slipping it from my shoulders so it fell in a soft pool of silk at my feet, kissing and biting my shoulders as she did. L's jacket was tossed onto a chair, the tie loosened, the studs of her shirt removed one by one. I unbuckled her belt and unzipped her trousers, slipping my hand inside and rubbing it against the stiff cock tight in her briefs.

My panties were torn off that night after the evening clothes were discarded and the sex was hot and hard in the cold apartment as we lay on the fur coat draped over my friend's pull-out sofa.

The next day dawned grey and chill and we lay nestled in the fur coat and each other's arms. We dressed for a new game and headed out to the Village, ready for a new adventure on the anonymous streets of New York.

The game evolved as we walked arm-in-arm through the Village. I was a wealthy woman from the Upper East Side; L was my boy toy. We headed into a sex shop—something with pussycat in the name—and looked at a range of products we didn't yet have in our arsenal. We played with the clerk, we played with each other, we drew the clerk into our game. We bought a few items and then we headed back onto the street, heated up from the exchange of sexual banter, improvisation and cash for sex toys. L pushed me up against a wall in a small alley and kissed me hard, her fingers pinching my nipples through my blouse, her hand slipping up underneath my skirt, underneath my panties. We had swift, covert sex right there—her fingers deep in my cunt, pumping me against the wall, my hand pressed hard between her legs as she moved against me, kissing me ever more insistently. It was midday in Manhattan, the big fur pulled around us and no one seeming to notice a woman and her blond boy toy kissing in a picturesque alleyway off the strand.

The afternoon faded and we wandered through the streets arm-in-arm, back to the apartment. We packed and headed for the train to Philadelphia and home, our night at the opera over, but its melody lingering on.

.

Postscript: L and I spent several years together, before we parted as dramatically as any grand opera leads. But despite our problems, bed death never overtook us in our years together; we were always operatic lovers, our bedroom larger than life.

In the years after we parted, our adventure at the Met remained a story we would both tell, a bel canto moment of seduction, excitement and risk. Two years ago L died, far too young, of cancer. I told the story at her memorial service. Her passing as a boy, and of course, the romance—not the sex. The tale exemplified who she was—big and bold, a risk-taker, an opera-lover—and everybody smiled.

Tuesday Night
Joy Parks

"If I write about this, can I tell them the truth?"
"Sure," she said. "But which one?"

What I remember. We all looked pretty much the same back then. Angry. And tired. If you came here to meet a woman, tough luck. Might as well go home now. Alone. All talk, no action. The personal is political. Being a lesbian isn't about sex. Sometimes it made my head hurt. Maybe it was just squinting into the light, the artificial heat beating a tattoo against my brain, headache building in cheek muscles held too firm, don't smile, not now, probably not ever again, this is serious business, this changing the world. It is 1984 and stranger than Orwell could have imaged, the movement is winding down, getting strained. We must, no, we will, destroy the patriarchy, gut it like a fish, chop off its head. And we relish the work. At least in front of each other, at meetings like this, we're all sisters here, the holy appointed turtleneck-and-flannel-shirted chorus of she who will not be silenced.

I am younger than most of the women here, the youngest I assume, in fact most of them are probably old enough to be my mother, but I don't think about that, too large a leap to make. My mother would never be here, she'd hate the way we're dressed and that no one bothered to fix her hair or, for god's sake, put on a little lipstick. Just 'cause you're a lesbian doesn't mean you have to look like hell. I can see her standing under the greasy yellow light; hand on her chic pant-suited hip, hair "done" and freshly dyed, giving makeup tips to the attendants of the Tuesday night lesbian feminists separatist discussion group. She doesn't care that her first-born daughter is a dyke, she just wishes I'd dress better, lose the fatigues, the dumpy sweatshirts and about ten pounds. Jesus, you were brought up better than that. Weren't you?

Actually, *yes.*

It's the first time she's been here. But she's not new. There's nothing new about how she walks, how she leans forward with her shoulders, nothing fresh practiced newly out about how she takes up space, the way she sits with her legs open wide, the way she moves her arms when she talks. She knows all the tricks, could teach the rest of us a thing or two about how to make our presence known, how dare you assume I'm straight, no one would with her. Not an issue. That's just it. That's what this is all about.

We're the ones making an issue out of it.

Most meetings I have something to say. Usually, I join in on the litany of slights against our existence; all of it exaggerated so I can feel I belong. Truth is, I don't really notice if the bag boy at the grocery store looks at my breasts. I usually don't even notice if there is a bag boy; I don't pay that much attention to men. I work part-time for a gay newspaper, and read manuscripts freelance at home for a publishing company, which is pretty much staffed by women, so I don't have a boss who calls me "honey" or "babe" or tries to feel me up when I work late. I got the university to let me do an independent study on lesbian writing. So there goes that. In fact, I feel pretty lucky, like things are actually going my way. But I don't let on. You can either be oppressed, which seems to be what everyone else here is, or privileged, which gets you put in your place. Apparently I can't avoid it, with my white skin and fresh-minted university degree. Even though there are plenty of wimmin here with graduate degrees. Doesn't matter that my grandmother was Cherokee or that there were times I had to work three wait-ressing jobs at once and eat plain spaghetti with melted margarine and salt for days just to pay rent and tuition and books. I'm still privileged. I'm not on welfare, I'm not losing custody of my kids. I'm not selling myself on the street, but then again nobody in this group is either, even though we talk about how just about every-thing is prostitution. A lot. But still I'm privileged and I get told about it. So to take the sting out, I make up oppressions.

But tonight, I don't want to say anything at all. I don't want to risk looking stupid or weak or privileged in front of her.

I don't want to stare either, but I can't help it. No fatigues, no buttons with lesbian messages, no wimmin's symbols dancing on a chain. Just soft-looking tight white jeans that meet a pair of tan suede desert boots. It's the boots that gave her away. She's wearing a white oxford shirt neatly tucked inside her pants, with a nice wide belt and a smooth caramel-colored suede vest that brings it all together, hides her breasts from those who might try to figure out what she is. My first girlfriend (and I use that term loosely) in high school did the very same thing. No backpack or bag. Certainly not a purse. Bet she carries a wallet in her back pocket.

It's the first night that I haven't said a word and still I'm more comfortable here than I've ever been. I sit cross-legged on my chair and pretend to stare into space, listening to the meeting buzz around me. There's a wimmin's dance on Saturday to benefit the Lesbian Mother's Defense Fund. A Take Back the Night March next month. The abortion clinic still needs more volunteers. Her fingers are long, the nails short and neat and trimmed. Her hands are small, smaller than mine maybe, but there's something about them, the way they rest one to a leg, not folded, not put away, but out and on display. The way her knuckles rise, tiny veins knotted tight, she does some form of work with these hands, something to make them look a little rough and used. But gentle. And the rings. I've never seen rings like that. They're art, abstract shapes with dark onyx and tiger eye and then the tiny one, silver and a purple stone, delicate but not at all feminine, sitting on her pinky finger. I'm staring again, my eyes stroking her hands like a caress. I remember reading about that, probably in one of the books my great aunt had hidden in the bathroom laundry bin—her secret stash of sleazy lesbian paperbacks. I know they were there because I read them all. How the women in those books checked out each other's hands, as if they were sizing them up. Thinking about what they'd feel like inside them.

I feel warm and look around, as if I'm afraid these wimmin can read my mind. I'd catch hell for sure if they knew I was thinking about that. Radical lesbian feminists aren't supposed to think about sex, at least not that way. We don't objectify women. Thinking about having sex with a woman I don't know, not respecting her whole being, her mind, that would definitely be viewed as sexist male behavior. And anything that even seems slightly related to male behavior is bad, bad, bad.

Funny, when I look at her, men are the last thing on my mind.

"So how long have you been out?"

I'm still shaking a little. I told her it's because I'm cold, and that's safe because it's freezing out, but it's warm inside the diner, almost too warm, and I can feel a trickle of sweat working its way down my back. I'm shaking because I don't know what to say and I can't believe I'm sitting here across from her. I guess she must have noticed I was staring at her most of the meeting. She did a good job of not letting on, but she was waiting for me when I came out of the community centre and asked if I wanted to go have coffee. Me. Out of all the women in the room who are so much more mature and certainly know more about politics and the movement and everything, she wanted to have coffee with me. So I'm nervous because I don't want to blow this, make a mistake, sound too young and dumb and boring.

Truth is, I'm not sure if I am out. I wear all the buttons on my knapsack, like "Lesbians are everywhere" and "A womyn needs a man like a fish needs a bicycle" but the truth is, I haven't had much experience. I spent a whole year of high school sneaking off to the first-floor girl's bathroom during study hall to be felt up by one of my high school friends who confessed to me once while she had her fingers in my underpants that she'd always wanted to be a boy. That and a few nights in university when a dorm mate stayed over late and we laid on the bed and start kissing and touching each other, while she kept telling me over and over that she wasn't a lesbian. She wasn't much of a kisser either, kind of limp and lazy and disinterested, and, truthfully, I had preferred my high school experiences. At least that had been exciting, especially knowing there was always a chance of being caught. But something told me me I shouldn't tell her that.

"A while. You?"

She leans back and stretches her arms out along both sides of the fake red leather seat. Cocks her head to the side, looks at me and smiles. A little sheepishly. She has blue, blue eyes and tiny streaks of gray in her short brown hair. I watch the smile lines around her mouth, trace her lips with my eyes. She starts to laugh.

"Honey, I think I was out before you were born." Then she looks at me, real serious. Like she's waiting for me to react.

Honey. She called me *Honey*. Like a man would. I wish I could think of something indignant to say, something that shows my awareness of how language oppresses us. How it objectifies me, makes me a sex object.

But the truth is, I like it. I really like it. A tiny bubble of desire rises in my stomach. I wonder what it would feel like to sit close to her when she called me that. To lie back inside the "L" of her arm that's thrown over the seat. A shiver of heat courses through me. I try to ignore it. We talk some more, or she talks, mostly about this book she's thinking of writing and how she's come to the group because some friend of hers thinks she should. Because, as she says, the world is changing. And I listen and think of her arms and her lips and being called *Honey*. And when she walks me to my subway stop later that night, she leans over and kisses me quick on the forehead without even asking if it's okay and while I wait for the world to stop spinning, I watch her walk, no, hop, dance, bop away, light snow shimmering around her like tiny disco mirrors under the bright street light.

The following Tuesday, I get to the community centre early so I can rearrange the chairs so she can sit beside me when she gets there. If she comes. I'm hoping. Finally, she does and I smile and she smiles back, but it's a little smile, like I'm just a friendly stranger, like we didn't talk for three hours and drink four coffees each and finally order big messy pieces of coconut cream pie because the waitress kept giving us dirty looks. Like she hadn't called me *Honey*. Or talk about how long she'd been out and how many women she'd dated and even lived with and how it had seemed like a lot, but I didn't say anything because it felt like I was judging her. Besides, she's almost twice my age, so she's had time to do all that. She didn't sit beside me but right across from me, and from time to time through the meeting, she would look over to see if I was looking at her.

That was even better.

The night's topic for discussion was gender constructions. About how thanks to feminism lesbians have started understanding their oppression and how they oppressed each other by playing roles. How now that we know better, they don't have to act like straight heterosexual couples anymore, don't have to ape the patriarchy, like one of the wimmin said, to pair off in couples where one would be more feminine and one would be more like a man. Butch and femme they called it. Now that we are so much more aware. Free to be what we want to be. There's no need to do that anymore.

She was waiting for me, head down, looking at her desert boots. She looked up when I came out, and smiled a small awkward smile. "Coffee?" she asked and I nodded and we started walking toward the diner we had gone to the previous week. After a block or so, she slipped her hand around my arm.

"It's slippery here," she said very matter of factly. "I don't want you to fall."

After we ordered, I pulled my knapsack off the floor and pushed it along the length of the bench seat. She watched me intently.

"I keep meaning to ask you what's in the bag?"

I really don't want to tell her my secret but I can't outright lie.

"It's my clothes."

She waits for more details.

"My work clothes. I had a meeting today so I had to dress up in a skirt and heels. I change in the subway bathroom and wash off my makeup and perfume before I get to the meeting. I know it isn't really that honest, but I can't walk into the publishing company looking like this." I motion down at my jeans and turtleneck and navy wool pea coat.

She leans back and traces her finger along the metal edge of the table. I'm worried I've offended her because I wear stuff like that to work. I put my hands on the table to stop them from shaking. She still has that effect on me.

Finally, she looks at me and says, "I'd really like to see you in those clothes."

I smile. Nod a little nervously. I think she's making a joke, but she's looking at me intensely, like she's waiting for more of a response. I keep smiling, but she's making me nervous. She leans in closer. Slides her hands over mine. Whispers in a low voice that's almost a growl.

"I mean it. I really would like to see you dressed like that."

Within minutes, she's paid for both coffees, which probably isn't very feminist, and is sitting beside me on the subway, solid and warm, just as I had expected, but silent as we rock and sway our way to my apartment.

❤

I'm almost afraid to come out of the bedroom. I didn't change back into my work clothes; I wanted to put on something fresh and clean. I'm wearing a gray houndstooth straight skirt, with a side slit to make it easier to walk in, my favorite deep rose silk blouse with tons of little buttons that presses tight to my breasts; sheer stockings—the good ones that cost a lot so I don't wear them everyday—and a pair of black patent leather heels. I lean closer to the mirror, unbutton one more button. Almost instinctively I think I know what she wants from this. I spray on a little bit of "Bluegrass" perfume, touch a tiny bit of Revlon's "Wine with Everything" to my lips. I look like I do when I have to go into the office to drop off reports or pick up more manuscripts. No, better than that. But I look so different from what she's used to seeing. I steady myself on the heels; take short steps so I don't trip out of nervousness.

The room is dark. I had lit a couple of candles before I went to change, for effect and to make her not notice how tiny my little apartment is, that the furniture is secondhand at best, some of it found on the street on trash day. I want everything to look as good as it can right now. Including me. She sits up straight and pulls herself to the edge of the couch as I walk through the archway. She doesn't say a word. But there's nothing shy about the way she's looking at me, starting at my face, slowly moving her eyes over my shirt, down over the round swell of my breasts inside a lacy demi-cup bra that pushes them upward and out. Past the curves of my hips under the skirt, down, down to the slit that reveals my legs, the heels that make my legs look shapelier. She still doesn't say a word, but her eyes grow wider and softer and she closes them for a moment. Looks away, then looks back at me. And before I can say a word, she's next to me, she pushes me backward until I feel the wall behind me. She lifts my arms above my head, anchors them back with her hands, so I can't push her away. She kisses me, my neck, my shoulders, her lips wetting the soft silk of my blouse, whispering *yes, yes, yes*. She stops. Looks at me. Whispers again.

"This is what I wanted. I knew it when I first saw you. The way you looked at me. Like you knew what you were looking at. No woman's looked at me that way in so long. I didn't think they made 'em like you anymore."

She grasps my shoulders with her hands, kisses me again, this time on the mouth, her tongue exploring mine, needy and wanting. She slides her hand lightly over my breasts, and my nipples harden instantly. I feel like I'm falling, but she's holding me too tight. Her breathing changes. She moves her lips in a trail down my neck. With one hand she twists open a few of the buttons, her mouth grazes the edge of my bra, she licks a line down between my breasts. My legs buckle. I can feel the wetness seeping into my panties and I try to press my legs together to stop it. But before I can, she pries my legs apart with her knee, presses tight against me, arches her back, starts to grind against me. Her hands are everywhere.

I can feel her breath, and I hear sighs and moans and I can't tell if they're hers or mine. There's an ache between my legs, the only time I felt anything like this was in the girl's bathroom during my study hall escapes. And never this strong. I think the word. *Cunt.* Yes, inside my cunt, I'm hurting for her. I want to feel . . . something. She's whispering my name; her hands slide over my hips, pushing me higher. I'm not sure if I'm still standing on my own, or if she's holding me up against the wall with her body. Her hand is between my legs now, stroking me through my panty hose, through my underpants. I push down, to feel her closer. She stops. Smiles. "That," she whispers, "is what I liked about the old days. Stockings are easier." And she laughs and I'm not sure I get it, but I don't care, I just want to keep feeling like this. Finally, she reaches down, lifts me—she's stronger than she looks—my legs slung over her arm so we look like some stupid honeymoon scene. She whispers, "You got a bed in this place?"

She spreads me out on the bed, turns on the small light on the night table. I look panicked. She whispers, "I just want to see you." She takes off the flannel shirt she's wearing over her T-shirt and arranges it on the lamp, diffusing the light. Smiles. Then she lies down beside me on the bed, finishes unbuttoning my blouse. Grimaces at the number of buttons. Slides her hands over my breasts and reaches behind to unhook my bra. My breasts tingle in the air. With one hand, she grasps one nipple, hard, takes the other one in her mouth, and bites me, just a little. My hips buck up off the bed. She smiles down at me, reaches behind me. In seconds, my skirt is off, the panty hose gone. I feel exposed. *Vulnerable.* For a second, I think about all I've read about lesbian sex, about sharing and equality and no one being in charge, but she is, she is leading this, doing the doing and I'm ready to explode. This is what was missing, I can't explain it, I have no words for it, but this is it. *She* is it.

She rolls on top of me, slides her thigh further between my legs, grips my hips, and presses hard against my wetness. Her body is amazingly strong. I feel like I'm swimming in the heat beneath her. Then she rises up and starts to slide her thigh against my wetness faster and faster and I know I'm crying out, moans and sighs and noises I've never made before. She's watching me lose myself in this, she must know it's my first time really, it's pride I see, pride that she can make me feel the things I'm feeling.

She slows for a moment, rolls onto her side beside me, strokes the lips of my cunt with her fingers. I want to scream. I keep rising up off the bed, as if I'm trying to trap her fingers inside me.

She whispers. "Tell me what you want."

I can barely hear her. I can barely think.

"Tell me," she says. A little firmer. "Tell me if you want my fingers inside you. Tell me if you want my mouth."

She stops. Hesitates. She's doing it on purpose.

"Tell me you want me to fuck you. Tell me you want me to make you mine."

I nod. *Yes, yes, yes.* Yes to it all, I want her and whatever she wants to do to me. *Yes.*

"No." She stops. Her fingers stop moving. "Say it. Say what you want."

I reach up to her, touch her lips. I want her to kiss me. I don't want it to stop. I pull her toward me. She resists. Smiles just slightly, but it's a hard smile. Bare with lust.

"Tell me," she says again, this time arching up away from me.

So I do. I do. I scream out for her to take me, to fuck me, to eat me and suck me. I beg her to put her fingers inside me. Beg her to fuck me hard, harder, harder and she does and I scream because I've never had this before and it hurts just a little, but it's a sweet pain and I want more. I feel so open, I want to take her whole hand inside me, I want to wrap my legs around her, pull her inside, and I tell her all these things, and that I am hers and hers alone. And I am panting and screaming and crying and I come and I come and I've never done that before either really, so I scream and speak words I couldn't imagine saying to anyone.

When it's over, her fingers are still inside me. She pulls them out slowly, so not to hurt me and I feel a gush. The wetness streams out of me. Her hand is full of wet creamy fluid. I never knew there would be so much. I look at her hand and feel embarrassed. I whisper, "I'm sorry, I'm sorry."

She wipes her hands on the already wet sheets and puts her finger to my lips. It smells like me. She lays her head down on the pillow, pulls me close inside her arms.

"Listen . . . don't ever apologize for that. For being that wet. It's beautiful. It's a gift. A gift to me. To whomever you're making love with. It means what they're doing is giving you pleasure. And a woman like you is going to make a lot of butches want to do just that."

I'm still a little groggy. "A lot of what?" I ask. I've heard the word she said. I can't remember where.

"Nothing," she whispers. "You're tired. Rest. I think you earned it." There's something so caring and gentle about her voice now, so different from the way she spoke to me when we were making love. *Protective.* That's what it is. And it works on me because I fall sound asleep beside her.

❤

Later, much later, it must have been the middle of the night, she woke me to tell me she had to go home and get dressed for work.

After I locked the apartment door, I fell back to sleep right away. When I woke up in the morning, I realized I had nodded off before I had a chance to do anything back to her. But she seemed perfectly okay with that.

Between that Tuesday and the next, she came over every night. She didn't call, she just appeared at the door, as if she knew I'd be there and let her in. Knowing she was coming, I started dressing up for her. During the day, I'd sneak away from work to buy something new, a long silky nightshirt, a lacy teddy and finally, a pair of stockings with a real garter belt that stung my thighs, but made me get wet whenever I put it on, just thinking about where her hands would go. That was on Friday and because she didn't have to work the next day, she stayed all night. In the morning, I made us coffee, real coffee with real cream, and we laid in bed and finally, I got the courage to offer to make love to her. I reached over to touch her breasts under the T-shirt she always wore in bed.

But she stopped me.

"No," she said. "That's not necessary."
I was confused. I didn't want to do all the taking. I told her that.
"Oh honey, you aren't. You have no idea what you're giving back to me."
And I left it at that because I didn't want anything to change.

The following Tuesday, I couldn't bear to put on my sloppy fatigues, my dumpy T-shirt. I couldn't look like that in front of her now, so instead I keep my work clothes on. Good dress pants that hugged my hips and legs in all the right places. A baby blue button-down sweater opened at the neck. And just a touch of lipgloss. The other women notice it too, stare a little. I don't let on.

But she doesn't look at me at all during the meeting. I keep looking her way, trying to get her attention. But she sits there like a stone. Tonight we talk about equality in relationships. Monogamy is bad. No one has any claims on a lover. No one can belong to anyone. And why chastity is an excellent option, how it makes it possible to have deep relationships on other levels.

She shifts uneasily in her seat most of the night.

When I leave, she's there, but something's different. She doesn't take my arm; instead she walks beside me with her hands in her pockets. Like she's afraid of touching me. Gets on the subway without saying a word and is silent all the way to my apartment. Finally, inside, she says we have to talk. About how I can't get sloppy, can't let them see what's going on. But I don't understand.

She sighs. "Remember when they were talking about lesbians before the movement?"

I nod.

"Well, who in the hell do you think they were talking about? Lesbians like me. They think I want to be a man because I want a woman who looks like a woman. Because I want someone who wants to be beautiful for me. Someone who wants me because of the way I am. And yes, someone who actually wants to have sex, wants to be made love to, not just talk about it in theory. Someone like you."

I didn't want her to know I already thought about this. Why she was different from the women in the group. And why I felt more comfortable once she started coming. So instead, I just nod.

"I mean, do you think I act like a man? I don't. And I don't want to be one. I don't want to be anything but what I am. But they just don't get it."

She's quiet for a long time.

I ask her why she's hiding what she is, why it matters what they think?

"It matters," she says. "It matters to me. You haven't been on the outside of everything your whole life. You don't know what it feels like. To inspire that kind of disgust. To have women afraid of being around you. Like you're going to jump them the first time you get the chance."

For a moment, I think I see a tear. I reach out for her and she comes to me, which I hadn't expected, and we hug and touch and I thought I was comforting her, but soon she has me out of my clothes, right on the couch and my legs are wrapped around her, and I feel her hips move, grinding harder and harder into my body, making me writhe and scratch her with my newly grown nails. Then she moves down my body, spreads my legs and licks me, her tongue moving in and out and up and down. Until I'm so wet that I cry out for her to fuck me, to take me, take me hard. To hell with what they said, at that moment, I do want her to possess me, I want to feel that she owns me, controls me. And she does, she does, her whole hand sliding deep inside me so slowly and I scream and buck and see lights behind my eyes. And after I feel as if we've broken through something, gone somewhere we're not supposed to be, but we're there now and we're in it together. Conspirators. She leans her head down at me, kisses my lips, bites my earlobe just a bit and whispers, "Now you do belong to me. You're mine."

Knowing that makes me want her even more.

That week, she comes over every night too, and stays almost all night most times. When we aren't making love, she tells me stories of what it was like when she came out in the '60s, the bars and the bar fights and drinking and drugs. The hidden clues, what you looked for to find other lesbians, what you wore, how you held a cigarette. And all the hiding and lies and why she wants a change, why it doesn't seem so much to ask for her to just hide her old gay ways, if it means being part of something she needs. If it means support and real friends and just a little bit of respect. I want to understand. I want to keep her secrets. But I don't see how it's much of a change from all the lies she had to tell before.

But I'm not that good at hiding. I haven't had the practice. I start wearing nail polish and lipstick all the time. Long dangly earrings and chains that sway against my breasts when I walk. I wear skirts and heels almost every day. And the following Tuesday, I decide I'm not going to let them do to me what they're doing to her, and I stride into the meeting in a short black leather skirt and red silk blouse, Revlon Red nails and lips and my hair in a soft French twist with loose little curls that make me look like I've just been ravaged.

I look like the poster girl for the patriarchy. But only if you don't know enough to know what you're actually looking at.

She wants me to believe she's not looking at me, but the truth is, she can't keep her eyes off me. She waits until she thinks no one is watching her, then sneaks a look my way. Her face is hard, she looks angry, in fact I'm sure she is, not just at me for being so defiant, but also at herself. That she let this happen, let me happen, that she couldn't keep things under wraps. Her fear of coming undone, doing the wrong thing, especially now, when she's making such progress at being accepted. Being tolerated. Being emasculated. Yes, that's it. There's no good gender-neutral word for it, but that's exactly what this is doing to her.

The topic of the evening is about being a willing victim to the patriarchy, about dressing to please men, being a walking advertisement for rape. I guess I've inspired this, but I don't join in, don't defend myself because I'm too busy watching her, too busy thinking about how I'd like to saunter across the room, hike up my skirt, climb on her lap and straddle her thighs. Open my blouse and slide one of my breasts from its lacy red encasing, caress my nipple with my own painted nails because I know she likes to watch me touch myself. Pry her mouth open with a lipstick kiss and feed her one of my breasts. Arch up against her so she can feel the heat between my legs, let her catch the scent of me, while she sucks, bites. Then guide her fingers under my skirt, past the scalloped stocking edge to the wet flesh above, no panties, no, just open wet cunt and all for her. Rock against her fingers. Flood her hand.

Whisper how I want her to make me come, that only she can fuck me this good, this well. *Seduce* her, I think. Just thinking the word makes my cunt contract. I want to make her want to possess me. Make her want me so bad nothing else matters. Just like I have before on my couch, but tonight I want to do it right here, right now, in front of all of these women who demand she be something she's not to win their acceptance. Those who want her to be less than what she is. I want to show them they can't touch us. That we are what we are and we don't need their approval. Their tolerance. No more than we need it from the rest of the world. And I get so lost in the fantasy of her spreading my legs and fucking me openly at the radical lesbian feminist group meeting that I don't even realize everyone has left and I'm sitting alone in the room.

She's waiting for me when I walk out and she's furious. She can't believe I was so openly defiant. Do I have any idea what these women think of me now? Or her? I want to tell her that from the way she treats me in the meetings, there's no way anyone could know we're lovers, but I don't bother. She tells me maybe they're right, that women shouldn't treat other women the way she's treated me and dozens more. They're getting inside her head. They've already gotten to her. There's no talking to her now, no way to explain why what they think doesn't matter. She needs their approval, even if it means living a lie. But thanks to her, I've learned I *don't* need it. And I don't want anyone who does. So I don't say a word. Don't ask to be forgiven. And she's not expecting that.

In the end, she hugs me, there on the street, in the yellow light in front of the community centre and whispers "this is about me, not you. It's what you make me want to be, what you make of me. And I can't let that happen. Not now. Not again."

I stand there in the dark, watching the first butch I ever fell in love with walk away and all I can think of is the stupid playground poem. *I'm rubber and you're glue, what bounces off me, sticks to you.* I take a vow to never let them, any "them" get to me. The world isn't ever going to tell me what to be or how to be it. But neither are the women of the Tuesday meetings. So I stop going to meetings, stop trying to fit in, eventually give myself full permission to wear the clothes I like and seduce the kind of women I want. I learn that if you're afraid of what's wild inside you, others will be too. And before long, I find my kind are actually in fashion again. For a while anyway.

But she did go back to the meeting and said and did the right things, and wrote the book she had talked about. Then another, and another and then finally one about how hard it was to be butch in the lesbian feminist movement. The things it did to her. The way it made her change.

Last Saturday, I drove nearly 200 miles to hear her read from it. I sat in the front row, with my legs discreetly crossed beneath my tight black skirt, my green cashmere sweater unbuttoned just enough. I am what I am. Thanks to her or in spite of her, I learned to be proud of it. To protect it. And in a room of mostly what were once Tuesday night women, she read of how the movement had done so much good. And about the cost to her and women like her, and how no one had wanted to talk about that. And she couldn't keep her eyes off me. Later, while she signed books for a crowd of her readers, I waited until it was my turn. I had to know how the story turns out. When she reached for my book, I leaned in close, as if to whisper "it's been a long time" or "good to see you again," but instead I brushed my breast against her shoulder and dropped my hotel keycard into the pocket of her black denim shirt. Good choice. Her eyes are still brilliant blue, her hands still look strong. I grazed my lips, soft in Sephora Sheer Mauve #87, against her neck, her cheek. Then I turned on my heel and felt her eyes on me as I walked out of the hall.

I didn't get home until Tuesday night.

Going Down
Becky Arbogast

I always get a thrill out of staying in a hotel, mostly because I love the fact that someone else has to cater to my every whim. Unlike most people, I like the feeling of being away from home, and three days in a luxury hotel is enjoyable for me even if it means the days are full of boring business meetings. My first agenda after settling into my room on Sunday evening is to orient myself to the hotel. To my pleasure, I discover my daily commute will be two minutes down ten floors to the business center, and since I am not a morning person, I appreciate the valuable minutes of quality sleep this and room service will provide for me.

Monday morning, my mind still hazy from sleep, I step into the elevator and my eyes are drawn to her immediately. She stands slightly taller than me with wavy, black, shoulder length hair. Her appearance is captivating. Standing across from her, I try not to stare but the thin material of her T-shirt stretches across her chest and I can see the outline of her breasts. Her jeans are molded to her body perfectly and the polished black boots convey a confident butch image. I feel my heart race as her gaze finds mine. She raises her eyebrows, acknowledging my perusal of her body, and I try to shift my focus to the numbers above the elevator panel. When the doors open to the business center, I catch her watching my exit, and her gaze is so intense my breath catches just at being the focus of her attention.

I dream about her the entire day, returning again and again to the vision of her sexy stance, and it keeps my body in a constant state of arousal. Fantasies about what her hands could do to me haunt me throughout dinner and during the elevator ride back to my room. I hold my breath at every turn, hoping she will appear again.

Tuesday morning, I step into the elevator to find her leaning against the rear wall as if waiting patiently for me. Pushing my way through the crowded elevator to the spot directly in front of her, then turning my back, I glance up into the mirror above the doors and watch her eyes devour my body with a gaze filled with desire. She finally looks up and catches me watching her. Again she raises her eyebrows in a question, and I want to scream *yes, yes, whatever you want.*

When the elevator stops two floors down, I can barely contain my enthusiasm to see more people waiting to file in. The temptation to press against her is almost more than I can resist, and the space between us radiates with heat from her body. I step back, creating room for the new occupants, and feel her hands on my sides pulling me into the security of her arms. I search for her eyes in the mirror to reassure myself she is more than a fantasy. Her body is warm and hard, her breasts firm against my back, and I push against her, craving to be closer. The elevator bell signals our arrival at my floor, and I sigh as she releases me. Looking back as I step out of the elevator, I long to return and let her ravish my body. Instead, I resign to spend another day dreaming of her caressing every inch of me.

By Wednesday morning, my entire body is humming with anticipation. I watch the clock, hoping to match the time exactly to the last two morning encounters. Will she be there? It hurts to even imagine that she might not be. As I walk to the elevator, the seam of my khakis pushes my body into a heightened frenzy. I consider returning to my room but I know that my body craves more than my own touch. Every part of me aches to be molded by her strong, delicate hands.

The elevator doors open and there she is relaxing against the rear wall. Though this morning there are only a few people in the elevator, no one seems to notice how close we stand. Facing the doors, directly in front of her, the heat from her body washes over me. My muscles quiver as she pulls me firmly against her, resting her head on my shoulder and pressing her lips against my ear.

"Be patient," she whispers softly.

Nodding, afraid to trust my voice, my body relaxes into hers. When the elevator stops at the business center, she tightens her grip, holding me in place while everyone exits, then steps around me pushing the button to make the doors close. When she turns to face me, I slide my arms around her waist and pull her into a tight embrace. She presses her lips against my neck and the heat of her mouth melts my flesh. Her hands slip between us to caress my breasts, stroking my aroused nipples. I inhale deeply, trying to catch my breath.

"Do you have somewhere you need to be?" she asks in a husky voice.

"Only here with you," I manage to say.

Struggling to remain standing on my trembling legs, she senses my weakness and slides her leg between mine, providing support for both of us. Her body moves in rhythm against me as she presses her soft, warm lips hard against mine. Her tongue gently explores the inside of my mouth, and we both moan as the kiss deepens. I can imagine running my tongue over her entire body, tasting all of her. She moves to my zipper and deftly opens the front of my khakis. As she slides inside, the elevator bell announces another stop. Quickly, she turns her back to me, blocking my partially undressed state from the other early morning travelers.

Several women step in but none seem to notice the shiver that courses through my body as I think about how little it would take to bring me to climax. My lungs scream for oxygen, and I am overwhelmed with an undeniable hunger for her. Sliding my hands under her shirt, luxuriating in the softness of her skin, I gently rake my fingernails along her rib cage. I gasp softly when my fingers discover her naked breasts; they mold perfectly to my hands and my thumbs stroke a circle around her nipples. She shifts slightly to conceal her hand sliding between us and into my open khakis. Burying my head into her back, I am unable to conceal my excitement as her fingers explore the wet folds between my legs.

The elevator bell reminds me that we are not alone. As the women exit together, the last one gives us a backward smile and a knowing wink. Without moving her hand from inside my boxers, my companion presses the stop button as soon as the doors close.

"Where were we?" she whispers, turning to face me.

I pull her against me; kissing her in answer, then gasp as she begins to move her fingers again.

"You are so wet."

"Only for you," I whisper back.

As her fingers stroke me gently, her other hand unbuttons my shirt and slides it off my shoulders. She easily maneuvers the front clasp on my bra and pushes it out of her way, allowing her tongue to flick back and forth across my nipples. The passionate moan she coaxes from my body is deep and filled with desire.

My fingers scrape down her back, sliding around her body and over her stiff nipples to the fly on her jeans. The buttons open easily and my hand travels down her stomach, seeking the heat that awaits me inside her briefs. The sweet smell of her pushes me closer to the edge. Sliding my fingers through her wetness, I'm careful to avoid the rigid tip of her, knowing she won't be able to hold on. Her upper body presses into mine, holding both of us up against the side of the elevator. I thrust one finger, then a second inside her, and she pushes her hips hard against my hand. My palm slides across her clit, matching the rhythm of her hand on me.

"Oh yes."

"Please don't stop."

My spinning head and the explosion of light behind my eyes keep me from knowing exactly which of us is speaking. She slides a finger into me as we both go over the edge. We cling to each other, holding on to the moment.

"Wow," I murmur into her neck. "You are so hot."

She rests her head on my shoulder, breathing deeply. I apply pressure with the palm of my hand and she squeezes me tighter. As she gently slides her fingers across my clit, I push hard against her hand, begging for more, and she strokes me gently, bringing me quickly to another orgasm.

We wrap our arms around each other, waiting for our desire to subside. After a minute or two, she releases me, putting space between us and begins to adjust my clothes.

"Your meetings are over today?" she asks.

I nod.

"Then I guess I'll see you when you get home tonight," she says with that devilish smile I love so much.

"I can't wait," I whisper eagerly.

Just One Night
Tanya Turner

"Are you a porn star?" she asked as I took my seat, preparing for the screening.

I looked at this older woman, her hair sprinkled with gray, her eyes crinkled in a friendly way, and laughed. "Me? No, but I know people in the film." I was wearing a plunging corset top that showed off my ample boobs and the miniest skirt I could find, and was flattered that she'd even think to ask such an outrageous question. Then again, we were about to watch a snippet of a XXX film, and the entire crowd of partygoers was salivating with anticipation. I sat alone, near the woman and her friend, and tried not to feel self-conscious while on-screen all manner of sex took place, men and women and women and women in various contorted positions, in full view. I knew some people in attendance, but they were seated far away, and I could tell this woman was checking me out. I tried to set that aside and just enjoy the movie, as the scenes got more and more outrageous. None of it really phased me until the end, when I saw one girl balanced on her hands and feet, raising her ass into the air in a modified push-up. Exercise had never looked sexier.

The mood of the party got even more risque as the night wore on. I mingled with women whose breasts were bared, people getting spanked, people getting propositioned all over the place. A roaming photographer managed to snap my picture with the mystery butch, and while we chatted a few times throughout the night, nothing much happened. I wasn't sure if she was with her friend, and besides, I felt slightly out of place, like I didn't belong with such a glamorous, kinky crowd.

I didn't think too much about my new friend until I ran into her a few weeks later at another party. She really laid it on thick, but she had to, because I was so slow. Even though I'd once again managed to dress in my sluttiest attire, I felt like a prude compared to all the wild women around me. She bought me a drink and I even sat on her lap, but still, it took me forever to figure out that she was flirting with me; at twenty-one, I was so young and inexperienced, and she seemed older and suave, but eventually I managed to pick up on her clues when she simply jumped in to the middle of our bumbling conversation and asked if she could go home with me. A shiver of excitement ran through me, along with a feeling of truly being an adult—getting picked up by a stranger who thought that I was worthy of this kind of attention.

We went back to my ultra tiny dorm room, but I didn't even have the presence of mind to be embarrassed about its miniscule size or the extra-long twin bed we found ourselves on. She toyed with the chain link necklace I imagined so tough and cool back then, tugging on it, staking her claim on me. Then she kissed me, her hands lifting my shirt, kneading my breasts, and making me moan. I surrendered to her touch, no longer worried about what was proper or what she thought of me, because her hands were sending a very strong and direct message. She pinched each nipple, and when I exclaimed, she did it harder. I closed my eyes, put my head down, the ultimate pillow queen demanding her due, my curvy body a contrast to her steely, muscular one. She was a stone butch, not stern but not full of endearments either, which was fine because I didn't need those. Knowing she wanted to fuck me was more than enough, and I let her, panting and writhing as she tugged on the metal necklace looped around my neck, the cool surface digging into my skin. I arched my neck, giving myself to this stranger as she calmly claimed me.

I was half afraid to look at her, knowing she was probably twice my age and very likely ten times as experienced. Looking back, I wonder what she saw in my youthful innocence, my uncertainty and need, but at the time I was so raw and eager for any new experiences that I didn't think to question it. Her teeth sank into my shoulder as she pinned me beneath her, her short nails trailing along my skin. She stripped me down, pulling my clothes off with as little fanfare as possible until I was stark naked on the narrow surface of the bed. I could feel her looking at me, examining me with her eyes and her hands in the dim light as she traced a finger along my spine, pressing the vertebrae as she went before pausing as she reached the curve of my ass. She kept going, though, her finger pausing to dip along the surface of my asshole, testing my reaction, perhaps, before her other hand plunged into my center. Her fingers were small and efficient, pressing against me with powerful thrusts as I pushed back against her. I hardly knew a thing about her and yet there she was, working my most sensitive folds into a rip-roaring orgasm. I was incoherent, babbling something that must have made sense to me but that she wisely ignored, doing what she wanted to do instead.

She leaned down, resting her head rather sweetly on one of my cheeks, her breath warm along my curves as her fingers sloped and slid inside of me, rhythmic lunges that I quickly became accustomed to. What had seemed strange at first as we moved from the fun flirtation of the bar to the quieter solitude of my dorm room morphed into something else, a coming together as we both eased into our roles. She tugged on the chain, letting my tender neck feel her desire for me as she twisted her practiced fingers inside me while I struggled to stay on the bed. For a few minutes, I tried to hold on to some semblance of the good girl I'd always strived to be, the law student *who didn't do things like this*, but I couldn't, not when I'd taken home a virtual stranger, one who clearly cared more about my body than me. We liked each other on one level, yes, but it was clear from the start that this would just be a one-night stand, nothing more, nothing less.

She was fiery, hot, snakelike as her fingers practiced their experienced magic on me, moving in ways I could only begin to grasp as I drooled onto my pillow, tossed my long hair, feeling young and glamorous and invincible as she proved just how easy I was. In hardly any time at all, her fingers were coaxing forth my climax, like my body was a maze whose secret trapdoor she'd discovered long ago. I didn't marvel at her quickness, though, just twisted against her, moaning, pushing back, feeling full and high and wanted. She'd made it clear this was a one-way street, that she was one of those stone butches I'd only read about, stilling my hand as I tried to remove her shirt. Once I'd been refused, I'd stopped longing to touch her, had quelled all desires of that nature in order to fully enjoy her touch, her fingers slamming and twisting, her other hand pressing down against my body, appreciating it like a national treasure, something you're not supposed to touch but do anyway, sneaking reverent, mischievous strokes. She wasn't tentative, but since we both knew the score, knew we were as entranced by each other's age and (in)experience as we were by our chemistry, we could go to a level that was purely physical. It was all over in probably half an hour, but certainly one of the longest half hours of my life. We didn't speak much during or afterward, and any details she told me about herself have long since been forgotten.

Weeks later, the party's organizer gave me a photo from that night, of me and her and her friend. I'm glowing, beaming, while they're smiling normally. I still have it around here, somewhere, but I don't know where it is, just like I once knew her name, and now it's faded into obscurity. But I still remember my initiation into the world of lesbian sex for the hell of it, without any kind of soulmate kidding ourselves, without anything deeper than hunger and connection and desire, just a quick and dirty one-night stand, one of only a handful to come.

Us
Nell Stark

I'd always thought my first time would be with a man, on our wedding night. That I'd be thinking about it all week up until the day, and during the ceremony, and the reception, and in the limo back to the hotel. That I'd be suffused with anticipation—nervous and excited and eager and happy.

Then, I saw through a glass, darkly. Now, face to face.

It's Saturday. Two weeks exactly from the day I first kissed her. She made me do the kissing, of course—I'm the one with the baggage, here. If my parents knew how my lips feel against the back of her neck while she brushes her teeth in the morning . . . well, they'd say it's wrong. That *we're* wrong. Hell, even I thought it was a sin, when I first arrived on campus as a freshman. Such a good girl—so smart and nice and proper. And now, here I am—a bona fide lesbian. I never asked for the label, but if it's the cost of loving her, then I'll take it and own it. I'll do anything to make it so we can stay right here, lying side-by-side on my bed in our pajamas, both reading books as the chill October wind blasts sporadically outside the window.

It's taken me three years to need her. Three years of gradual shift, tectonic plates slip-sliding under the surface of my being. Rearranging. Preparing a way in the wilderness. We were best friends almost immediately, but the rest came slowly—filling in around the edges, drip-dropping into the cracks, sealing them up, one by one.

She sets her book down on the nightstand and turns toward me, tucking an errant curl of my hair behind one ear with a gentle hand. I smile into her face, so familiar, so beloved.

"I think you need a massage," she says, a slight grin playing at the corners of her mouth.

My eyes get a little wider and I feel my smile change shape. Eager. I love how her hands feel on my back—smooth and steady and gentle. Safe. She takes my expression for the acceptance that it is, and shifts so she's kneeling on the bed. "Turn over."

I flip obediently and am rewarded a moment later by the gentle, circular pressure of her hands against my shoulders. I let myself sink into the mattress with a long sigh. The warmth of her palms soaks through my shirt and into my skin.

"Feels so good," I murmur, allowing myself to drift. No thinking, no worrying, just floating—basking in her soft, confident strokes, arching a little against her touch when she hits a sore spot. My eyes are closed but I won't let myself sleep; no, I want to remember every moment of this, every touch. Once in a while, I make sure to hum just a little, low under my breath, so she knows how much I love this. Love *her*.

Suddenly, I feel the hem of my T-shirt being lifted up, and then her hands are splayed over the small of my back. I exhale involuntarily. Her skin on my skin—comfort, closeness. And something else, something a little dangerous. Heat stirring way down deep, uncoiling and stretching. Hungry.

"Is this okay?" she whispers, remaining motionless.

"Yes," I reply. My voice sounds deep, even to my own ears. "That feels amazing."

"Good," she murmurs, and remaps my entire back with the soft pads of her fingers. I'm lost again, floating, reduced to nothing but sheer *feeling*. When her hands finally stop, I can't tell whether it's been minutes or hours since she began to touch me.

"Wow," I whisper, rolling over with an effort. My body feels languid, fluid. Have I ever been this relaxed? "That was the best massage I've ever had. Amazing. Thank—"

I'm looking at her face but she's not looking at mine. The movements of her hands have bunched up my shirt a little, and she's staring at the revealed expanse of my pale belly. She slides down toward the foot of the bed, and suddenly, I can't breathe. Her head lowers slowly, so slowly—giving me time to change my mind, I dimly realize—until her lips connect with my skin. One kiss, featherlight. Two. Three. So loving, so careful. I feel like porcelain. She covers the patch with tender kisses, then reaches for my shirt to hike it up a little more—and freezes.

"I think I'm trying to seduce you," she whispers. Her voice sounds young, uncertain.

Seduce me? Really? Does she really want me like that? She said so, back on that night when she first told me she loved me, but it's so hard to believe. Should I stop her? The heat between my thighs flares again, and now I can feel an ache in my breasts, too. Her lips are so good, so *right* on my skin—and suddenly, I realize that I don't want her to stop. I want her to touch me, so much more than she already is.

"If I'm uncomfortable, I'll tell you," I say a little breathlessly. "But that feels really good."

"Okay," she murmurs, and bends her head back down to my stomach. Gradually, she pushes the hem of my shirt up, higher and higher, going so slowly for my sake. I love her for it, even as I want to beg her to really touch me—but the words won't come. Ironically, my greatest fear is that I'll scare her with the intensity of my desire. There are other things to be afraid of, of course, but right now they couldn't matter less. And then her index finger connects with the soft underside of my right breast, and I can't help hissing at the jolt that storms from my skin to the focal point between my legs.

She pauses, and I feel the fine tremors of her fingers against me. "Too much?"

"No," I rasp. "No, it feels great."

"Okay," she whispers again. And then, "I love you."

"I love you back," I reply, voice trembling. Not out of fear or even nervousness—every touch of hers is so clearly another "I love you." Out of *want*. I am aching, aching so badly and I need her to—

Her hand closes gently around my breast and I let out a humming sigh. Yes, *that*.

"Good?" she asks, and I nod, my breaths quickening as I feel her other hand slide up my belly. And then she's kneading, kneading and rubbing and sometimes her fingers rise and pinch my nipples ever so lightly before sliding back down and around. Her mouth presses sucking kisses into the indentations of my ribcage, and my body comes *alive*, back arching involuntarily.

"Oh . . . feels so amazing." I'm throbbing now, pulse beating in time to the pull of her hands. The way she touches me, firmly but so gently—I want those long fingers to explore every inch of me. Do I dare tell her that? Will she think I'm being too forward? But our honesty—it's important. It's everything. We've promised each other to tell nothing but the truth, and I can't hide it anymore, can't deny that what I want, what I need so desperately, is for her to—"I want you to touch me everywhere."

Instead, she stops. *No, please!* I force my eyes open, lift my head to regard her anxiously. "What—what's wrong, love? Did I say the wrong thing?"

"No," she says, shaking her head vehemently. "No, not at all, but—" She pulls down my shirt and slides up to rest on her stomach next to me. "What exactly do you mean by that?"

I freeze. "Um, uh, I don't know," I say lamely. Which isn't true at all, but not even my interior monologue can verbalize what I really want. I know what it's called, and I know that I need her fingers there, but what if saying so is too bold? What if, what if—

"Well," she tries again, "How, um, how far have you gone?"

My swallow is audible. This is my best friend, the woman I love, the one I trust above all others. I can talk about this with her, and I *should*. I clear my throat, grab a fistful of blanket as an anchor, and finally manage to speak. "Pretty far."

"Okay," she replies slowly, as though musing over a puzzle. The back of her left hand brushes against my cheek, and I know she is trying to soothe me. "Have you ever had an orgasm?"

My face must register shock, but she just lies there watching my widening eyes, looking at me calmly. This is emotion-overload—I've gone from highly aroused to panicked almost instantaneously.

What it all comes down to, of course, is that I'm afraid to answer her—afraid that maybe she'll think differently of me once she knows how much experience I've had. How needy I truly am. Will she still want me? And besides, it's surprising to hear her say that. It. *Orgasm*. We haven't exactly talked about sex . . . ever. Not like this. I know she had a girlfriend in high school, and one serious boyfriend here at college, but I never asked for details and she never volunteered them and now here we are and I want her hands on me more than I've ever craved anything in twenty-one years of serial obsessions, and what if she thinks I'm some kind of monster because I have to touch myself nearly every night just to get some sleep?

Her face is both serious and gentle as she looks down at me, and all of the sudden, it's so very clear what I have to do. So I wind up, suck in a breath, look her straight in the eyes, and say, "Yes."

She blinks. "Really?"

"Yeah," I confirm, no longer able to meet that surprised gaze. "Lots, actually." I pick at the checkered fabric of my blanket and risk another peek at her face. No disgust, no disdain, nothing but curiosity and that deep, abiding tenderness that I love so very much. "I've never had sex, though."

"I figured that," she replies, nodding. Her right palm cups the side of my face, briefly.

"You asked how far I've gone," I say into the silence, suddenly wanting to tell her everything—from discovering masturbation in the fourth grade to reaching second base with my high school boyfriend, to hooking up on a pool table with some random frat boy this past summer in a desperate attempt to get her out of my head. "I guess I've gone as far as you can go without actually having sex."

"Really?" she asks again. "That's a surprise. You always seem to get a little uncomfortable whenever anyone brings it up."

"Yeah, well, some of that's an act," I confess. If I wasn't blushing before, I sure am now. "But most of it's not. I guess I get nervous talking about it, for some reason."

She leans over to press a lingering kiss on my forehead. "We don't have to talk about it if you don't want to."

"No, no," I reply, forcing myself to look at her again. "I do want to, with you. It's good to be honest. Necessary." I roll onto my side so it's easier to see her face. "So, uh, have you?" I ask, tentatively. "Ever, y'know, had . . . one?"

"Yes," she answers, just as firmly as I did, then laughs at my expression. "We're both shocking each other tonight, aren't we?" She reaches forward to comb a stray lock of hair away from my eyes. "With Cheryl, after we'd been together for about a year."

"Oh, okay," I stutter weakly. I've seen a picture of Cheryl in her high school photo album, and all of the sudden, my spinning brain can't help but see them lying on a narrow bed curled around one another, black hair mingling with blonde on the pillow. The mental image sends twin surges of jealousy and desire rocketing under my skin, and I have to struggle not to shiver. What would it be like to touch a woman? I'd always been afraid of touching guys—afraid because I didn't know what to do. But a woman would be familiar. Soft—she'd be so soft.

"Nothing like that ever happened with Matthew, though," she finishes, and I feel my head jerk up at the revelation.

"Really?"

"Yep, really." She grins at me, a little mischievously, and I some-how manage to smile back. How can she be so at ease in this moment, when I can feel my forearm muscles knotting under her hand? "You sound relieved."

"I think I'm beginning to understand what my jealousy was *really* all about," I say wryly. "I loved you even then, and just . . . didn't know it." There must be something in my voice—some tone or hitch or stutter—that lets her know I'm not quite finished, because all she does is stroke my arm and wait. I have to swallow hard before I can speak again.

"I went to the frats a lot, while you were with him," I mutter, turning my head away. "I'd go and drink, fool around with guys . . . it wasn't good."

I'm waiting for her to pull away—to tell me that I'm just too *much* for her, that she'd rather be with him after all—but instead, she leans in close, wraps one arm around my waist and lightly kisses the side of my neck.

"I'm sorry you were so lonely," she whispers against my skin. "You need touch. It's one of the things I love about you. I promise I'll try my best to give you what you need."

"You," I murmur, hugging her even tighter. "I need you."

We lie still for a little while, then, reveling in our closeness—physical and emotional. And as I hold her, I smile into the twilit room because she loves me, she really does and not even my past can interfere with that. Now that the secret's out, I feel so much lighter inside . . . but even so, there's one other thing I want her to know. At least the words are easier, this time.

"Have you, uh," I begin awkwardly, and pause. All right, maybe this *isn't* easier. It seems ultra-taboo for some reason—even though I know that it's normal. Healthy.

"Have you ever touched yourself?" I finally blurt out. "Because I have . . . and, and recently—this past week—when I did I, um, thought of you."

Silence. Great—I've gone and done it now. Now she thinks—

"I have, too," she says suddenly, almost too quietly for me to hear. "I've always been ashamed of it, even though there's no reason to be." She pauses and sighs. "And yes, I've thought of you sometimes. Even before this past week."

"Oh," I say weakly, because the throbbing has started again. She's thought of me? Of me touching her?

"That was my last secret," she admits. "The last thing I hadn't told you. I'm not sure if I ever would have, either. So . . . thank you."

We lapse into stillness again, except for her hands. They move—slowly, carefully—down my sides to my waist. The throbbing speeds up as I realize her destination, and I feel my breaths quicken. Her hands—I need them on my skin. Badly.

She tugs and I obediently roll away from her so I'm lying on my back. She bends down to kiss me while slowly hiking the hem of my shirt up my stomach, up and over my heavy breasts. The slide of cotton across my nipples makes me shudder, and I think a little noise—sort of like a whimper—escapes my throat. And then her mouth opens over mine and I follow her lead, moaning when our tongues touch tentatively. French kissing had always just been the thing to do, but it's so different now, so profoundly *sensual*, every light brush of her tongue against mine sending pulses of heat down my spine to pool between my legs. I *want* to taste her, and to be tasted in return.

She finally pulls away, only to bring her hands back to my breasts. My head jerks back on the pillow as the breath leaves my body in an explosive sigh. Hands clenched at my sides, I try to understand what she is doing to me even as my body becomes a riot of sensation. A moment later, I feel wetness against the sensitive skin around one nipple, and my eyes flash open to behold the most incredible sight they've ever seen: her tongue flicking me back and forth, then circling, just before she pulls my nipple into her mouth and sucks in, *hard*. I can't help it—I cry out—especially when she does it all over again and mirrors the motions of her tongue on my other breast with her fingers.

The tightness between my thighs is an ache, now—pulling, throbbing, almost painful. The power of her mouth and fingers burns away my self-consciousness and embarrassment, purging me until all that's left is white-hot desire.

"Oh, god," I cry softly, throat rough from so many harsh, gulping breaths. The swirling motions of her tongue stop and I shudder involuntarily. "I need you to touch me," I rasp, "or else I'll go insane."

Pause. My body pulses, a firecracker, spark halfway down the fuse. *Please!*

"Okay," she breathes. "I love you." She slips her right hand under the elastic waistband of my boxers, and I'm gasping, gasping and trembling as her fingers find me—hot and swollen and liquid.

Light at first, light and teasing, then more firmly as my gasps become whimpers. I hear them. There is nothing but this—her scent enveloping me, her long hair brushing against my collarbone, her fingers dipping down into my wetness and then returning up to circle my clitoris. Swirling, dancing—so gentle, so loving. My body tightens, thighs trembling as my hips arch into her hands. I'm close, so very close, and it's right there—just beneath the horizon like the predawn sun, ready to burst above the skyline in a shower of red-gold sparks.

Her name explodes against my lips as I come for her, shuddering against her hand for the first time. "I love you, I love you," she whispers, continuing to massage me gently until the last of the spasms are past—until I finally regain enough strength to open my eyes and look up into her beautiful face. There's a tiny crease between her eyebrows that I'd smooth out with a finger if I could raise my arm.

Some distant part of me realizes that my cheeks are tingling. I've hyperventilated.

"Are you okay?" she asks quietly, stroking the sweaty wisps of hair back from my forehead.

"Oh," I manage, my voice sounding faint through the roaring in my ears. "Th . . . that was—there are no words." I can still feel the staccato pulse of my heart against my ribcage and I take a few deep breaths to slow it down. "Incredible d-doesn't even come close."

She launches herself at me, then, and I hold onto her and murmur "I love you" over and over, and in between she keeps saying "thank you, thank you for letting me do that." *She* is thanking *me*? I'd laugh if I could find the strength, but my entire being is limp and heavy. Sated—for the first time in my life.

It would be so easy to fall asleep in her arms—to surrender to the overwhelming lassitude she has brought to my body. But I won't—not yet, not when I can touch her in return. I need her to feel how much I love her, and I want to repay her for the amazing gift she's just given me. Want to feel her softness, everywhere. Only, I'm nervous. Guys had always been content with exploring my body, so I don't have much experience touching anyone but myself. And what if I can't please her? I *need* to be able to make her feel good, to give her what she's just given me.

"I—I want to touch you, if it's okay," I finally whisper. "But I don't know how."

"It's more than okay," she answers, voice catching. "And don't worry about it—just do what feels good to you."

"All right," I reply. "But can you tell me what . . . what you like?"

"Yes," she whispers back, stroking my hair. "Love, you don't need to—"

"I want to," I interrupt her. "I want to. Please."

She lowers herself to the mattress and turns onto her back. "I love you," I murmur, and kiss her.

The anxiety doesn't last long. It all feels so good, so right, so sacred—circling licking kisses around her bellybutton, rubbing my face against the softness of her breasts, teasing them gently with my tongue. And when I finally slide my fingers into the narrow valley between her legs, she shows me how to move them against her—how to make her writhe and even moan a little—until she arches against my hand and I drink in her gasps with kisses. I fumble a few times, I know—and everything takes a little longer than I think it *could*—but that's okay. I'll learn. What's important right now is that I can make her happy. That we're together, loving one another, unafraid.

Later, when she turns her back to me so we can spoon, I slip my hand beneath her breast and squeeze gently. She hums. What a privilege it is, to be able to touch her like this. To be able to show the sheer intensity of what I feel.

"We made love, didn't we?" I whisper, my voice thick with fatigue.

"Yes," she murmurs back, pushing closer to me. I imagine that I can feel the atoms of our skin blending together so that there's no longer a barrier between *her* and *me*. So that there's only *us*. "That's exactly what we did."

Working the Night Shift
Therese Szymanski

"Hey, nobody's allowed in here." The big, burly man I had never seen before started to yell at me, then stopped himself. "Oh. You're a girl. Go on."

The naked woman whose ass I'd just been admiring as she bent over, stood, turned and smiled unabashedly at me. She was blonde, but I couldn't tell if she was a natural blonde because, well . . . she was completely shaved between her legs.

I was glad my family wasn't exactly normal. I mean, really, how many folks go to help a hospitalized brother in another state and end up in a situation like this?

"I'm Leeka," she said, coming up to me, running a finger along my collar, and tightening my tie. There'd been a chill in the women's restroom earlier, which the two bachelor party dancers had apparently tried to alleviate by turning both showers on to hot, so the scalding water would heat the air. The result was a much warmer changing room that was rather quite steamy, enough to cause little beads of water to collect and roll down smooth, curvy, luscious skin. "Hey, this isn't a real tie," Leeka said.

"Uh, clip-on," I said. "I never wear clip-ons but if a guard's going to wear a tie she'd better wear a clip-on 'cause otherwise somebody can grab you by it and strangle you. That would be really bad." I could feel my cheeks flush, and that was just one of the places my blood was rushing besides my brain. Her breasts were perky, her nipples hard, and she wasn't exactly crossing her legs in front of me.

"Hm," the other girl, a brunette, said. "You don't have a gun. How're you gonna protect us from all those joes out there?"

"She's got this really big stick," the blonde said, caressing the nightstick that hung at my side. My brain went to some very bad places and I got a bit weak-kneed with the way she ran her soft hand up and down my, er, nightstick. Little did I know at that moment how much time I'd waste during the rest of the night keeping the boys from my big stick, because they wanted to "borrow" it as soon as they saw the girls.

It wasn't even *my* nightstick—I'd had to borrow it from my brother, since I'd left mine in D.C. They'd really have been all over my stick and 'cuffs, since mine were much nicer. "And I've got these," I said, pulling out my borrowed handcuffs.

"Oooo," the blonde said, running a finger over the hard metal.

"Leeka," the brunette whined. "You have to help me decide what to wear!"

"I, uh." I pointed at a stall.

"Heather. Leeka," the boy said, his arms crossed over his broad chest, "you have to get ready. Let her do what she came here to do."

"Oh, Brian," Leeka said. "You never let us have any fun."

I have to admit, I was grateful as a wino who'd just been given a quart of Boone's Farm that the showers were running. Otherwise I'd never be able to do what I'd gone there to do.

I raced from the restroom as soon as I was done, never looking back. It'd been a wicked long time since I'd been around dancers, and these two were just so young and . . . nubile . . . and . . . and . . .

apparently my inner stud had gone out to pasture sometime during the intervening years.

Plus there was the entire "I'm here to do a job and not get some nookie" bit of it all.

I stopped by the bar to grab a bottle of water, which I ensured was not opened before it came to me, even as I observed the male bartender (obviously the boss) with his arm around a female employee. Slender, with long dark hair and eyes; lush, full lips; and just-right makeup. She reminded me a lot of the hot, bad-girl lead from the movie D.E.B.S.

But I didn't like the way they were acting around each other—him grabbing her waist, her giggling and flipping her hair, showing cleavage and pushing against him. So I went back to the office, hoping the boys would be able to behave themselves and not trash the building. After all, I was only there to ensure the safety of the building. I was paid by the party-throwers, but only because the apartment complex made them hire a guard from my brother's security agency if they were to rent the community building for an after-hours party.

Mostly I was here because my sister-in-law really didn't want to be, since she found bachelor parties extremely tiresome to work, because the boys'd get all testosteroney and all. Once she'd found out I'd still be in town, she asked me to work the job (making sure to mention there'd be strippers, because she knew that'd get bonus points with me).

I was there to help the fam, so of course I was both feet in.

Now, I could do without the misogynistic, patriarchal Chaldean men, however. I knew their sort all too well from all the years I'd worked and gone to school here.

And I wanted to get busy with being my old, bad self, a person I'd left behind years before. I wandered out of the office and the bouncer they'd hired, a big, big guy, grinned at me and nodded me in to see the dancers.

Once I stepped into the room, some dude walked up to me. "Here," he said, handing me a hundred dollar bill.

I stared down at it.

"Just look the other way when we smoke," he said.

I brushed past him, ignoring the bill.

Brian, who was overseeing everything while manning the music, grinned at me. "Go on. They do a real good show."

I moseyed on over, but couldn't really see anything through the mass of oversized boys. My presence was soon noticed, however, and I was pushed through to the front of the throng. It was as if the boys liked seeing even a uniformed butch like me watching two hot women stripping and dancing and rubbing up against each other. I really didn't want to be a part of their entertainment.

"Can I borrow this?" some guy said, trying to snag my night-stick, which I instinctively grabbed just before he did.

No matter how much the boys wanted to watch Heather's and Leeka's show—their naked forms, their bodies . . . They wanted also to watch me watching the girls touching each other, caressing each other, French kissing each other and licking each other's skin . . . flesh . . . sweat . . .

Okay, so maybe it was kind of hot.

But really, when they let the boys touch them, hold their naked forms and squeeze their tits, it got a bit too much for me. Boys were rough. Unappreciative. Just squeezing and touching and showing off for each other. Not wanting to make the girls feel good. Not enjoying what the girls were showing . . . giving . . . offering them.

I walked away.

"They always act like they've never seen a naked woman before," Brian said, just as the girls started taking money toward a toy show.

"I am *so* stressed out," Leeka said, following my direction into a corner a few minutes later. "I need a cigarette."

"Really, just five minutes," the short, hairy dude said, following me and grabbing at my nightstick again. "I'll give you twenty bucks!"

Brian pulled out a pack and a lighter. I went to fetch a glass of water from the bartender that the girls could use as an ashtray in this nonsmoking atmosphere.

"Oh, sure," a couple of guys said, moaning and whining. "You're gonna let them smoke inside."

"You want me to make them go outside?" I asked, keeping my back to the girls, giving them some privacy in their nudity. I used my body to keep the boys away from them.

They really had no reply to that.

"So are they your type?" the female bartender asked.

I was one of four females amidst more than a hundred guys but I was The Guard, which was to say that I was The One Wearing Far More Polyester Than Any One Person Ought To. Ever. When I was younger, I felt as if such a uniform gave me power. Now that feeling was gone. I used to be able to make boys in situations like this, and in any fast food restaurant, respect me. Now I used my powers for other reasons, and had lost this particular ability.

Also, I wasn't at my sexy, most confident best. I was wearing my brother's pants. And I was sure the gun belt made me look fat. "Uh, they're okay." I'd been figuring this bartender was straight, given the way she'd been hanging with that other dude earlier, whom I had assumed was her boyfriend. Now, the party was supposed to be a bachelor party, but until I saw the dancers paying special attention to the groom, I'd become sure it was just a blind pig, set up just to charge admission to a drinking party, so no matter what, I reckoned I wasn't scoring tonight.

"Just okay?" she asked.

"I, uh, well, I don't do dancers. It's a long story, really. And quite boring. But I kind of like women with brains and not quite so much silicone and . . . who likely don't have so many social diseases. I prefer to come away from relationships—or even one-night stands—with something other than venereal diseases."

"Well, that's frank and to the point," the woman said, leaning forward on the bar and bringing her arms forward to squeeze her breasts together and show off some mighty fine cleavage. "I'm Angela, by the way." Her gaze suddenly darted to just behind and to the right of me.

"A hundred bucks for just five minutes!"

I beat the dude to the nightstick yet again. He was old enough to be *my* dad, and all these girls were more than a decade younger than me. No wonder he needed my stick. "No," I said, yet again.

He slunk away and I went back to Angela, who was giving me a little, secret sort of smile. *There go my knees again.* "Uh. Hi. Reese. Is me," I said. "That's my name. Think peanut-butter cup." I was sure I could blither just a bit more.

"Ooo, I like Reese's."

I knew I should look at her eyes—into her eyes. Not . . . somewhere else.

"You're gonna miss the toy show," Brian said into my ear.

Angela was straight. I'd seen her with that boy, her boss, after all. "Uh, yeah. Right."

"You go," Angela said. "Come back after, though. When you're done watching."

Just to think, right before I'd left D.C. I'd stood in my bathroom and felt terribly middle-aged as I flossed my teeth. I mean, really, who flosses, except those in dire need of a real life? I'd suddenly realized I needed something to happen to help keep me young and alive.

I needed An Adventure again. *Be careful what you wish for.*

I was careful not to block anyone's view. That meant I stood aside so they'd stop trying to put me front-row center. Hearing the wolf calls was enough to make me want to distance myself from all that was happening around me—that and still having the image of boys holding the girls by their tits in my mind.

"C'mon, why won't you let me borrow it?" the dude-with-no-penis asked reaching for my nightstick again.

When other people visit sick relatives in the hospital, they bring flowers and cards. When I went from D.C. to Detroit to visit my big bro' in the hospital, I took my combat boots. Turns out, I should've also brought my nightstick and handcuffs. Lord knows, my stick wasn't as easily grabbable as this one was.

There really was no response to such a statement—I mean, "No, you cannot use my nightstick to replace the penis you don't actually have," or "I know my stick's bigger than yours," just isn't something I could say in that situation. It'd only instigate a fight or someone trying to strut his nonexistent stuff.

It was only after all of this, and a few guys offering quite repeatedly to buy me lap dances that I finally gave in to one particularly tenacious fellow. I wasn't sure if he was paying for the dance himself, or if he'd taken up a collection, but he kept coming back to me, offering me a dance, and not asking anything of me in return. Really, someone offers you a lap dance with a hot chick when you're really getting hot and bothered, what are you going to say?

So I ended up in the room I'd earlier helped setup for lap dances. Brian told me and the other john the rules (if I'd known another "john" would be in the room, I likely would've kept declining the dance, but . . .), we could touch breasts and ass and . . . well, there was just one area off limits.

Truth be told, I wondered if the laws had changed, or if this particular company just had different rules than what I was accustomed to from my days of managing an adult theatre in the early nineties.

And then the music came on and all those thoughts left my head.

Leeka was naked and on my lap, sliding herself against me. She kept her legs spread over me, the entire time. She started by rubbing herself down on me, grinding on me. She reached for my nightstick as it got in the way, and I removed it.

When she spread her legs around my face, I saw that she was becoming increasingly wet and turned on. And I had yet to touch her. She had to push my face into her breasts, guide my hands down to her ass . . . pull them up over her inner thighs and up to cup her breasts.

I realized what was expected of me and I teased her nipples and looked into her eyes.

She leaned backward, putting her hands on the floor and placing my head between her thighs. I could smell her. And I could see her excitement. She brought my head as close to her pussy as possible without forcing my face into her.

She wiggled and moved ever so slightly to the music, going through the moves she usually went through while giving someone a lap dance.

Maybe her increasing arousal was because I didn't grab, grasp and pinch like others did. I knew, as I quite clearly saw her get wetter and more aroused, that she was getting more turned on— and that it wasn't merely that she was naked with her legs spread around my head.

She gave me what I'm sure most guys would love: An up close and personal look at all of her most private parts. Which she'd already been displaying for everyone present that night. Maybe I got something extra special, but it lost meaning because she shared so much so casually.

I was hot and disgusted with myself when I left that room. I'd just had my face between the thighs of a stripper. Bought for me by a man. But she was hot. I couldn't help my physical responses, so . . . I was in a right wicked Catch-22.

It made it really easy to turn down another lap dance, but then my dance patron slipped me a couple of bucks and told me to get a drink and tip the bartender.

So I got a bottle of water and tried to walk away, but he sent me back.

I said I couldn't.

He didn't accept that.

So I went back to Angela and said, "I'm supposed to do this." I leaned forward and stuffed the bills into her cleavage.

"Then I should do this," she said, taking a deep breath as she pushed her breasts together with her arms, really showing off her cleavage.

I stared for a moment. Then I looked away. She was really hot.

"I'm new to this," she said, reaching out, over the bar, to lay a hand on my shoulder. "I've never flirted with a woman before."

"So why are you now?" The words were out before I could double-think them.

"Because you're hot."

I think I chortled. Whatever noise I made, I can't spell. But then I said, "I look short, squat and polyestered in this uniform."

That's when my sister-in-law showed up and all the boys were big with the "It's all good," lines and lies and my night got a lot more difficult. If I had been myself when I was 18 it would've been no big, but now, her checkup had me trying to cover-up any mistakes I'd made.

But later on, near the end of the night, after so many folks had been kicked out, and most of the cleaning was done, I realized I could smell Heather, Leeka and Angela on my uniform. *Little did I know I'd remember that when my sister-in-law commented two days later that she didn't need to wash that uniform.*

It was when my hands were chapped from the cleaning, when my mind was boggled from looking for cleaning stuff, when the illegal card game was down to a dozen folks in the lobby and I'd blocked the front door from the wandering gaze of passing police, that I was posting something fun online that I felt someone enter my space.

I could see her reflection in the monitor, so I kept at my posting. Even as she walked up behind me, wrapped her arms around me, and rested her chin on my shoulder.

"You've turned down all drinks," she said into my ear. "I haven't."

"So what does that mean?"

She slid her hands down to cup my breasts. "It means I'm horny as hell and I know none of those boys out there can take care of it."

I pulled her hands away from me and turned around to face her. "So it's just the alcohol talking, eh?"

"Like hell you know," she said, reaching up to twine her fingers in my hair and pull my face to hers. "You have no idea how much you've been turning me on all night long. I saw how you were around Heather and Leeka: Protective." She ran her hands up my arms, under my short-sleeved shirt. "And you're strong, with nice muscles, but you didn't get all stupid around naked women like everyone else here."

"I'm really running out of self-control for tonight, though," I said, putting my hands on her waist—to hold her away or pull her closer, I didn't know.

"Good." She leaned up, flicked her tongue out to lick my lips, and as soon as she slipped it between them, I nipped it.

"Bitch," she said, caressing my lips with her smiling ones.

I gave up. I kissed her back. Wrapping an arm around her waist and pulling her in tight, I kissed her, then went inside her, running my tongue alongside hers, playfully nipping. With all of the blatant and open sexuality of the night, what I'd really wanted was this sort of intimacy—kissing and gentle, easy touching.

"So you want me, huh?" I said.

"God, yes," she said, pushing herself up against me.

She was just a straight girl playing with me, but I'd call her on her bluff. I kissed her roughly, shoving my tongue into her mouth as I picked her up, pushed my thigh between her legs, and threw her against a wall.

She rode my thigh as I kissed and suckled on her neck.

"Yes, Reese, yes," she said, pushing my hands down to grab her ass, then slowly drawing them up to her breasts, even as I pushed harder and harder against her cunt, so hard that her feet left the floor. It was like she wanted me all over her. And this time, I wanted it—she wasn't the A-ticket ride at Disney.

But it was also as if she was emulating one of the dancer's lap dances. Like she was making me be the man to her woman, but I was a woman as well. This woman was letting me somewhere special, giving something to me even as she wanted what I could give her. What she really wanted was to dance in a give-and-take.

I tried to control myself as I lowered her to the floor, trying to overcome my own urgency and horniness as I reminded myself how good she felt, how soft she was, how wonderful she smelled. I ran my lips lightly over her earlobe. "What do you want?"

"You."

"So you say. You ever been with a woman before?"

"N-n-no," she gasped, exposing her neck to me. She kept trying to control my hands, so I held hers by her sides while I kissed and nibbled on her neck and earlobes, licking along her collarbone and back up until our lips met again.

Almost.

She'd been running on alcohol and adrenaline earlier, but now I was making it all stop, making it all real.

I pulled back from her, looking into her beautiful green eyes. I released her arms so I could take her face in my hands. I brushed my fingers back through her hair. "Angela . . . Are you sure you want this?"

"Reese, I'm no virgin or little girl. As soon as you walked in . . . Well . . ." She took my hands in hers and intertwined our fingers. "I saw your hands." She unzipped her tight jeans. "Fuck me. Hard."

I met her gaze, then grabbed both her wrists in one of my hands, holding her arms up above her head, and shoved my thigh between her legs so she opened her legs further and moaned. Hard.

I didn't need to hold back. I knew what she needed, and I'd provide it. I shoved up her top, pushing her bra up with it, so I could fondle her naked breasts, feeling her hardening nipples under my palms as I continued kissing her ears, neck and lips, even as I slid my hands into her panties.

She pushed herself against my thigh even harder. "God."

"Don't call me god. Yet." I loved how soft and warm and wet and accommodating she was.

"Somebody could . . ." she gasped, "walk in." She didn't push me away, she didn't stop riding my thigh.

"Yes, they could," I said. I pushed her jeans and panties down to her knees, and shoved my leg into her cunt again. She smelled so good. I knew what she wanted, and I'd give it to her. My need was centered on making her feel really, really good, and I had a great big need to fulfill.

"Oh fuck."

"They can walk in anywhere here, now. Are you more worried about them seeing you naked, or about them seeing you with another woman's hand in your cunt?"

"God, Reese, I've wanted this . . . for so long—"

I left a nice hickey on her neck, and raced my right hand down her body, tickling lightly over her skin, down to her pussy. I wouldn't make her come too soon, after all, the teasing is half the fun.

"When I saw you tonight, I knew I needed to have you touch me like this." She pushed my hand between her legs.

I pulled my thigh back and slipped my fingers down to fondle her swollen pussy. I slid them up and down her wetness, slowly coating them. Coating my entire hand with her juices.

I kissed her lips, her neck, down her cleavage till I sucked and nibbled at each of her tits, lightly biting each nipple in turn. I kept my free hand moving over her flesh, reminding her just how naked and exposed she was.

And I slipped a finger, two, then three into her, even while flicking her clit with my thumb, feeling it up and down and pushing it back and forth as I fucked her and sucked her.

I stood and whispered into her ear, "I'm about to shove my entire fist into you."

"Ahhhhh . . ."

"And you're gonna like it. A lot." I bit her ear lightly. "I'm gonna fuck you like you ain't ever been fucked before." I mighta been polyestered, but I still knew what she wanted.

"Uh!" She struggled slightly against me, but I kissed her and bit her neck while slipping a fourth finger into her and tweaking a nipple, hard.

She groaned in pain, but didn't struggle against me. Didn't push me away. I thought about worrying, but, she didn't stop me.

I dropped to my knees and licked her pussy—all the way up, then all the way down, before flicking her clit with my tongue and teasing it with my teeth.

Then I shoved my fist into her.

All the way.

And she pushed away. She pulled from me and slammed herself against the wall. But I was all the way inside her.

So I continued to lick her, playing with her clit, her pussy, even while I moved my fist around inside her warmth, feeling her surrounding me, feeling her soft insides all around my fist.

She was rigid against the wall. Her eyes shut. Her legs spread.

She was on the brink of orgasm. Her coming for me was a gift to me, and I intended to take it for all it was worth—I'd make her gift pay back. Triple. After all, my sexual/pleasing-woman sense was driving.

I caressed a tit with my free hand, feeling her up and then playing with her nipple.

Her eyes were glued shut and a tear dropped from one. "Yes," she said.

I opened my hand inside her.

"Please."

I fondled her insides.

"Fuck."

She was all but squatting on my arm, sweat pouring off her. I went to town with my mouth. Licking, sucking, flicking.

She rode my fist, my face.

I started fucking her with my fist, pulling almost all the way out before shoving it back in, down past my wrist.

"Oh god, oh god, oh god!" She screamed, her insides tightening on my fist so hard I thought she might break my hand, even as her come drained out of her.

"I think—oh, no, not in here," Leeka said from behind me. I

turned briefly to see her and Heather stop in the doorway, keeping anyone behind them outside of the room.

I glanced up just long enough to see Angela notice them as well. They obviously just wanted to see her come.

So I made her come.

Maybe I shoulda told her my real name and number.

I'm sure the next time I floss I'd wish I'd done just that.

Unrequited
Kristina Wright

What I remember most about that weekend with Julie was the couch. Even when I refuse to let myself remember the other stuff, because remembering the good also makes me remember how I got my heart broken, I still remember that damned couch. It was bright orange vinyl, a glossy, saggy relic left over from the seventies and destined to finish out its life as the crash pad for Julie's friends. I spent one long, agonizing night on that orange couch and I can still remember the crackle and smell of the vinyl.

"It came with the apartment," Julie told me as she showed me around her small one-bedroom place. "Is it okay?"

I tried to smile, but the couch didn't look very comfortable. Still, it was the best, the only, choice I had. "Awesome. Thanks."

Julie had been the first one I'd called when I hit Atlanta. Truth was, Julie was the only one I'd thought to call, the only one I'd wanted to see. I was twenty-two and running south—nine hundred miles away from a nasty family situation to the one place I felt safe—Julie's arms. I'd been in love with her almost since the day I'd met her, but she had no idea how I felt. As far as she was concerned, we were best friends.

Only friends.

"I'd let you share my room, but Kevin moved back in last night." She gave me a lascivious little wink that made my stomach flip-flop.

Kevin was her on-again, off-again boyfriend. Things were on again, apparently.

"The couch is great," I said, eyeing the orange monstrosity dubiously. "I won't stay long."

That last part cost me a lot to say. I wanted to stay forever. I wanted her to want me to stay forever.

"Oh, please. You can stay as long as you want." She handed me a pillow and blanket and grinned. "I'd better get to bed. Kevin wants to make up."

I tossed all night, the vinyl couch squeaking with every restless movement I made. Behind the closed bedroom door, I heard Julie and Kevin. The walls were as thin as my flimsy cotton T-shirt, so I heard every whimper. Every giggle. Every moan. I pulled the pillow over my head, pressing my cheek against the cool vinyl couch. God, I was tired, but the sounds coming from the next room—and the continuous loop of images playing in my fevered imagination—wouldn't let me rest.

It was a long, long time before I fell asleep to the soft sound of Julie's breathy moans. I dreamed I was trapped inside my own heart, pounding out the rhythm of my heartbeat as I tried to escape. My heart was made out of orange vinyl.

I woke at dawn, blinking away the panic of not knowing where I was. Then I remembered. Julie. A moment later, I felt like I'd been sucker punched in the gut. Kevin. I lay there on the couch, my sweaty cheek still pressed against the hideous vinyl, pillow flung halfway across the room. I rolled onto my back and groaned as every muscle in my body protested.

I heard a soft sound, little more than a catch of breath. For a moment, I thought they were fucking again. My stomach clenched until I realized what I was hearing. Crying.

I didn't know what to do. My first instinct was to go to Julie, but I knew better than to get into the middle of a lovers' quarrel. A couple of minutes passed and those soft crying sounds were tearing me to shreds. I couldn't just sit there on the couch and wait for them to come out, so I padded to the bathroom and started the shower. The water did little to soothe me. I needed to know if Julie was all right.

I finished my shower and pulled back the curtain. Julie was standing in the open doorway, staring at me. She quickly looked away as I reached for my towel and wrapped it around me.

"Damn, girl. You nearly gave me a heart attack."

Her eyes were red-rimmed and puffy, her jet black hair pulled back into a tight ponytail that made her look younger. She forced a weak smile. "Sorry." She balled up the hem of her faded black Journey concert T-shirt in her hand, then smoothed it out again. "I didn't mean to scare you."

I could feel her gaze on me as I stood in front of the sink. "Forget about it. Everything okay?"

She met my eyes in the mirror as I combed the tangles out of my long hair. "Kevin's gone. He never intended to stay. He just wanted to get laid."

The breath whooshed from my lungs, but the relief was bittersweet as I watched Julie's reflection crumble. I turned to say something comforting. What, I didn't know.

She didn't give me a chance to say anything. She reached for me and I pulled her into my arms, my wet hair trailing down her shoulder as she sobbed against my neck. I hugged her awkwardly, unused to the feeling of her body against mine. We'd been friends for five years, but neither of us was a touchy-feely kind of person. She clung to me like she was drowning and I was a life preserver. I held on, feeling the softness of her small breasts against me, the sharp angle of her hipbone where it pressed against me. There was nothing sexual or intimate about our embrace, but a small part of me thrilled to be able to hold her like this, to comfort her.

"Come on, you need to sit down," I whispered softly when her wracking sobs threatened to shake the fillings loose from my teeth.

She whimpered and shook her head against the crook of my neck.

"It's okay," I said. "I won't let go. Okay?"

She just nodded.

Wrapped around me the way she was, it took some maneuvering to get us out of the bathroom and across the hall to her bedroom. The sheets were tangled and the room smelled of male and sex, but I'd be damned if I was going to haul her out to that hideous orange couch. I sat on the edge of the bed and half dragged her across my lap, cradling her against my chest as she cried.

"Ssh, it's all right," I soothed, making gentle circles on her bony back. "It'll be okay."

She shook her head against me and I realized my towel had slipped below my breasts. "No," she breathed against my skin. "It'll never be okay."

There was no way to adjust my towel without moving her and I wouldn't move her until she didn't need me anymore. So we sat there, her face against the swell of my breast, her arms wrapped tight around my waist. I rocked her like a child, even though she was four inches taller than me, as if I could give her something she needed.

Sobs gave way to soft tears as I stroked her hair and whispered nonsensical things. My skin had become desensitized to her touch to the point that I didn't know where she stopped and I began. It was only when I felt the gentle, insistent tugging on my nipple that I realized Julie had stopped crying.

A quick intake of breath, my hand stilling on her back, as I tried to figure out what the hell had just happened.

She released my nipple and looked up at me, wide-eyed, tears filling her eyes and spilling over to slide down her blotchy cheeks. "I'm sorry. I don't know why. I just—"

I pressed her head gently to my chest so she wouldn't see I was crying, too. "It's okay. I'm here. Whatever you need."

I meant it.

Silently, her mouth closed around my nipple. I sighed, holding her closer, my hand still making gentle circles on her back. She tugged harder and I whimpered, feeling a corresponding tingle in my clit as her lips and tongue coaxed me to feel things I shouldn't feel.

Somehow, we ended up stretched out on the bed, my damp towel balled up in the small of my back, Julie's leg thrown over mine. She let my nipple slide out of her mouth with a wet slurp and covered my breast with her hand. I twisted toward her, our legs tangled, my cunt throbbing.

Julie's T-shirt rode up and I reached out to tentatively stroke the curve of her hip, aroused beyond measure by the contrast of her olive complexion against my pale skin. I stroked her hip, then slid my hand up under her T-shirt and let my fingertips glide up over her rib cage to her breast. Unsure of her response, I pulled back, my hand settling in the curve of her waist.

"Don't stop," she murmured into the hollow of my throat. "Touch me. Make me forget him."

It was all the encouragement I needed.

Dappled sunlight fell across the bed, across our bodies, as I reached under her T-shirt and caressed her breasts, feeling her nipples harden under my fingers. She whimpered and arched against me and I tugged her shirt up, over her breasts and stared at her tight, brown nipples. She pushed against me and I leaned down, sucking first one nipple, then the other, in my mouth and squeezing her breasts as I did. I could have lain there all day, doing just that, but she reached for my hand and guided it under the waistband of her panties.

I will never forget how hot and wet she was. So fucking wet and hot I could barely stand to touch her.

"For me," I whispered softly, trailing kisses down her body, wanting to tattoo her skin with my lips. "For me."

I hooked my fingers in the sides of her white cotton panties and tugged them down her long legs. I settled between her thighs, breathing in her scent, a combination of arousal and latex. I blocked that last part from my mind as I stared at her cunt. Her pretty, pretty cunt, opening for me, swelling and darkening for me.

"For me."

I reached out and traced the lips of her cunt—from where they met at her clit, down to her perineum and back up the other side. My finger trembled on her clit, my breath coming in quick little pants. It was part arousal, part fear. I was so afraid she would make me stop, change her mind.

She didn't.

Her mouth opened wordlessly when I closed my lips around her swollen clit and licked. Gently at first, then harder, until my entire world was this succulent bit of flesh against my tongue.

"Mine," I breathed against her clit, as if saying it could somehow make true.

She arched against me, trapping my head between her legs as she clawed at the sheets. Wrapping my arm around her thigh to anchor her to my mouth, I plunged my tongue into her cunt to draw her juices back up to her clit. I thrust two fingers inside her and fucked her hard while I licked and sucked her clit. When I whimpered, she trembled at the vibrations of my mouth.

Her body quivered beneath me. Her hands fisted in my hair as she moaned, pulling me closer, not pushing me away. Almost unconsciously, I was grinding against the sheets wadded up between my legs, my clit as hard and sensitive as hers. I sucked her clit as I worked myself toward orgasm, in the same bed she'd fucked her boyfriend. I moaned into her cunt, my mouth all but devouring her as I came.

She went still then. Silent. I panted, my body still throbbing. I licked her steadily with quick, firm strokes until the walls of her cunt contracted on my fingers and her juices flowed over my tongue. Then she was coming, and coming hard. Coming for me.

She gasped something as she came. One word. One name.

Not mine.

"Kevin."

Forever
Amie M. Evans

After nine years, I still stand behind my cocky promise to Wendy of "forever." And I relish the way I offered myself to her that night. Nine years. Incredible, because when we first met, neither of us was looking for more than some good sex and maybe a casual relationship. Both of us were cautious—her even more so than I—about committing to anything more than dinner. We dated, á la carte, for six months before finally acknowledging that we were, after all, a monogamous couple. The irony in this is neither of us had actually dated anyone else in four months.

Our relationship has always been the kind in which you feel you've known the each other forever, and yet there is something new to discover about the other every day. Even now, after nine years, when we can repeat verbatim each other's favorite childhood stories, finish each other's sentences, and anticipate correctly 99 percent of the time each other's reactions to any given situation, we surprise each other with new facts about our lives and tastes. My mother says Wendy and I are linked through a past life—old souls connected throughout time—and this is why we have come together. A truly romantic friend of mine argues that we were fated to be together, destined to meet—that it was preordained.

But I am neither a traditionally romantic person nor an Eastern spiritualist; I simply believe we were lucky. Lucky to find each other. Lucky that things worked out at all. And lucky to have had it hang together so well for so long. When you think about all the tiny, mundane things that affect a meeting, a coupling, a long-term relationship, it becomes clear that nothing short of pure luck mixed with hard work and a little chance could ever possibly explain success.

The odds were, after all, stacked against us. For starters, she's 13 years older than me. To put that into perspective, I started kindergarten the same year she started college. It is more probable she would be dating my mother than me. Also consider that I had just moved to Boston, where we never ran into each other in social situations because we didn't travel in the same circles. So, if it wasn't for my complete inability to navigate Boston (navigating new cities is a skill, I might add, that I normally excel at), I would never have purchased anything at the upscale pet boutique where she worked, let alone have become a regular customer. But as it was, I had four cats who needed food. Wendy's pet store—where I first saw her—the only place I ever saw her—was the *only* pet store I knew how to find with any consistency. She never noticed me until I resorted to an underhanded femme trick: I sent her a red pepper plant with a request for a call and dinner. She thought the whole thing was an elaborate joke by her co-workers. So, perhaps it was destiny that brought us together, because the very fact she called is incredible.

Tonight, I slipped a black, lacy skirt with a late forties white petticoat over my thigh-high stockings and garter belt and a button-down black cashmere sweater over my push-up bra. I remembered that, back then, when dressed in jeans and a T-shirt—desperately hoping to pass as a "real lesbian"—Wendy had dismissed me as not being potential dating material because she was looking for a femme. It's silly now, when I think back on it, that I wanted her to see me as something other than what I was, and even sillier that what I was was what she wanted. Silly, until I remember how even now femme is often read as straight or, worse yet, as a traitor co-opting heterosexuality. Silly, until I, once again, am not taken seriously by my sisters because of my lipstick and high heels. So maybe it was two old souls recognizing each other that allowed all of this to get started. For us to work through and overcome the misconceptions, misrepresentations and general folly that is identity under pressure.

But now, nine years later, no one would suspect we weren't meant to be together as Wendy slips into her blue, shark-skin dinner jacket, a tie and freshly pressed black dress shirt and pants. She is adorable to me, with her slender, hipless body, shockingly blonde spiky hair, piercing blue eyes and callused hands. In all her punky butchness, she is the love of my life.

Our nine-year anniversary was special. We decided to exchange rings in a private ceremony, just us. This is before gay marriage in Massachusetts when our friends were having lavish or simple public ceremonies to exchange vows. It is Boston in early November 2003. The days can be deceiving with their sun-filled skies and mild breezes, but the evenings, when the sun goes down and takes its warmth with it, are chilly and crisp and full of the promise that winter and snow will soon arrive—a gentle reminder that this is, after all, Puritan New England.

In the entryway to our home, Wendy helps me into my floor-length, fake-fur coat and picks up the bag containing two cham-pagne flutes, a small bottle of Brut and a box with our rings, fresh from the engraver. The word "Forever" and our names are carved into the inside of each ring. "Forever . . ." arrogant perhaps after only nine years, but our confidence isn't blind, joyful youth. We are both wide-awake, experienced adults who entered this relationship with slow, deliberate steps. I am now in my thirties and she is in her forties. We are comfortable with the arrogance of forever.

We go out into the cool air and get into our 1983 Datsun 280 ZX. It's a family heirloom her father first purchased as a midlife-crisis car. Her brother-in-law drove it afterward, who then passed it down to her. Wendy is lovingly restoring it, and we seldom drive it because it is designed for speed—low to the ground with a long, aerodynamic hood and bucket seats with a console between them. It is much less comfortable than our Ford Taurus with a bench seat in front, which is perfect for sex in the car.

But I have a plan and have insisted we take the Z.

When we were first dating, we spent a lot of time at Manray, a hip, trendy club in Cambridge with a goth/fetish theme on Friday nights. Dressed in sexy fetish wear made of leather or latex, we'd go for drinks, dancing to trace and industrial music, and to-see-and-be-seen. Evenings at the club always ended with sex in the car in the parking garage two blocks away. We seldom go there now, having lost the need for activity-driven interactions years ago. And while I sometimes miss the excitement of the club environment and the fun of dressing up in costumes, I more often miss the sex in the car that ended the night of dancing. It is to this garage I direct her to now.

She takes the time-stamped ticket from the machine and the gate opens, allowing us access to the first floor.

"Go to the roof," I tell her.

The garage is made up of four stories of concrete ramps with parking on either side. We drive past rows and rows of empty spots as the daytime workers have already left and the nighttime club goers have not yet arrived. There are two other cars parked on the roof. Most likely, at this time of night, they belong to the garage attendants because who else would park this far up with so many open spots below? Wendy pulls into a space facing the river and turns off the car. She looks at me, raising one eyebrow in question as I hand her the bottle of Brut, first pouting then flashing her a smile. Wendy smiles back, shakes her head, then opens the car door and places one foot on the concrete floor. Leaning out she holds the bottle of champagne against her thigh and with both thumbs pushes on the cork until it finally gives way with a familiar pop. Turning back to me, she hands me the cork, which I drop into

and the other bent at the knee. I let go of her arm and support my upper body on my left elbow. I cock my head and pose again, knowing she can see my cleavage at the top of the sweater and if she were to bend just slightly she'd be able to see up my skirt where the stockings and garter belt frame my bare cunt. "Then look," I taunt her, "if you can't guess."

She laughs, then steps closer, grabbing both of my ankles and pulling me toward her so my legs are on either side of her. I rest my feet on the bumper as she pushes my knees open and slides her hand up the length of my stockinged leg. When her fingers encounter the strap of the garter belt, she pauses to pull on it gently, then moans and continues up my thigh and into my bare, wet cunt.

"Fresh," I say, slapping at her, but she catches my wrist with her free hand and pins it to the hood before I am able to make contact with her face.

"No panties? Where could they have gone?" she says as she slips one finger into me.

I moan.

"You're so exposed without panties, so open and wet." She inserts another finger, thrusting into me harder this time. "Such a bad girl. Someone who didn't know better would think you wanted to get fucked." She pulls both fingers out and works my clit in a hard circular motion.

"Someone who didn't know better would think you wanted to fuck me," I say with mock sarcasm.

"Hmm." She removes her hand from between my legs and releases my wrist. As I look up into the dark sky full of stars, I can hear the zipper on her pants slide down and imagine her pulling the 8-inch dildo out of the zipper opening and rebuckling her belt to hold it in place. "Luckily for me, you aren't someone who knows better," she says, grabbing both of my ankles and sliding me to the end of the hood.

I am exactly at the correct height for her to fuck me, which isn't luck at all, because I had checked last week to make sure of this fact before insisting on taking the Z, just in case she decided to pack.

I place my legs on her shoulders and she leans into me, unbuttoning the front of my cashmere sweater. With the help of my push-up bra, even on my back I have cleavage. Wendy buries her face in the valley of my breasts. Her flesh is warm against mine. She pulls the lace demi-cups to the side, exposing my hard nipples and the soft fleshy, swells of my breasts. Wendy takes a nipple into her mouth, sucks on it, pulls on the ring that runs through it, and bites the hardening flesh gently. She licks and kisses her way across my chest to the other nipple, where she repeats the process. In her wake she leaves wetness that the cold air turns into a stream of goose bumps across my excited skin.

I feel the head of the dildo against my labia, then the pressure as it enters my cunt. Wendy slides in slowly until the whole length of it is inside of me. She grabs my hips to hold me in place and prevent me from sliding, then slams into me. Her strokes are firm and sure. She's familiar with the terrain and the tool. Wendy pulls out until just the tip is inside of me, then plunges back in, once again burying the entire dildo. I moan more loudly with each stroke. I am excited by the fact that we are breaking the law by fucking in such a public place and even more excited by the sensation her belt buckle causes on each inward stroke when it hits my clit.

"Fuck me," I say, grabbing her hair and pulling her closer to me, and she grunts as she pounds into me harder. I feel the width of the dildo fill me up, then leave me empty with each stroke. I am sure the next inward plunge will make me come as my clit swells from the contact with her buckle. She locks her mouth on my nipple. Sucking hard, she works it with her tongue as she thrusts into me. The car rocks slightly with each inward stroke she takes.

"Come for me," she orders, and her words push me over the top as she thrusts into me. I come hard, squeezing my fingers into her arms as she thrusts one last time before collapsing on top of me as my orgasm pulses through me.

The car shakes and her glass, half full, tumbles to the concrete ground, shattering on impact. We both look in that direction, startled at the noise and suddenly how unaware we have been of our surroundings. We laugh, realizing what has caused the glass to fall and create the distraction.

"We should go before anyone catches us," I say.

"Yeah." She kisses me, then pulls out.

I button my sweater as she removes the dildo from her pants. Wendy helps me off of the car and wraps the coat around my shoulders. She opens the door and tosses the dildo into the empty bag, then grabs the box containing our rings while I grab my champagne glass. We return to the front of the car and I place the glass on the hood. She kisses me on the forehead, then opens the box. Our matching rings sit inside on a velvet lining. Wendy removes the one with her name on it and hands me the one with my name on it. Placing the box on the hood, she pulls me in close to her.

"I pledge my love to you forever," Wendy says, slipping the silver band on my finger.

"And I pledge my life, my love, my everything to you forever," I say, slipping a nearly identical ring on her finger.

We kiss with our bodies pressed against each other's—a lifetime together before us, the possibilities endless—then each take a sip of the last of the Brut.

Wendy deposits the empty champagne bottle and the bits of glass into the trash near the stairwell exit while I add the box and the remaining glass to the dildo in the bag. We get back into the car. As she drives down the ramps, I notice more cars have filled up the spaces that were empty before. People have started to arrive to go to the clubs or to eat. She hands the attendant our ticket and $3 and he opens the gate. We have a dinner reservation at an Italian restaurant in the North End that is the home to the city's best lobster ravioli and a wandering accordion player who serenades lovers. Our anniversary celebration and our lives together have just started.

A Night Like No Other
Lynn Ames

I waited in the airport and paced, unsure what I would say or how I would react when I finally saw Marina in person for the first time. My stomach fluttered with nerves. I knew I wanted her to be The One even though she'd told me we had no future together and that she didn't want to hurt me by leading me to believe otherwise. I knew I wanted her to be the one because her e-mails already had me desperately in love with her mind and her heart. I knew I wanted her to be the one even before she'd sent me that incredible picture of her coming out of the surf in the black bikini, water droplets beading on her perfect skin.

The crowd coming out past security was thick, but I would've known her anywhere. She was even more beautiful than her picture. I was instantly wet. She smiled and I was lost—lost and irrevocably in love.

"Hi. Nice sign," she said, pointing to the piece of paper I held aloft. "And that's Queen Marina to you. Princess, pfft, really." She winked and, catching me completely off-guard, drew me into a body-tingling hug.

"Hi," I breathed into her nearby ear. "I can't believe you're really here." It was a start.

"You've got a beautiful smile, anyone ever tell you that?"

My whole body was still singing from the hug, even after she pulled back. Those incredibly expressive brown eyes, the high cheekbones, the body to die for and the heavenly smell. I realized she was smiling at me knowingly, waiting for me to say something. What had she asked me again? *Oh, yeah*. I blushed.

She shook her head. "You are too cute for words. Shall we?" She took me by the arm and led the way out of the airport.

It was late when we arrived at the hotel in midtown Manhattan. She had made me promise there would be two double beds in the room. Somehow I hoped she'd changed her mind. She hadn't. To say I was mildly disappointed would've been an understatement. Still I waited for Marina to choose a bed, and I dropped my duffle bag onto the other without complaint. I thought I was doing pretty well until she came out of the bathroom wearing red silk boxers and a matching top.

My mouth went dry, all moisture in my body having pooled elsewhere. I crossed my legs tightly and stifled a groan.

"Your turn," she said brightly.

"I . . . I think I'll take a quick shower," I said, hastily throwing together my toiletries and nightclothes. Two nights of this. I didn't know if I could take it.

I let the cool spray wash over my trembling limbs. I reminded myself that she only wanted friendship. What was it she'd said?

"Justine, we're at different places in our lives; I love you, but I can't go back where you are, and you shouldn't try to jump ahead to where I am. It just wouldn't work."

That was all well and good, but it did nothing to diminish my love. Not only that, I was incapable of controlling my body's reaction to her. I wanted her so much it hurt.

I soaped my torso, my nipples taut and sensitive as my fingertips brushed over them with the body wash. I gasped, pinching my right nipple. My left hand stroked its way down to where my clitoris throbbed painfully.

I nearly came at the first touch. Seeing her that way, as I had imagined her so many times in my dreams, hit me hard. I'd thought I was prepared for the proximity. Clearly, I'd been wrong. A vision of her emerging from the bathroom played in my mind's eye, and I swore I could smell her perfume. The climax ripped through me, and I bit my lip to avoid crying out.

When I returned to the room half an hour later, having done my best to compose myself, she was asleep. Her hair, long and silky, played across the pillow, the darkness of it in sharp contrast to the white pillowcase. Her leg, sun-kissed and golden, was thrown carelessly over the covers. She looked like an angel.

I tiptoed to my bed, pulled back the covers, and slid in, snapping off the light over the headboard. In the darkness, I heard her mumble, "Sorry I'm such a party pooper. I'm whipped."

"That's okay," I said, as the huskiness of her voice seeped in through every pore.

I dreamed that she came to me. I watched in amazement as she slowly unbuttoned her top, cradled her breasts in her palms and licked her lips seductively. She knelt on the bed and crawled toward me on all fours, her breasts swaying. The look of intent in her eyes was unmistakable.

"I want you, Justine," she said seductively. "I want to be the first to really make love to you, the first to bring you to orgasm."

"Yes, I want that, too. I want you more than I've ever wanted anything in my life. Take me, please," I begged. As I felt her mouth close over me, I arched into her and moaned.

"Hey. Hey, Justine. You okay?"

"Mmm." Her hand was warm on my shoulder. *My shoulder?* I shot up in bed, narrowly avoiding a collision with her face. "Wha?"

"Shh. It's okay," she said, laying a hand on my shoulder.

Did she know what I'd been dreaming? *God.* I swallowed hard, still trembling, my body thrumming with desire, demanding satisfaction. I didn't trust myself to speak.

She stroked my hair, whispering soothing words in my ear. I thought I'd go mad.

"I . . ." I cleared my throat. "I'm okay."

She backed away but remained sitting on the side of the bed facing me, her thigh pressed against mine. "Do you have nightmares often?"

"Nightma . . . Oh, um, sometimes." It was the truth, although the only thing bad about this dream was being awakened too soon.

"Are you gonna be okay now?"

"Yeah. Yeah, I'm fine. Thanks." I smiled at her briefly. "I'm sorry I woke you."

"No problem. I'm a very light sleeper. If you need me, I'll be right over there." She inclined her head toward the other bed, concern etched in her features.

If I need you, will you stay with me? I wanted to ask the question out loud but knew I'd be taking shameless advantage of her. I couldn't bring myself to do it. I nodded and watched her return to her bed.

I spent what little was left of the night tossing and turning—afraid to fall deeply asleep lest I have another mind-blowing dream.

"You sure you're up for a show and dinner?" she asked as we brunched at Ellen's Stardust Diner.

"Of course, I've been looking forward to it."

"You must be exhausted."

I was, but I wasn't about to admit it. Looking into those sparkling eyes, I wanted to give her the world. The idea to see a Broadway show had been hers, and I would've done anything to fulfill her wish.

We went to the TKTS booth in the middle of Times Square

and queued up with hundreds of interesting characters. Marina, an expert on New York City, assured me it was the best way to get half-price same-day tickets to Broadway shows, and the people watching was well worth braving the long line. She let me pick the show; I went for *Beauty and the Beast*. It mirrored how I felt about our relationship.

Not that I considered myself a beast, but I felt as though I'd been a prisoner in my own castle until Marina came into my life. For the last several years, I'd been wondering if I was frigid—I'd never found anyone who could move me. Marina, on the other hand, could make me wet with a word in an e-mail. I sighed. Having her by my side for thirty-six glorious hours was both a torture and a joy. I wouldn't have traded it for anything in the world.

We sat in the third row center; I'd never been so close to the stage. When she took my hand during the second act, my heart stuttered. The softness of her skin, the way our fingers naturally melded together—it felt so right.

I asked myself why she would make such a gesture if all she wanted was friendship. Was it friendly to hold someone's hand in the theater?

When the show was over, she withdrew her hand. I felt the loss all the way down to my toes. She bumped my shoulder. "Did you enjoy the show?" she asked, her eyes twinkling with excitement.

"Very much. I especially loved the second act." I winked at her. She just smiled and led us out the side exit. I knew she wasn't trying to tease me intentionally—at least I didn't think so—but she was driving me insane. I wondered if she knew that and was enjoying the game.

We shared a marvelous dinner at Carmello's around the corner from the theater. Twice she leaned over and fed me from her fork. I returned the favor, my eyes mesmerized by her tongue, her lips, her throat. I spent long minutes lost in her gaze, daydreaming about what could be, if only she'd let it happen.

Afterward, on the way back to the hotel, she held my hand again. If I hadn't wanted her so badly, it might have been enough.

When she came directly toward me in the hotel room wearing those red boxers and that button-down top with the top three buttons undone, my heart stopped beating.

"I had a great day, did you?" she asked, standing less than a breath away from me.

"It was magical," I managed to reply.

"Thank you." She reached up and kissed me softly on the forehead, enveloping me in a sweet hug.

I closed my eyes and savored the sensation.

"Is this okay?" she asked.

"Mmm hmm," I answered, afraid my voice would fail me if I actually tried to form words. My heart, which had begun beating again, was practically jumping out of my chest. I was sure she could feel it against her breasts.

"Good night, Justine. Sleep well."

"You too," I said, even as my body was screaming at her to stay.

I lay awake for several hours. My body was impossibly aroused by that one simple hug, and no matter what I tried, I couldn't quench the fire that burned within. She'd said we had no future together. I accepted her position, even as I disagreed. She'd said it wouldn't be fair to me. Was that her decision to make? I would've given anything—everything—to lay with her for a night, to know the taste of her, to hold her in my arms. I listened to her soft, even breathing . . . and made up my mind.

Quietly, I pulled back the covers, swung my legs over the side, and crossed to the empty side of her bed. For several minutes, I simply stood there on shaky legs, watching her sleep. My palms were damp. So were my panties. I reached out, wanting to brush a stray hair from her face. I pulled back before making contact. Finally, I looked at the digital clock on the bedside table: 2:46 a.m. I was running out of time.

As carefully as I could, I slid underneath her sheets. I was afraid to breathe, lest I wake her and send her screaming into the night. I propped myself up on my elbow and memorized her face. The strong jaw, the cute little nose and those full, luscious lips. Unable to contain myself anymore, I reached over, gently tracing the sensuous curve of her lips.

Taking perhaps the biggest risk of my life, I whispered huskily, "I'm so hot for you."

I'm not sure what I thought would happen, but her next move both shocked and aroused me beyond words. Slowly, she opened her lips, running her tongue over my fingers, drawing my index finger into her mouth. She caressed it with her tongue, closed her lips and began to suck. My body trembled. I'd never felt anything half as sensual.

"Can't leave a girl hanging, can we?" she asked.

Before I knew what was happening, she was hovering over me, still sucking my fingers, her thigh pressing against my center. I closed my eyes in ecstasy, even as my stomach churned with fear.

"Are you sure this is what you want, baby?"

Her look told me there was a second part to that question. She was asking if I really wanted this, knowing it would only be for one night. "Y-yes, it is." I nodded, my eyes heavy-lidded with desire for her. I could think of no one I would've trusted more with my body or my heart.

"Remember, you can stop me any time. If there's something you don't like or . . ."

"Shh." I put my fingers over her lips. "I'm nervous, that's all. I want so much to please you, and I don't know how."

"A good lover listens to her partner's body. That's how she knows what her partner wants. Right now I'm listening to yours."

I could smell the sweetness of her breath, the intoxicating scent of her perfume mixing with another, equally intoxicating scent.

"Tonight is all about you, sweetheart," she continued. "I want to please you in every way you can imagine. I want to make your dreams come true. If you're sure . . ."

I nodded. *God, am I.*

"Tell me what you want," she breathed, her mouth inches from mine.

I couldn't speak. She lowered herself just far enough to brush her lips gently over mine, before kissing me full on the mouth. My limbs went weak. She nibbled at my lower lip, sucking it into her mouth. I sighed with pleasure. She urged my lips open, exploring my mouth with her tongue, challenging me, capturing me in the rapture of the perfect kiss.

As our tongues danced together, I felt her hands begin their own exploration. Her fingertips caressed my skin everywhere—shoulders, collarbones, arms, belly, sides. My body was awash in sensation. My breasts ached for her touch, but she did not go there.

"Is this okay?" she breathed against my mouth.

I understood. She didn't want to scare me. "Wonderful," I answered honestly.

"Do you want to go further?"

"God, yes. I want you so much."

"Tell me what you want," she commanded. "Tell me how you want me to make love to you."

I closed my eyes tightly. I'd been dreaming of this moment since the first time we corresponded. Now that it was here, I had no idea where to tell her to begin.

She must've known that. She kissed my center through the satin of my panties. I levitated off the bed, my very being on fire. Carefully, she removed the barrier as she brushed her fingers over my sensitive skin.

Her mouth hovered over mine again. She sucked my lower lip into her mouth once more, making me shiver. She kissed and licked her way down my body, pausing to nibble on a collarbone, nip at a pulse point and press her tongue into the dimple on my chin.

"That's incredibly sexy, you know."

"My dimple?" I managed to wheeze out.

"Yes," she said. Her voice flowed over me like honey.

I'd never felt sexy before, or attractive, but she made me feel as if I was the most beautiful woman in the world.

Her fingers grazed my breasts, and my body arched off the bed.

"So soft," she murmured, as she rubbed her cheek against the side of my left breast. Her tongue reached out and flicked my nipple; I gasped as it contracted painfully. Slowly, she lifted my shirt off. "May I?"

"Yes," I breathed, astounded at the care she was taking with me. I'd told her once in an e-mail that I was shy about my body. My love for her grew even more.

"You're very beautiful, you know."

"No," I managed to whisper, as she drew my nipple into her mouth, her teeth closing gently over the tip.

"You're wrong," she said with her mouth full. "Gorgeous, in fact, and I'm going to show you just how gorgeous."

She kissed her way down my body, finding sensitive points all along the way. I felt as though I was in a dream, every inch of my skin was on fire, every nerve ending ablaze yearning for her. "Marina," I moaned, "take me, please."

"Oh, I intend to," she answered. "Tell me what you want, love." When I didn't answer her, she lowered her mouth and ran her tongue up the length of my clit. "Do you want this?" She did it again.

I felt a ripple spread through my body, beginning at the base of my toes and working its way upward.

Hearing no audible response, at least not an intelligible one, she continued her slow torture. "Or do you want this?" I felt her fingertips brush against my clit, dipping into my center.

"Mmm."

"That's not an answer," she said. "This." She stroked me again with her tongue. "Or this." She squeezed my clit with her fingers, then pressed them into my center.

I was incapable of speech. My body was singing with a desire it had never known.

"Well, since you can't seem to decide . . ." She began exploring my folds with her tongue, licking, sucking, teasing.

My hips rose off the bed in supplication. I didn't know what I wanted, but I wanted it with a passion.

"Does that feel good, baby?"

"God, yes," I said, as I felt the universe tilt.

"Or perhaps that's not enough?" Gently, she massaged the base of my clit with two fingers as her tongue continued its dance.

"Yes." I moaned, although it sounded more like a shout to my ears.

"Is this what you want?" she asked, as she sucked my clit into her mouth.

I hovered on the edge of the stratosphere.

She dipped two fingers into my center, matching the rhythm of her tongue, and I was lost. Or maybe I was found. I felt my body explode, a billion bright lights burned behind my eyes. It was like nothing I'd ever experienced before and like everything I'd ever dreamed of.

She held me, stroking my arms, my hair, my breasts, my pelvis. She cooed gentle words, her voice soft and low. When my breathing had returned to normal, she asked, "Are you all right, baby?"

"Fantastic," I answered, barely able to speak.

"Was it everything you wanted?"

"Almost." I rolled on top of her.

"Almost?"

"I want you," I said plainly, trying to convey my desire in my eyes.

"That's okay, honey. Tonight was about you, not me."

"No, I want you. I want to make love to you."

"You don't have to—"

"I know I don't. Please, baby. Please let me touch you." I could see her resolution wavering. I kissed her mouth, tasting myself there. It was a heady sensation. I felt my belly tighten all over again. "Please."

She lay back on the pillows in invitation. With shaking fingers, I undid the buttons on her top, stopping to kiss each exposed bit of flesh. She was exquisite—even more beautiful than I had imagined.

"I'm not sure what to do." I hesitated, nerves finally getting the best of me.

"Listen to what my body's telling you and follow your heart. It'll never lead you astray."

I closed my eyes, breathing in her scent. I ran my palms over her hardened nipples. It wasn't enough. I feasted with my mouth and felt her hips seek mine. I lowered my hand between us and found her center, stroking her. I felt her body tense. *Listen to her body*. It was telling me she wanted something else.

I looked into her face. "I want to taste you."

"You don't have to do that."

"I know—I want to. Please." I knew oral sex was something women enjoyed having done to them. Certainly, I'd loved it when she'd just done it to me. I didn't expect to like the taste, but I wanted desperately to bring her pleasure. My mouth hovered over her center. "Please," I said.

"If it's what you want."

I didn't wait for any further invitation. I breathed in her unique scent, nuzzled her clit with my nose and trailed my tongue through her wetness. She tasted like the nectar of the gods. "You taste delicious."

"You don't have to."

I lowered my mouth to her again. I was intoxicated by her. I wanted to explore everywhere. With each stroke of my tongue, I felt her draw closer to orgasm. Her clit swelled in my mouth and I thought I would melt. Her wetness soaked my cheeks and I was elated. I felt her lift off the bed and begin to tremble. I knew a feeling of joy like none I'd ever experienced before. I flicked my tongue over her clit, then dipped deeper into her center. I massaged the sides of her clit with my thumbs and drank of her again. As she came hard the sound of her cries echoed in my ears, reigniting a blaze in my core.

With a strength I didn't believe she could possess, she pulled me up, wrapping her legs tightly around my middle as her body continued to quake. The feel of her hot center against my abdomen was almost more than I could bear. My whole body began to shake.

"You need me again," she whispered in my ear as I supported myself over her with my arms.

I was helpless to do anything but nod. The feel of her, the taste of her, was the most powerful aphrodisiac imaginable.

She flipped me onto my back, her thigh pressed tightly against my center. She kissed me with purpose, her fervor nearly equal to my own. I felt her hand slide between us. She stroked my center and my body rejoiced.

Her eyes stared at me intently as she reached blindly for something on the nightstand. When she pulled her hand back it was shiny with a wetness that smelled of cinnamon. Had she been expecting me all along?

The thought barely registered, as with a gasp of surprise, I felt her fill me completely. My body exploded again, my core red hot. She was deeply inside me, her fist buried in me, and I couldn't get enough. I felt the fingers of her other hand beg for entry at my puckered opening, and I quivered. She filled me from every angle. Within seconds, I was beyond thinking, beyond imagining, beyond knowing. I was simply a ball of white-hot sensation, streaking toward a place beyond anything I'd ever dreamed possible.

When I came back to Earth, she was stroking me gently, kissing my chin, nose, forehead and cheeks. I smiled at her and ran my fingers through her hair.

"Okay?" she asked, concerned.

"It was so much more than that," I whispered, overcome. "I never knew—"

"I'm so glad I could give that to you," she said, tears forming on her eyelashes.

"Me too," I answered sleepily, my body still trying to catch up, my mind at peace.

When I woke several hours later, I was wrapped securely in her arms, her breasts pressed against my back, her pelvis hugging my ass. I smiled into my pillow, knowing that for the rest of my life I'd be wet every time I thought of Marina and this night. It would have to be enough.

Out of the Crowd
Kate Sweeney

Okay, that's the third time she's walked by and looked at me. Or am I paranoid? I asked myself as I sipped my drink.

Having come out to the bar on a whim on a humid Friday night in August, I stood outside in the beer garden and leaned against the wrought iron railing. Waiting for an open table, I had time to think. I just hate when that happens, because I usually think about Karen.

Karen was like a popcorn kernel. You know that little piece that sticks in the back of your throat? You're constantly trying to hack it up, but the fricking thing just hangs on?

I laughed as I took a drink. Maybe I'm the one who's hanging on. I'd gotten so used to blaming Karen for everything, I couldn't do anything else.

Gee, Monroe, how about dealing with it and letting it go? Now there's a novel idea.

I took another healthy drink, beating down the inner voice that has nagged at me for nearly a year. Perhaps if I get it drunk, it'll leave me alone.

With the help of a few dear friends who love to butt in, I realized just what I was doing—allowing myself to fall into the dark abyss of self-doubt and despair, over what? A gorgeous woman who ripped your heart out through your nose? Yep, that would be she.

So I decided enough self-loathing and pity. I tried the dating game. I preferred the self-loathing.

After several months of the painful dinners and clubs, the "I'll call you. No, I'll call *you*," and waiting around for the phone call that never came, I decided that self-polluting, as the nuns called it, was better. At least I could trust my own hand.

After about thirty minutes wandering down Memory Lane, I was about to give up when two young women vacated the small table by the sidewalk. Scooting over quickly, I commandeered the table, pleased with my stealth move. I hadn't knocked over a thing.

There she was again, walking across the crowded street. I watched her this time, while she idly browsed the shop windows. I grinned slightly. The shops were closed and the windows dark. I wondered what she was looking at.

Watching her, I realized how different we were in our appearance. I'm on the shorter and stockier side of the scale. She was average height and weight. My hair is shorter and graying. She had shoulder-length, reddish-brown hair. I liked the way it blew in the light summer breeze. She wore jeans and a black tank top. Even from across the street I could see that she filled the top nicely. I chuckled to myself and sang—"*Standin on the corner, watching all the girls go by.*" That was exactly what I was doing.

The woman intrigued me, not because she was standing out in the crowd, but because I felt she was trying to get my attention. How egotistical is that? Shrugging, I turned back to my cocktail and watched the rest of the crowd on the busy Chicago neighborhood avenue.

The full moon was rising over the buildings now, and I sat there with my feet up and watched it drift across the sky. I realized how much I loved the city and how I didn't come downtown enough. There was always so much going on—

"Excuse me," a soft voice called out.

Shaken from my reverie, I looked over and there she was, smiling shyly.

"I wonder if you could help me. I'm looking for twenty-three twenty Hood Ave. I was told it was in this neighborhood but . . ."

I blinked several times. Her smile was contagious, and dimples cut lines into her cheeks. It was her soft, hazel eyes, however, that made me sit up and take notice. Her elegantly shaped eyebrows, dark and thick, arched in question.

"Uh . . ." I said stupidly, before quickly collecting my half-wits. "I'm sorry, but I really don't know my way around the neighborhoods. Is someone expecting you? I can ask the bartender. I'm sure she knows. Why don't you come in and have a drink. We'll ask her." I wondered how I suddenly became so chatty. Usually, I never get beyond my initial "uh." This was an improvement.

"Well, I don't want to intrude," she said.

I waved her off and pointed to the entrance.

"I'd welcome the company. Come on around the—"

She quickly hopped the guardrail and stood by my table, sporting a happy grin.

"—or you can just vault right into my life." I laughed openly at her antics, not understanding how true the statement was to be.

She laughed along with the other patrons and I offered her the chair. I sat opposite her as the waitress came up to the table. She ordered a glass of white wine. I got a refill for my gin and tonic.

I offered my hand. "Danielle Monroe. My friends call me Dani."

She smiled again and my heart tripped over itself. Good grief. "Genevieve Hastings. My friends call me Genny," she said and shook my hand. It was warm and soft. Geesh, as if I'd never shook another woman's hand before!

"That's a beautiful name. Would you mind if I called you Genevieve?"

She shook her head. "No, I wouldn't."

Our drinks came and I asked the waitress about the address. "It's about three blocks east. Then take a left. Should be in the middle of the block." She set the drinks down and left.

"Well, there you go. Are you meeting someone?"

"Yes, my sister. I'm in from Michigan and she phoned saying she was going to be late. I have a few hours to kill, so I thought I'd just have a look around but I forgot to get directions. She just moved here."

I laughed at my arrogance. *Right Dani, she was looking at you!*

Genevieve cocked her head to one side, looking at me in confusion.

"Okay, fill me in," she said and sat back.

Suddenly, I felt like an ass. "I . . . I noticed you walking back and forth and I, well, I thought you were looking at me," I admitted with a grimace. "I know, pretty arrogant."

She grinned a bit and looked at her wineglass. "I was."

My mouth dropped. I was a bit dumbfounded, which is my natural state. I said the most articulate thing I can remember saying. "Oh."

C'mon, it's better than "uh."

Genevieve chuckled and sipped her wine.

My curiosity got the better of me, as it usually does. "Why?" I asked.

I don't think I've ever seen a woman blush so deeply. It was endearing. I leaned on the table, resting my chin in my palm and waited.

"Well, I don't know. I suppose I just saw you and thought you looked interesting," she said as she looked into my eyes. "Now that I see how green your eyes are, I have to change that to captivating," she finished quietly.

Now *I* was blushing. Because I didn't know what to say, I wisely said nothing.

We talked for almost two hours about everything and anything.

I told her things I don't think I ever told anyone. Perhaps it was because she was a total stranger and had nothing invested. Perhaps it was the sincerity sparkling in her hazel eyes. And just perhaps I was tired of being alone and welcomed Genevieve's interest for however long it might last.

Around midnight, Genevieve glanced at her watch. "Oh, my God! I was supposed to be at my sister's thirty minutes ago," she exclaimed and flipped on her cell.

"Cinderella?" I asked with a sad grin.

Genevieve smiled at the comparison. "Sis? Shit, sorry. No, I'm fine. No, I'm right around the block. No, I . . . I'm not alone. I—" She stopped, glanced at me and turned to the street. "I'll tell you later." I heard her whisper. "I'll be there in a few, bye," she said, then flipped the phone closed. She gave a nervous chuckle. "That was my sister, Marilyn."

"I gathered," I said, grinning.

"Well, I should be going," she said in a hesitant voice.

I was actually sorry the evening was over. I hailed the waitress and signed for the bill.

"Please, let me—" she said, but I shook my head.

"Nope. I had far too much fun. You're on vacation, of sorts. How would it look in the travel guide if I let a visitor pick up the bill?"

Genevieve laughed and stood. I gently grabbed her elbow.

"Ah, let's take the conventional way out, Miss Hastings."

She smirked a bit. "Killjoy."

"I'll walk you to your sister's."

"I don't want to intrude on you any further," she said.

I stopped and looked into her hazel eyes. "Intrude? Genevieve, this was the most fun I've had in quite a while and, honestly, I really don't want it to end," I said, meaning every word.

Genevieve nodded and we walked down the quiet neighborhood street.

I walked with my hands in the pockets of my shorts, wanting

desperately to hold her hand. It's not that I *wanted* her to trip or anything, but when her sandal skipped on the pavement and she reached for my arm, I was in heaven.

"Better hold on to me," I said seriously, offering my elbow.

She smiled as she slipped her arm in mine.

"How long are you in town?" I asked.

"For the week, then I have to go back. School starts in a few weeks and I haven't even begun my curriculum for the little urchins."

I chuckled and she held my arm tighter.

"Here's her house," she said quietly.

Frowning, I looked at the little bungalow and let out a dejected sigh. Genevieve released my arm and I stepped back. "Well—" she started.

"Genevieve, maybe if you have some time this week . . ." I began, taking out my wallet. "Shit, do you have a pen?"

She fished one out of her small purse.

I scribbled away and handed it to her. "If you don't have time, I truly understand. However, if you have some free time this week and you don't call me . . ." I wagged a threatening finger in the air.

Laughing, she looked at the card. "Hmmm. Home, work, cell, e-mail."

God, my face was hot with embarrassment. "Well, I . . . I mean I, well, if I'm not at home. I—"

Genevieve reached out and put her fingertips against my stupid lips. "You are sweet, Dani Monroe. Thanks for a great evening. I will call you if I have time."

I took her hand and kissed the warm palm, and heard her breath catch. She caressed my cheek. I looked her in the eye and smiled. "Damn, I want to kiss you."

She grinned, the dimples spreading across her face. "I *want* you to kiss me."

So, I did. I cupped her pretty face and kissed her softly. No rush, no great passion. Just a kiss. Okay, it was a long kiss.

I felt her body tremble as my hand rose to her waist. I pulled back and tried to focus.

"Whoa." I was breathless.

"That was nice, Dani. Goodnight."

"I guess," I said, disappointed that the night was over.

When she turned to go, we both noticed the blinds moving in the living room window. Genevieve hid her eyes with her hand. "Oh, God," she said. I walked up behind her and kissed her head.

"Tell her I said, hi," I whispered and kissed the back of her neck, smiling when I heard her soft groan. "I'd better let you go before she comes out here with a shotgun. Goodnight. I hope we can see each other again, Genevieve. If not, I had a wonderful time."

"So did I. Goodnight, Dani," she said and walked up the steps. She turned and waved, and entered the house.

Then, she was gone.

I slipped between the sheets and let out a sigh. *Figures, an attractive woman literally vaults into my life and I'll probably never see her again.* I drifted to sleep with visions of the dimpled smiling face invading my dreams.

The shrill sound of my phone nearly catapulted me out of bed. I reached over sleepily. "H'lo?" I mumbled, my heart racing. I hate to wake up like that.

"D-Dani?"

I was immediately awake. I bolted up and swung my legs over the side. "Genevieve?"

"Yes, I . . . I know it's early," she started in a soft voice.

I glanced at my clock. It was six thirty.

"Doesn't matter. Are you all right?" I asked as I wiped the sleep out of my eyes.

"Oh, yes, I'm fine. I didn't mean to scare you."

"Too late," I joked and lay back down, pulling the sheet over me. "How are you?"

"Well, I couldn't sleep. I've been . . . well, I've been thinking about you," she said quietly.

I grinned like an idiot. "Really? That sounds good. I've been doing the same thing."

"You *are* an egotist," she said.

"No, funny girl. I've been thinking about *you*." I grinned and nestled into the pillows, putting my hand behind my head.

"My sister got called back to do a double shift at the hospital, which means twenty-four hours. She won't be back until Sunday afternoon. So . . ."

"You'll be all alone in Chicago and that just won't do."

"Well, I wouldn't want to report you to the travel guide."

"I guess you're stuck with me for the weekend. Give me a bit to get ready and I'll pick you up by nine. How's that?" I offered as my heart hammered in my chest.

"That sounds wonderful. I'll be waiting." I heard the smile in her voice when I hung up the phone.

I nearly killed myself trying to get out of bed.

We spent the morning by Lake Michigan. I did my best to show her the magnificent Chicago lakefront. I tried to avoid holding her hand while we walked along the sand. It was extremely difficult. At lunchtime, I took her to a nice little restaurant at Navy Pier. When we finished, I sat back and took a deep breath.

"So, where would you like to go next? The Art Museum? The Adler Planetarium? What would you like to see?"

She leaned back. "Oh, I don't know." She sighed. "I'm not sure if the travel guide would allow this."

"Hey, I'll take you anywhere you want to go."

An elegant eyebrow arched dramatically. "Then I'd like to go to your place and see your bedroom."

Is it actually possible to swallow your tongue? I sat there, once again, sporting the dumbfounded look. It took me a nanosecond to gather my dim wits before I called out, "Check please!"

I'd never driven so fast in my life. Genevieve had her hand resting on my upper thigh. I was glad for the stick shift. The constant motion of my hand on the gearshift took my mind off her warm caresses.

Of course, I had to stop at the red light, didn't I? I waited patiently for the green and glanced at my passenger. The lust in her hazel eyes made my mouth bone dry.

"Geezus woman, don't look at me like that right now. I have to drive," I said helplessly.

She grinned evilly, leaned over and kissed my ear. I shuddered violently.

When I felt her hand under my shirt, I nearly came. "Genn—" I gasped, and my treacherous legs instinctively parted. I felt her hand slip into my shorts and I let out a deep groan when her fingers slipped in and touched my clit. I leaned forward and clutched the steering wheel like a lifeline.

"So wet," she said as her fingers danced.

My head was now on the steering wheel, but when a horn blared behind us, I jumped and put the car in gear.

Genevieve still kept her hand in my shorts while I drove. I chuckled nervously. "Genevieve, I don't think I can drive with your hand in my pants."

"Try," she said.

I shot her an incredulous look when I heard the challenging tone in her voice.

The normal drive to my suburban home takes a good thirty minutes. I rolled into my driveway in just under twenty.

I jumped out and ran to grab the giggling Genevieve by the hand, practically dragging her to the door. Of course, now I was fumbling with the fricking keys while Genevieve kissed my neck, her hands roaming all over my ass.

"You're distracting me, woman," I said, finally getting the stinking key in the door.

No sooner did I get us in than one hundred-twenty pounds of highly aroused high school teacher slammed me against the door.

"My God, Dani. I want you," she said and kissed me deeply.

I groaned and eagerly returned her kiss, easily parting her lips with my tongue. Moaning deeply, she welcomed my tongue and sucked it hungrily into her mouth. Hands fought against one another while we hastily unbuttoned each other's clothing.

In the heat of pure lust, I ripped her blouse. *Oops.* I tried to apologize and got kissed for it.

"Fuck it," she said, in a low voice as her hand roughly kneaded my breast.

Okay, let's slow down here. I pulled back, panting, and tried to get some air. I took her by the arm and we got as far as the couch. "Living room," I gasped out my tour.

Genevieve laughed and I easily unhooked the front clasp on her bra—thank God I hadn't lost my touch—and quickly slipped it off her slim body.

"God, you're beautiful." I kissed her deeply and slipped my hand between us to unzip her shorts, sliding them and her panties off in one swift movement. "Genevieve, I can't believe how soft you are," I whispered. My hands slowly roamed all over her body. They came to rest on her ass and I pulled her close.

"Dani," she pleaded. I saw her body break out in gooseflesh. I gently sucked on the soft skin of her upper breast, pulling the flesh between my teeth. "Ahh!" she cried out and held my head in place.

I struggled out of my shorts and kicked them off, all the while kissing her heaving breasts. Genevieve fell back onto the couch and her legs trembled. When I moved toward her, she put her hand up.

"Wait. I just want to look at you for a moment," she said and her look of lust was unmistakable. Now, my body is not the best, certainly not the worst, but . . .

"Okay, that's enough," I said and quickly slipped in between her open legs.

Both of us sighed when our bodies touched. For a moment, we just looked at each other. I moved my hips into her, balancing my upper body on my arms. I let out a deep groan as I felt her smooth legs wrap around my waist.

"Genevieve, you feel so good," I whispered.

"God, Dani, so do you." She reached over to palm my breasts.

A shiver ran through me and, as she tweaked both nipples, I arched my back, pressing my hips harder into her.

I kissed and nibbled my way to her small, firm breast. Taking the hardened nipple into my mouth, I sucked ravenously. Genevieve's hands were first in my hair, pulling and scratching, driving me wild, then they were on my shoulders pushing me downward. I was slick with my own arousal as I kissed and licked my way down the length of her slim torso. I stopped at her navel, lazily sweeping my tongue in the small depression.

"Now, Dani. Now . . ."

"Yes, now." I let out a deep groan while her hands eagerly pushed on my shoulders.

She parted her legs so wide I thought she'd split in two. I lowered myself between her soft thighs and moaned, breathing in the scent of her arousal. "I'm going taste you now, Genevieve," I whispered softly. I placed my hands under her thighs and lifted, pushing her legs back toward her. "Hold yourself open for me."

Genevieve quickly placed her hands behind her knees and pulled back. "So beautiful," I mumbled as I gazed at the offering before me. I slowly licked up and down the length of her.

"Ohhh," she groaned in a raspy voice and twitched. "Don't stop, Dani."

Like I could. I slipped my tongue deeper between her folds. I nibbled at her sensitive clit and heard her whimper as she pulled her legs farther back.

"Genevieve, my God," I mumbled against her wetness as I drank all she offered me.

"Deeper, please Dani. I can't believe how good this feels," Genevieve begged, her body now glistening in sensual sweat. "I need to come, Dani. Please let me come."

She bucked her hips against my mouth. I pointed my tongue and thrust it deep inside her. Her musky, heady scent and taste drove my arousal off the charts. I felt my clit throb in empathy.

As my tongue darted deeper, my nose touched her swollen clit. Moving back and forth, driving my tongue deep into her, I brought her to a screaming orgasm.

Her body tensed and she held onto her legs, drawing them close to her chest.

"Coming! God, I'm coming!" she screamed. "Oh God! Again!" she cried out as I continued.

She dropped her legs over my shoulders and twitched convulsively. I continued to lick the length of her. She cried out again and grabbed for my head. "I can't . . . I can't . . . No more . . ." she begged and tugged at my head.

I pulled back and kissed the inside of both thighs, causing her to jump. "Please stop!" she cried out, and I relented. I scooted up next to her, on my side, to hold her close. She latched onto me and curled up, her body trembling and quivering. I reached over and slipped the small afghan off the back of the couch to cover her. "Sweet Jesus, Dani Monroe. I have never had such a powerful orgasm," she whispered. "I can't move."

I grinned and kissed her damp hair. "Well, it's been a while for me. I wondered if I still had it."

She looked up sporting an incredulous look. "How long?"

I shrugged. "Almost a year."

She groaned and cuddled closer, kissing the top of my breasts. "I can't imagine you being any better," she whispered tiredly.

I grinned evilly. "We have another twenty-four hours, Genevieve. You'd better get some rest."

"Twenty-four hours. I don't think I can take much more of you, Ms. Monroe." She sighed, and drifted off to sleep. I soon followed.

When I woke, it was nearly four in the afternoon. Genevieve was breathing deeply. Wore you out, huh? I thought happily. I am such a child. I leaned over to kiss her forehead and she stirred. She moved her lovely body into mine. Her eyes fluttered open and I gazed into the soft, hazel eyes.

"Hello," she said sleepily. "How long have you been awake?"

"Not too long. How do you feel?" I asked and lightly kissed her warm lips.

"Hmm. Wonderful," she sighed and pulled me close.

"We'd better get off this couch. It's seen better days," I said seriously. I eased off, and offered her a hand. "How about a tour of the rest of the house?" I whispered into her ear, delighted when she twitched once again.

"Oh, okay," she sighed dramatically, and followed me to the bedroom. "You travel people sure are bossy . . ." She let out a shriek of laughter as I tossed her onto the bed.

She lay there laughing, while I reached over and opened the nightstand drawer. She watched as I took out a harness.

"Oh God, you're gonna kill me," she said. I saw her pupils dilate as I slipped into the harness.

I picked out a suitable attachment and crawled between her legs. *God, I hope I haven't forgotten how to do this. Oh well, time to see if the "like riding a bike" theory works.*

"I have a feeling you're going to enjoy this," I whispered and kissed her breasts, pulling the nipples between my teeth. Her back arched into the touch and she held my head in place. I reached between us and ran my fingers through her copious wetness and ran my wet fingers over the head of the dildo. She did something I did not expect. She sat up and pushed me on my back. The bike theory was put on hold for a moment.

"Lie still and nobody gets hurt," she said in a sexy voice I hadn't heard before.

She reached in and parted my legs and knelt between them. I lay there, amazed, trying to figure out what she was about to do. She lowered her mouth over the flesh-colored dildo and flicked the tip of it with her tongue. I twitched as if I could feel it. For that one moment, I actually envied men. She took it into her mouth and moved her head back and forth, causing it to slide over my clitoris.

"Oh God!" I moaned.

I cried out as she lifted my leg over her shoulder. I nearly exploded when her wet tongue slid between the straps of the harness. She pulled at the phallus and I arched my back. "Shit!" I groaned helplessly.

"Dani, look at me," she ordered, and my eyes popped open. She slipped her hand down between her legs and gathered the moisture there, smearing it all over the head of the dildo. My mouth went dry as I watched. She straddled my legs, positioned herself, and slowly slid down.

I watched the arousal on her face. Her eyes fluttered as I watched the phallus disappear deep inside her. This was almost too much. I nearly came at the sight. She rocked back and forth slowly, making me groan as the base slid across my clit.

Genevieve lowered completely and gasped. "So deep," she moaned, slowly riding back and forth.

I placed my hands on her hips and moved her faster. She grabbed my forearms and cried out, arching her back, her nipples taut and straining; her abdomen quivering. She was . . .

"Magnificent," I said in a raspy voice. My mouth was bone dry.

Suddenly, the urge to have her was overwhelming. I needed to have her, immediately. I flipped her onto her back, still buried deep inside her.

"God, Dani!" she cried out as I pulled back and drove quickly in. "Yes!"

Thrusting against my hips, Genevieve grabbed my ass and pulled me close. "Harder Dani," she said, and I complied. I worked my hips, both of us groaning and grunting.

I pulled out and urged her first onto her stomach and onto her knees. I entered her from behind and continued thrusting. "Yes, don't stop," she grunted as I reached over and held onto her shoulders.

I was panting wildly and my heart was pounding as I leaned down and kissed her sweat-soaked back, licking the salty skin.

"Come, Genevieve." I couldn't believe the pure lust I felt for this woman. I had never wanted to fuck someone so bad.

As if she read my mind, she turned and looked at me.

"Yes, Dani, harder," she begged, and I obliged. I held one hand on her shoulder and one on her hips and I ground into her. "I . . . need . . . to . . . come . . ." she whined desperately.

My hips moved rhythmically. With every thrust, she cried out, begging me to continue. Then she cried out her warning.

"Gonna come!"

I leaned over her back, driving the phallus deeper. She growled deeply. I knew she was on the edge and what she needed to tumble right over it.

"Genevieve, touch yourself and come for me now," I said.

I never saw a hand move so fast in my life. It shot down between her legs. I couldn't help myself. I reached around and joined her fingers, rolling her clit between my fingers and hers, and that did it. She squealed and bucked back into my hips, calling out my name over and over. I was in heaven. I wanted her to come hard and she did just that. Finally, she collapsed onto the bed, completely sated and exhausted.

Both of us were panting and sweating. I leaned over her smooth back and kissed her. She moaned in a low voice, her body jerking and quivering as I pulled out. She groaned and moved her hips back onto the dildo. I grinned evilly as I took it out very slowly.

"Oh God, Dani, if you don't quit that I'll come again!" she screamed as I pushed it back in quickly. Her body shook and, all at once, she was on her knees again. I was amazed at her stamina.

"Another go?" I whispered playfully into her damp hair. A helpless moan was my answer. I slowly eased back in all the way to the base and bucked several times, her body jumping each time. I could feel her orgasm building. I reached around once again to tweak her sensitive clit. With two or three strokes, Genevieve came again. This time it was slow and long. Genevieve was now lying flat on her stomach, motionless. I slipped the harness off and scooted next to her, lying on my side. Her face was turned toward me, but her eyes were closed.

"Genevieve?" I whispered, pushing the wet hair off her face. *Shit, I killed her!* "Um, Miss Hastings?"

Her eyelids fluttered opened. "I still have my hips, don't I?" she whispered.

I laughed quietly and reached down to caress said hips. "Yup, all seems to be in order," I assured her. "Did you, um . . ."

"Yes, damn you. I nearly fainted. I couldn't take anymore and I couldn't speak. You beast," she said and tried to rise up, but her arms were too weak. She flopped back down. "You did this to me. I hope you're proud of yourself," she moaned helplessly.

"Very. If I had feathers, I'd be struttin' like a peacock," I laughed and lifted her so I could scoot under her. Her head rested comfortably on my breast, her arm flopped across my waist.

"I've never been so satisfied in my life," she said in a dreamy voice as she cuddled close.

After a few moments, she kissed my breast. "Seems you have all the toys . . ." she said and raised herself up on her elbows. "Hmm," she said thoughtfully and hopped on top of me, straddling my abdomen as I let out a deep laughing groan. She leaned over and rummaged through the open drawer.

As she moved, I felt her wetness coating my abdomen. I let out a deep sigh as I caressed her soft hips.

"Ahha! This is what I need," she said triumphantly and held out a long silk scarf. "My turn," she whispered and kissed me deeply, her tongue snaking into my mouth. I felt my hands being tugged over my head and the silky material holding them to the headboard. Genevieve leaned back and grinned evilly. "Now . . . Let's test your resolve. I do not want you to move."

I wriggled my wrists and laughed. "Well, this is a good start," I said, trying to get some moisture back into my mouth.

With her soft legs straddling my hips, Genevieve ran her fingernails over my breasts, scratching at my nipples. I groaned and bit my lip.

"No moving," she warned and I felt beads of sweat forming on my brow. She raked her nails underneath my breasts, then up and down my sides as she slid her hips across mine, coating me with her wetness. "God Dani," she whispered as she leaned in for a kiss. "You make me so wet."

I love erotic talk, and Genevieve was doing it just the way I liked it right then. I groaned into the kiss as she darted her tongue in and out. Her nails were causing me to quiver uncontrollably each time they made contact with my overheated skin.

"Shit," I hissed and arched my back.

"No talking either," she whispered in my ear, sensually running that wicked tongue around my lobe.

I shook like a dog as her tongue snaked down my neck to my breasts. Just with the tip, she flicked my hard nipples, first one then the other. A heart attack was imminent as I tried desperately to play her dastardly game and not move.

"You're being very good, Dani," she said against my breasts.

Sweat dripped down my neck. It felt as though my entire body was on fire. She dragged her nails down my sides to my hips and across my quivering stomach. She followed her nails with her tongue, kissing and licking her way down my overheated body. I was throbbing so badly I thought I'd explode. Instinctively, I bucked my hips, hoping for some contact.

"Ah, ah, I said no moving," she whispered. I groaned and shook my head. "Am I teasing? You may speak," she said.

"Yes!" I said in a raspy voice.

She chuckled quietly and slid down my body, her tongue slicing and darting along the way. I parted my legs and she nestled between them. I tried to close my legs but with her kneeling there, I was helpless, but I liked it!

She pushed my legs wide and I heard myself whimper. Totally exposed with my hands tied, I felt extremely vulnerable.

"You're so wet, Dani," she murmured as she kissed the top of my quivering thighs. She inhaled and sighed. "Hmm, intoxicating. I can't wait to taste you," she said, and I groaned. "You do want me to taste you, don't you, Dani?" she asked in an innocent voice. My eyes bugged out at the question.

Was she nuts? I nodded furiously. I was so hot, wet and throbbing I thought I'd spontaneously combust.

I never thought of myself as a very emotional person. Reason and logic ruled my day. However . . . when I felt her nail lightly raking over my unbelievably hard throbbing clit, I nearly cried like a baby. I would've sung Swanee River if she asked—I was that gone with a need for release. I could feel my arousal cascading from me, seeping down my thighs, which twitched in an attempt to close, trying to get some contact from somewhere.

The sweat ran down my face as Genevieve turned me into a mass of quivering begging flesh.

Muscles convulsed in places I had no idea I had muscles. My arms strained as I frantically tried to get out of my bonds to grab that head and hold it between my legs. *Boy, she was good!*

"So, Dani," she said.

Panting like some wild dog, I looked down at her, the sweat running into my eyes.

She reached down and slipped her fingers into her own wetness, crawled up my body and presented the saturated fingers to my mouth. "Suck," she said in such a sexy voice I nearly came.

I eagerly took each finger and sucked it clean as she toyed with my breasts with her other hand.

Suddenly my mouth was watering as I bathed her wicked fingers with my tongue. She pulled them out with a resounding 'pop' and grinned as she lay completely on top of me. Our breasts compressed together as she sensually slid her body over my overheated torso. Her knee nudged between my legs.

"Hmm, I can feel your heat, Dan," she said and kissed me, sucking on my bottom lip. She pulled at it and let it go, once again sliding down my body. "Be right back," she whispered against my breast.

My legs were so far apart, I nearly dislocated my hips.

"Ready for me, baby?" she said.

Ready? Baby? Oh, shit . . .

I nodded and whimpered. My body was not my own. It was this trembling mass of exposed nerves and it belonged to Genevieve.

She nestled between my legs and pushed them open even wider.

It happened. She took pity on my jelly-like state and slipped her cool tongue across my overheated flesh. The jolt of electricity that shot through my groin could have lit up the entire North Shore of Chicago.

"Shit!" I screamed.

I felt her warm breath, her cool, wet tongue and her teeth as they nibbled at my lips. I was squirming and writhing as she licked me like the proverbial starving cat. Lapping up and down the length of me, from my clit to my, well she was coming dangerously . . . when my ass twitched I knew I was gone.

"I'm sorry, Dani," she mumbled.

I didn't understand as I raised my soaked head and looked down between my legs.

She reached under my thighs and raised both legs and pushed them lewdly apart. "I can't let you come yet. You taste too good."

"OH GOD!" I screamed as she rammed her tongue deep and licked from the inside out. I bucked. I writhed. I twisted against her. I wasn't at all sure I wouldn't rip the headboard right off the bed.

She reached over, rummaged through the drawer and took out a very large black dildo. I groaned and twitched with anticipation as she liberally coated it with lube. She held the tip of the large phallus by my entrance and my inner muscles contracted automatically.

"Gonna fuck you now, Dani," she growled and slammed the entire dildo home.

I lifted off the bed and cried out as I felt her mouth once again sucking at my clit. Pumping the dildo in and out, suckling my clit,

I came with such an explosion I honestly thought I would pass out. I felt it building and building and I came. Repeatedly. I couldn't move to stop her. The pleasure was unbearable.

"Stop," I begged as she continued.

"No . . . Not done," she mumbled.

Okay, she's the devil. My body convulsed again.

"C'mon, Dani. One more time." She leaned in and licked the sweat off my breasts, purring as she did so.

"So full," I grunted and trembled. God it felt good as she slowly pulled it back and slid it home again. I felt my orgasm building again as she pushed the phallus deeper.

"So good," I said.

"So good," Genevieve whispered.

"Genevieve!" I cried out my warning. I started panting uncontrollable.

"I know, love," she whispered and slid down my body once again. She pulled the dildo out so slowly I thought I was going to die right there.

"Ahhh . . ." When I felt her tongue on my oversensitive clit, I erupted again. "Easy, easy," I whispered.

Genevieve lay with her head atop my thigh, gently kissing my curls. I jumped, but when I was certain that was all she was going to do, I relaxed.

"Genevieve, could you do me a favor, please?" I asked, exhausted.

"Mmm, anything you want, Dani," she whispered as her fingers caressed my thighs.

"Could you untie me, please? I'm losing circulation."

"Oh, God I'm so sorry!" She scooted up and untied the scarf.

The pins-and-needles sensation lasted for a few moments as she massaged my arms. Chuckling, she kissed my sweaty forehead and lay between my legs. It felt so good to feel her body on top of me.

As the feeling crept back into my hands and arms, I put my arms around her waist and held her there. She rested her head on my breast and I wrapped my legs around her.

"That was incredible," I said.

Genevieve nuzzled close. "It certainly was," she mumbled, then both of us took a well-deserved nap.

I woke with the oddest sensation. I was completely aroused, for something different. Glancing at the clock, I saw it was seven thirty. I looked down and laughed; Genevieve, sound asleep, was still on top of me. However, my right nipple was in her mouth.

As I moved, her eyelids fluttered opened and I chuckled quietly. She realized her position and looked up. She looked like a kid with her hand caught in the cookie jar.

"Hungry?" I asked. Laughing she released my breast and I slapped her rump. "C'mon."

After showering together, which amazingly did not evolve into sex, I handed Genevieve my robe as I slipped into a pair of shorts and a tank top.

"Okay, I'm starving!" I announced and headed for the kitchen.

Sitting at the tall barstool by the counter, Genevieve nibbled on cheese as I prepared steaks for the grill.

Over dinner, we talked about our lives and our loves and past relationships. We found we had a great deal in common.

"I like you, Dani. I really do. How is it that you're single?" she asked as she ate dessert. "This is good!" she exclaimed, delving into the root beer float. "Answer my question please."

I sighed and shrugged. "Just lucky I guess."

She gave me a curious look. "I don't believe you. I think you'd love to be in a relationship, Dani Monroe."

"How about you?" I asked. "You're extremely attractive and very intelligent. Why aren't you with someone?"

Genevieve sipped through the straw. "I guess I never found someone who really just liked me for me. I've been in love but they never seemed to want more from me. Maybe it's me."

I shook my head. "It's not you. I've only known you for a short while but I think I'm right on this. You haven't met the right one.

Maybe neither of us has," I said. I looked up to see tears in her hazel eyes.

"What's wrong?" I asked. I reached across and took her small hand in mine. "Tell me."

She sniffed. "Shit! I don't know why I'm crying. I'm happy. I have a great job. A family that loves me. I just had the best sex I've ever had . . ." She stopped and blushed horribly and laughed at my dumbfounded expression. "Yes, Ms. Monroe, I have never had better sex."

I thought for a moment, as I watched her. Smiling like a jackass, I noticed so many things about her that I'd overlooked in the heat of passion.

There was a tiny scar on her left eyebrow. She hummed quietly while she ate. Her eyes lit up when she talked about her job. She had an annoying habit of sucking her teeth when something, like a bit of steak, was stuck there. I chuckled inwardly and shook my head. *Figures, Monroe, you started to fall for someone who lives in another state, who's only here on vacation.*

"Wow, what are you thinking?" she asked, leaning her elbow on the counter and resting her chin on her hand.

I looked into the hazel eyes and grinned. "I'm thinking I really like you and I wish you didn't have to leave, but I'm glad we have the rest of the night," I said. Genevieve blinked and swallowed hard.

"I feel the same," she whispered.

I took the dishes and placed them in the sink. As I turned back to her, I looked into her eyes. Sadness flashed through them. I flipped off the light in the kitchen, took her by the hand and led her back to the bedroom.

She watched as I lit several candles by the bedside, then smiled as I walked up to her.

Standing by the bed, I reached over and cupped her face. "I don't want sex tonight, Genevieve. I want love. I want to make love to you slowly and completely." I kissed her.

I was shocked when I felt her lips trembling. I slipped the robe off, and it fell in a muffled heap at her feet. I threw back the quilt and settled her into the middle of the bed.

I stood before her and slowly took off my top and my shorts. She smiled, and I could see her body trembling as I slid next to her. Looming over her, I gently kissed her. I reached down and cupped her small breast, running my palm over it before tenderly capturing the hard nipple between my finger and thumb. Genevieve sighed into the kiss and arched her back into my touch.

My hand wandered down her torso. I memorized every line, every curve, and every adorable dimple.

"God, you're soft," I whispered against her lips as my hand found its way to the dark curls. She sighed and parted her legs, welcoming me once again.

This time, it would be slow and tender. My fingers pushed back the defensive folds and she gasped.

"A little sore, Dan," she warned. I nodded.

"I know. I'll be very gentle, Genevieve," I assured her.

We held a gaze as my fingers softly wandered through her moisture. She was still swollen, but I easily and slowly slid my fingers up and down the length of her; her arousal instantly saturating my fingers.

"My God, Genevieve," I whispered still looking deep into her eyes. The candlelight flickered and danced in them. "Beautiful."

I slipped one finger into her and my heart skipped a beat as I reveled in the warmth. "Heaven," I sighed. Genevieve bit at her bottom lip as she arched her back slightly. Gently working in another finger, I rolled them around inside her, slowly stretching her walls. I curled my fingers, finding that one spot and gently massaged. Her breathing became labored as she closed her eyes and whimpered slightly.

"Dani," she said and grabbed my shoulder, pulling me close.

I softly kissed her cheek and her mouth before I gently nibbled her earlobe.

Her fingers dug into my shoulders and when her body tensed, I pulled back. I wanted to watch her succumb and slip over the edge.

She went rigid. I felt her inner walls tighten and swell around my fingers. As I tenderly pressed my thumb against her swollen clitoris, I leaned in.

"Look at me, Genevieve."

Her eyes opened. She looked lost as she tried to focus.

"Please, Genevieve," I whispered almost as a prayer. "Come for me."

She came in slow sensual waves. "Oh God," she whimpered as she smiled and held onto my forearm. "Wonderful," she sighed and flinched as I moved again. I eased my hand away and kissed her deeply.

"Thank you," I whispered against her dry lips.

She rolled me onto my back, smiling as she returned my tender kiss. Without a word, she moved down my body and turned around, offering herself as she parted my legs. It'd been quite awhile since I enjoyed this mutual gratification. I tucked the pillow under my head as she rocked back to my awaiting tongue.

I groaned deeply as her cool tongue slipped over my clitoris. We mirrored our lovemaking, stroke for stroke. Each swipe of our tongues was in unison, as if it were a choreographed, sensual dance.

We came together holding on tight, whimpering and exhausted.

Gently, I eased Genevieve up and into my arms. We kissed tenderly, and said goodnight to each other as if we said it every evening.

As I spooned behind her and held her close, Genevieve let out a long contented sigh. Kissing my arm, she pulled me incredibly close. She reached back and caressed my hip. I kissed the back of her shoulder as she fell sound asleep.

I lay in the darkness, listening to her breathing, feeling the slow rhythm of her heart beneath my palm. I smiled, remembering how I first saw her. How she had walked out of the crowd and into my life.

I have no idea what will happen tomorrow. I hope we'll make love, perhaps even be a little shy with each other.

Later, I'll take her back to her sister's to finish her short vacation. Then she'll be gone. I smiled softly as I drifted off to a peaceful sleep.

I hear Michigan is gorgeous in the fall.

Eva
Jean Byrnell

Whenever I remember the night I met Eva, I think of the dress Gilbert designed for me. Gilbert and I became friends in the fall of 1962 when he was giving a costume design seminar at Stella Adler's theater school in New York. He made his living designing drag. The gorgeous dresses he made sent a stream of Judy Garlands and Marlene Dietrichs out into the New York night.

I was twenty-one when I finished my two years with Stella and I moved to Montreal. Gilbert paid me a visit and brought me an amazing, dark raspberry, silk dress. He said we needed to jump-start my life out of the poor student phase.

The gift of the dress came the week that Dennis Russell, the person I hoped would soon be my boyfriend, had invited me to the Montreal opening of Carl Orff's Carmina Burana. Dennis had a contract to sing smaller roles with the Met during the season. The rest of the year he traveled and sang major roles out of New York. He was the leading tenor in this production of Carmina. I was desperate to jolt Dennis out of his gallant stage and lead him to something more intensely romantic. I hoped that with my new killer attitude, learned from Stella, and the raspberry dress, Dennis wouldn't stand a chance.

I did receive admiring looks from Dennis, who sang brilliantly. Following the performance we went to a reception at the home of the chairwoman of the Montreal Opera Society. The woman's home was one of the old Montreal estates set back behind protective hedges. Polished antiques were carefully displayed against a background of vanilla carpet and Wedgwood green walls. The long buffet was covered with trays of small, edible, works of art. There were tiny cheeses in brilliant colors and a tray of Chinese vegetables arranged like lotus blossoms.

Because of the dress I felt equal to the occasion. I was very aware that Dennis watched my progress as I smiled and mingled with the singers and opera goers. I stopped beside the smoked fish trays by a young man who told me he could have been the star of this production. He insisted he had the voice, but he couldn't seem to memorize the roles. He was sure that they would let him hold the score in some future production. I was relieved when Dennis propelled me into a small sunroom that opened off the main hall.

"Eva Deschampes insists on meeting you," he whispered.

I smiled because old ladies liked me. I often went to parties with high hopes of meeting mister right and ended up spending most of the evening talking to somebody's grandmother.

The woman standing in the sunroom was not an old lady. She was not like any opera society chairperson I had ever met. Eva Deschampes was in her mid thirties. She was tall and silver blond. Her beautiful, serious blue eyes were fixed on me.

"I'm so very glad to meet you," she said with an accent I remembered from a Swedish art film.

"Thank you for inviting me. I love Carl Orff." My mind raced for something sophisticated to say.

"Jeannie is here in Montreal looking for work as an actress,"

Dennis said. That sounded ridiculous. People looking for work as an actress were usually pathetic unless they recently completed a major run on Broadway.

"I did a little acting in Copenhagen when I was in high school," Eva volunteered. She was Danish not Swedish. "I was terrible but I had a crush on the person who was playing the lead so it didn't matter." She laughed.

"You must have been wonderful. I wish we could have seen you." Dennis was beginning to burble.

He was finding it hard to maintain his composure while he was in this elegant woman's company. I felt a jealous pricking at my skin. This was not how the evening was supposed to go.

Eva asked Dennis how he came to sing at the Met and he took a breath and began to talk about his favorite subject. I thought I might as well begin to clear up dirty plates or pick the dead leaves from the plants in the sunroom windows. Certainly neither of them would notice what I was doing. Eventually Eva was called away by her husband. I followed Dennis to the living room where he was quickly surrounded by earnest and adoring opera patrons.

I am not sure whether it was the smoked salmon on the buffet that gave me the terrible headache or the disappointment at not being the center of Dennis Russell's world. I thought that if I could find a bathroom I could raid the medicine cabinet for aspirin.

Down a short hallway that led from the dining room were swinging doors to the kitchen. I looked; the room was empty and mercifully quiet. I found a clean glass from a cupboard, got some water from the tap and sat with it at one of the long white counters.

"You're needing a little time away from the talk, talk, talk?"

Eva had come into the room and was standing behind me. I immediately felt awkward. I shouldn't have been helping myself in her kitchen.

"Yes, I guess I do."

"Me too," she said, and sat down on the stool beside me. "You know Jeannie, I think that is one of the most beautiful dresses I have ever seen and the person wearing it could stop my heart."

I blushed. I don't usually blush because I'm not fair, but right then, I could feel the color rise from my chest and change my face to Pepto Bismol pink. I stumbled out a thank you and looked at her more carefully. She was wearing a pair of sleek, black pants and a white blouse, which she wore unbuttoned in order to show three gold chains lying against her pale skin. I could just make out her nipples through the layers of silk blouse and lingerie.

"Have you gone with Dennis for a long while?" she asked. "He is such an interesting man."

"Off and on I suppose," I said. The jealousy was jabbing at my stomach this time but it wasn't clear to me why I was jealous. I think I wanted Eva Deschampes' exclusive attention as much as I wanted Dennis's.

We sat for some time in the kitchen. She asked me about my relationship with Dennis and my time with Stella Adler. I found out she had two sons at boarding school. She took me into the basement and introduced me to her elderly German shepherd before she was called back to her guests. I felt honored she had taken so much time with me.

She ushered me back into her living room and introduced me to a man who was actually looking for his wife and had little patience for party chatter. As soon as he backed away from me I looked for Dennis. I wandered from drink table to chesterfield back to the dining room without settling into conversation with anybody. Dennis was nowhere in sight. I saw two women descending the big staircase into the front hall. I hadn't asked Eva for aspirin and the headache was now taking over my life. I was certain these women, who were wearing freshly applied lipstick, must have come from a second-floor bathroom. I went up the stairs and found it at the end of the hall.

I opened the mirrored cabinet above the sink but there was only a row of extra soaps and some lotion on its narrow shelves. I went pee and sat with my head in my hands until I heard somebody outside the bathroom door. I figured they were waiting for a turn so I washed quickly and opened the door. It was Eva.

"Are you all right?" she asked quietly.

"Just a bit of a headache. I have to confess I was scrounging for aspirin," I said.

She looked at me as if she were puzzled.

"In your medicine cabinet."

She nodded and smiled at me. My hands began to tremble. "Maybe I can help, I'm pretty good at getting rid of headaches." She put out her hand and led me into a bedroom. It was a large, peach-colored room with a woven Persian bedspread. There wasn't anything personal on the dresser or on the tables so I assumed it was a guestroom.

She sat on the bed and I sat beside her, facing the wall. Her fingers found the back of my neck. She stroked and probed. She found the pain; I moaned. She pushed her fingers so deeply into the place that hurt, I thought I would cry and then she pulled back. She pushed into the pain again and again until I felt euphoric. As my body relaxed she kissed my neck.

"No, please . . . don't."

She found my mouth. This was the first time I had really been kissed by a soft mouth. There were women who made love to me. Lovely women who came from my imagination and disappeared the moment I fell asleep. I didn't allow them to surface during the day and I didn't ask questions about the reason I found them so compelling, but a woman would always come when I was alone in the dark. Several times in my life a man had been lying in the bed beside me, exhausted after his frantic gyrations, but my orgasm always came much later, coaxed to its peak by a woman I was never able to touch. Now I could smell a woman's spice and floral perfume. I could feel her skin. This was a person, pushing the straps of my dress away from my shoulders. I was horrified.

"I just want to make love to you," Eva said quietly.

I was frozen.

She pulled me up on the bed and switched off the light. I murmured 'no' as I closed my eyes and listened to her unbutton her blouse. I felt her naked body push up against me. I didn't want to be this, not in real life, but it seemed impossible to stop. Although I gently pushed her to move away, my body was aching for her to make love to me. The fire between my legs put an end to my confusion.

Eva talked to me. She murmured exactly what she was going to do as if she was afraid that if she startled me badly I would run. "Sweet girl, I'm going to kiss you there; hold my hand; yes, that's it . . . now." I could feel her fingers and kisses begin at my belly and travel with terrible slowness to where I waited. I watched her silvery hair come loose and brush my body with its softness as she kissed me.

I remember the startling realization of her tongue and how carefully it explored the country of my clitoris. Although that night I didn't actually know the word clitoris. In 1964 I had only heard the word orgasm once or twice. Once was when a jazz singer boasted he had given me one, when what he really had done was scare the hell out of me. There were few words spoken that related to a woman's pleasure in middle-class 1964.

Her tongue and hands became the center of the world until I lingered for a moment on that exquisite brink of orgasm and then let go.

When I lay in her arms I had a moment when I was afraid I wouldn't be able to make her happy. I was sure I wouldn't be able to do for her what she had done for me. It is astounding how quickly you learn. My fingers were accustomed to the feel of a vagina. It was familiar ground. I found her breasts with my mouth as my fingers coaxed her clitoris to become round and plump. I kissed her breasts and sucked her nipples as if I had finally come home. Eva's poise began to dissolve. I pulled away and watched her beautiful face relax, and tears fill her eyes.

I made circles in her pale, pubic hair with my tongue. I licked it slowly until it shone in the light coming through the window from the street lamp. She moaned and I lay on top of her, pushing myself onto her pubic bone to find some relief from the new ache that was growing inside me. She pushed me back and raised herself up on her arm. She took my hand in her own and pushed it gently up and down in the valley of my own cunt. She watched as I felt myself until another orgasm began to swell inside of me and I fell on her with a cry of pleasure.

I raised her hips in my hands and buried my face in her wet mystery. I remember it so well. She smelled like the summer sea. I took her clitoris in my mouth and I sucked until I was filled with her. She began to whisper demands as she came to the edge, her clitoris was firm in my mouth and I pulled back. I kissed the white skin between her thighs. She whimpered and begged me to love her. I took her in my mouth again and again. The power I felt was outrageous. Finally, we were at the place where there was no going back and I circled her with my tongue until her orgasm shook us both. I know the sounds that came from us were dangerously loud before we lay quietly in each other's arms.

I was drifting close to sleep when she took my face in her hands. "Please, put your number in the guestbook in the hall. I need to call you tomorrow. Please, don't forget," she said as she pulled on her clothes and quietly shut the door leaving me by myself.

I was sure everybody was staring at me when I came into the living room but it seemed nobody had missed me. Dennis was happily talking to Ronald Deschampes, Eva's husband.

"I've been telling Ronald about your acting career, that you had a part on Broadway while you were still in theater school."

"It was a very small part." I smiled as Ronald shook my shaking hand.

"You must have been enchanting," he said.

Before we left, I slipped into the foyer and put my address and phone number in the blue guestbook on the hall table. In the comments column I wrote, "Thank you."

How can I describe the terror when I went to my door at noon the next day to find Ronald Deschampes standing with a paper bag and a bottle of wine? I knew he had come to kill me.

As it turned out he didn't come to kill me. He had come to make a contract. He told me because he found me attractive he would pay my rent, find me work in the theater in Montreal, and I would be his mistress. I am sure I wouldn't have believed him if he had been the first middle-aged man to offer me rent for sex. I would have assumed he was playing a horrible joke. He wasn't the first, and so I listened to him for a few minutes; declined his offer as politely as I could and showed him to the door. I kept the bottle of wine and bag of croissants.

When I locked the door behind him I sank down on the floor to cry. I cried and laughed at the absurdity and cried again. I wondered if Eva would call and if I would I tell her about her husband's proposition. Did she know he did this kind of thing? Would I allow Eva to make love to me again? Was I a lesbian? Would I disappear into that dark world nobody talks about, childless, and reviled by everybody I had once known?

At three in the afternoon she appeared at my door. I told her immediately that Ronald had paid me a visit. She just smiled and shook her head. We sat looking out my window and talked until it was dark. We made love. We walked up the street and looked at the city lights from Mount Royal. I was so happy.

Being a lesbian in Canada in 1964 was against the law. If Eva's marriage ended because she was in love with a woman, her beautiful boys would certainly have been taken away from her. I began to tell lies to myself and to other people. The lies made patterns that criss-crossed everything I did. For nine months Eva and I loved each other. We were ecstatic and miserable in turn. One evening while she and I were having dinner in a restaurant we began to talk about the boys' Easter vacation and thinking about her sons gave me a surge of resolve. I knew it wouldn't last so I had to act quickly. I told her I was leaving because the risks we were taking were too great. I left the restaurant, took a taxi to my apartment, paid my landlady, packed a few things, got on a plane and never saw her again.

Thirty years and two heterosexual marriages passed before another woman made love to me. How lucky I am that in that thirty years there were people more daring than I am who spoke out. They created an environment where I can live openly with the love of my life. My partner Liz and I have been happy for sixteen years. I hope Eva fared as well.

Solo Hike
Bliss

The summer camp was my parents' idea. They wanted me to spend more time with kids my own age. I wasn't so sure about it, but looking back at the last two months, I'd had a great time so far. Like an Outward Bound program, the out-camping adventures were demanding and forced us to our limits—mind, body and spirit. We'd hiked on the Appalachian Trail, canoed on the boundary waters and bicycled in the mountains of New Hampshire and Vermont. The days were filled with strenuous physical activity that should have brought exhausted slumber, but for me, Elise was at the heart of my dreams.

Genuinely kindhearted and pretty, Elise was popular with everyone. Shorter than me and curvy, she had tawny, shoulder-length hair that fell in soft waves and a heart-shaped face bronzed by the sun. Gray-blue eyes changed with her moods, and her pale pink mouth looked so very kissable.

I often found myself staring at her lips. She caught me once, capturing my gaze as I memorized her features, and she smiled at me. A sweet, innocent smile that made me feel like a hungry wolf to her lamb. I was mortified. Still, I sensed Elise was different with me than she was with everyone else. Of course, that was probably just my imagination working overtime again . . . but then again, maybe it wasn't.

I didn't expect anything for my sixteenth birthday, but Elise set up a party for me in July. The party was fun, but I wanted Elise to myself. She got me when others didn't, she laughed at my jokes, and she touched me, a lot. Whenever I thought about her, my heart sped up, my mouth got dry and my palms got damp.

It was easy to daydream while bicycling, and Elise had been my favorite topic over the last 350 miles. I couldn't stop thinking about how she would feel in my arms . . . how soft her lips would be under mine. I was so lost in my fantasy that I nearly missed the turn to the cabin we would be staying in for the next few days. As I slowed in the driveway, I could see four tents already up. I hoped we'd be sleeping in the cabin, but it appeared that was not part of the plan.

Elise and a friend, Annie, greeted me as I stopped the bike and stepped off with rubbery legs. Elise reached out to steady me; her touch sent a spark through my body.

"You had a tough day," she said. "A broken chain this morning, and the heaviest load. You really must have pushed to get here, Lou. You did good."

I smiled tiredly. "Please tell me there's a shower with real hot water in the cabin." They both shook their heads. I was crushed. Elise immediately gave me a hug that made me shudder with want as more sparks exploded throughout my nervous system.

"There's a lake a short walk from here," she said. "Go on and get cleaned up; you'll feel better. Annie and I will set the tent up and get everything off your bike."

"Thanks guys," I said. I dug in my pannier to find some clean clothes, plus soap and a towel, then found the energy for another smile and headed around the cabin to the trail.

The walk was peaceful but my thoughts were in turmoil. She

had touched me again and hugged me. It seemed as though I could still smell her over the aromatic pines. The carpet of pine needles that muffled my steps just made my heartbeat seem all the louder. When I saw the lake for the first time, a light breeze rippled its surface, but the blues and greens of the sky and the surrounding trees were still reflected. A hill on the far side seemed to hold the lake, making the setting somehow more intimate. The water looked so inviting, I couldn't wait to get in to cool my ardor.

Putting my clean clothes and towel on a boulder beside the shore, I looked around to make sure I didn't have an audience, then peeled off my odious garments. I hesitated for a moment at the water's edge, but was surprised to find the water sun warmed to a pleasant, yet cool, temperature. As soon as I got waist deep, I slowly submerged my overheated, tired body. My nipples hardened when the water covered them; it felt like cool silk caressed my skin, enfolding me in its embrace.

I loved to swim; I felt powerful in the water. Swimming was easy and relaxing, and I reveled in the sensuous feel of the water surging over my skin with each strong stroke. A swim would rinse me and ease the effect of Elise's touch on my body.

Clean and relaxed, I tried to master my thoughts, but Elise kept rising to the surface of my mind. I could easily imagine her hands caressing me as our weightless bodies circled, met and parted in the water. Then, as if summoned, I looked over to see Elise standing on the shore, waving to me, sending my thoughts back into turmoil. Treading with just my head and shoulders above the water, I waved back.

Her expression softened; she smiled at me. I wasn't sure if I imagined her words or not, but I could swear she said, "You're beautiful, like a mermaid."

She raised her voice. "If you want solid food, you'd better come out now!" She laughed, waved again, and left me to get dressed.

I returned to find our tent up and my dinner in Elise's hands. "I had to get a plate together for you before the others ate everything in sight." She was grinning at me, and I thought I saw a sparkle in her eyes as she handed me my plate and sat down to keep me company.

Honestly, I was so tired, it was all I could do to chew and swallow the food. I felt bad that I wasn't very good company, but Elise seemed comfortable with the silence. When I finished, she just smiled again, took my empty plate from me and said, "Go get into your sleeping bag. You look like you could drop off to sleep at any moment."

Taking her advice, I walked to the tent and snuggled into my bag. I must have fallen to sleep right away because I never heard Annie or Elise come in.

Elise woke me the following morning. "Hey sleepyhead!" she said, nudging my foot with her toe. "I didn't wake you earlier because I thought you needed the extra sleep. The lecture is going to start soon, so you have to get up."

I sat up and rubbed the sleep from my eyes.

She burst out laughing. "You should see your hair!"

My hands shot up to my head. As I feared, my hair was standing on end. Even in the best circumstances, my hair was a challenge. It was fairly short and while there was a lot of it, it was very fine. I hated it. Somewhere between red and brown, it wasn't even a real color. Grumbling, I dug in my pack and found the baseball cap I kept for just such emergencies, jammed it on my head, and followed her out of the tent.

Shortly after lunch, I found out why the lecture focused on shelters, indigenous wildlife and first aid. We were going on solo hikes, allowed only a sleeping bag and what we could carry in a daypack. We were to hike a minimum of three miles, find shelter, and return to the cabin by noon tomorrow. I immediately thought of the hill on the far side of the lake.

I skirted the edge of the lake until the hill loomed ahead of me. Chuckling to myself, I thought, *At least I won't get lost on the return trip.* With my camp set up in a small clearing near the top where there was a good view of the lake, I settled in wondering what I should do next.

I heard noises coming up the hill toward me and somehow managed to cover my elation when I saw Elise walk into the clearing. "Hi. What are you doing here?" I asked.

"I followed you." She dropped her sleeping bag and took off her daypack. "The summer's almost over, and I wanted to talk with you, spend some time with you . . . alone." She blushed and looked at the ground between us.

"Really?" My heart soared, but my stomach clenched with nervousness.

Her gaze traveled from my feet, up my legs, pausing at my crotch, then to my breasts and finally to my eyes. "Yes." Her smile was uncertain, as if she didn't know what I would do, but the look in her eyes was smoldering, begging me to respond to her.

Her gaze burned my flesh, heating my skin as it passed over my body. My skin felt tight, as if sunburnt, but so sensitive. My stomach muscles tightened more, my breasts felt heavy, and sweat started to bead between them. I'd never felt so much from just a glance. I had to have more.

I closed the distance between us, stopping inches from her. Warmth radiated from her body; her skin was flushed. I raised my hand to touch her cheek. Her skin was satin smooth and just as hot as my own.

Her eyelids fluttered shut as she turned her face into my hand and brushed those perfect pink lips gently against my palm. How could so much sensation be focused on such a small area? My whole body responded to that simple caress. When our bodies touched, her warm hands slid around my waist and up my back, holding me. Our thighs met, and I could feel the jut of her hips and the rise of her small breasts pressing into me. I was thrilled that she was here. Although I was excited that she seemed to want me the way I wanted her, I was uncertain about what to do next when she tucked her forehead in the curve of my neck with a small sigh and rested against me.

Her action made me feel protective. I wanted her to feel safe. I pulled her quivering body closer, holding her tight and secure against me. Maybe she was as unsure as I? She always came across as being so confident, so sure of what she wanted and ready to go after it. It was that Elise I craved. I desperately hoped what she wanted was me.

Lifting her head, she looked first at my lips, then into my eyes. The smoldering desire was back in her eyes. Mesmerized by her, I barely heard her whisper, "Please. Please kiss me."

I lowered my head and touched her lips with mine. I'd had a lot of fantasies about kissing her, but the reality was much better. Hot, moist, and pressing back, our kiss fanned the embers in my belly. I grazed her lips with my tongue, begging for entry.

Cupping my face, she tilted it slightly, and finding that perfect angle, opened her mouth to me. I plunged inside of her. Our tongues danced, one sliding over the other at first, tentatively exploring, and then pressed against each other as if dueling for control of the kiss. We broke the kiss to breathe. We had to. Our chests heaving, we stared into one another's eyes.

"I've never shared a kiss like that, Lou." Taking the lead, she once again claimed my mouth with hers, gently biting my lower lip before sucking it into her mouth, stroking and soothing with her tongue. I took her tongue deep into my mouth, held and released it and then sucked it deep again. It was delicious, a mutual give-and-take between us that made the fire within me flare through my body.

I crushed her to me, and when her legs parted slightly, my thigh pressed between them. I stifled her moan with my mouth, and when I felt the damp crotch of her shorts molding to me, my hands moved to cup her ass cheeks, squeezing and pressing her harder against my thigh. The quality of her kisses changed, as if she couldn't get enough of me, as if she wanted to devour me.

When she broke our kiss, she leaned back in my embrace and opened her eyes. I'd always loved how her eyes changed color with her moods, but I'd never seen this color before . . . darker, more gray than blue, like a storm about to be unleashed. Her lips were fuller, swollen from our kisses, and raspberry in color.

"Can I stay here with you tonight?" she asked.

Mind racing, heart thundering, and stomach suddenly churning, I thought, *Can she possibly mean what I was thinking she meant?* "Elise, are you sure?"

She didn't hesitate for a moment, "Yes, I'm sure. I want to . . . stay here with you."

Everything was happening so fast. I needed a moment to collect my wits, to think about what to do next. She whimpered when I moved away from her. Taking a step back and a deep breath, I looked at her. "It's going to be dark soon. Let me set up our camp." I reached for her sleeping bag to unroll it.

While I was doing that, Elise unzipped my bag and spread it out over the ground cover. "I have an idea," she said. "Our bags are about the same size, do you think we could zip them together?" Her intention was unmistakable.

My breath caught at the thought of our bodies entwined inside of the sleeping bags. "If we can't zip them, we could just leave them open I guess."

Oh my God! Could I do this? Do I know what to do? Have I read enough to pull this off? As if she sensed my hesitation, she flashed a sexy grin at me and helped me to zip her bag together with mine to create a soft, warm nest.

The sun was about to set, and the sky looked as though it was on fire. The lake reflected the vibrant pinks, reds, oranges and yellows cast from above as we settled on our joined bags. I sat down behind her, wrapping her in a warm embrace. She settled against my chest and took my hands in hers. "This is nice," she said huskily. "You picked a great spot."

The dusk settled around us, the last light of the day waning. Elise took my hands and placed them over her breasts. They fit perfectly in my hands, molding to my palms. My heart rate doubled when I felt hard nipples pushing against my hands. I stroked her small, well-formed breasts through her shirt, and began kissing her neck.

As if my hands and mouth weakened her, she rested her head

against my shoulder, giving me better access to her arched throat. Her pulse quickened as I covered that throbbing spot with my lips and suckled. Her hands clutching my thighs, she gasped when I pinched her nipples between my fingers. Breathing hard, she faced me and leaned in for a kiss. Hot and urgent, our kisses were frequently interrupted with our need to breathe. I wanted her hands on my breasts, but she slowly explored from my waist and over my rib cage until she at last cupped my breasts in her palms. Her fingers played over my hardened nipples, sending a bolt of lightning through me, robbing me of breath and thought.

She took the hem of her shirt and lifted it over her head and off her body. Thunderstruck, I watched as she unhooked her bra and bared herself to me. My mouth watered at the sight of her full bosom and swollen nipples. She rose up on her knees as I pulled her closer, bringing her naked breasts to my eager lips.

The feel of her flesh changed as my tongue licked over her aureole to the hardened tip. Elise laced her fingers in my hair, pulling me tighter and holding me there. Gaining confidence, I sucked on her nipple, tonguing and nipping at it with my teeth, making it swell even more in my mouth. Arching her back, she pressed even harder against my mouth.

Groaning, Elise said, "Oh, that feels good. Oh God, so good!"

Her cries of pleasure urged me on, but when her body trembled in my arms, I left her breast to kiss and lick my way up to her neck. Feeling her racing pulse beneath my lips and hearing her say my name over and over, I thought my head would explode. I'd never felt this way before—amazed and aroused, just wanting to give her pleasure.

Letting my tongue run the length of her throat to her ear, I took her small lobe into my mouth and sucked it. A light sheen of sweat covered Elise's face and torso, her eyes were closed and her breath came in shallow gasps. Kissing her as passionately as I knew how, I lowered us onto our soft bed.

"Take your shirt off, Lou. I want to feel your skin on mine," Elise commanded.

Straddling her, I tore my shirt and sports bra off. Elise bit her lip as she smoothed her hands up my body to cup my breasts. The embers of my passion burst into flames as her thumbs toyed with my nipples. She pulled me down to take me into her mouth.

It was wonderful—her hot wet lips closing over my erect nipple stoked the fire to an inferno, consuming me. My arms shook from the wave of excitement I felt as her hot tongue circled and licked my erect nipples before she sucked them hard. I felt the wetness flow between my legs, felt the electricity course through my body from her explorations as she rolled us over to top me.

"Elise," I cried out. "I want you naked. I want us naked together."

Scrambling to our feet, we anxiously stripped off our shorts and underwear. As I pulled her panties down her shapely legs, I could smell her arousal; it made me dizzy with want. Shoes and socks dispensed with, I looked up at her. Illuminated by the nearly full moon, she was bathed in a silvery light that enhanced her contours with shadows. My hunger increased tenfold. I had to make her mine.

Standing, I embraced her, feeling her nakedness press into me, her heat warming my body. I covered her ass with my hands, pulling her closer, and up off her feet. She wrapped her legs around my waist, holding on as I lowered us to the ground. I kissed her, my tongue thrusting deep while my hips pressed her pussy rhythmically, unleashing at last the storm of passion she raised in me.

Her body moved beneath me, pressing up to meet my hips, inciting me to move faster, with greater urgency. Lifting myself for a better angle, I looked into her eyes. Her desire was blazingly obvious. She wanted me.

Voice tight and quaking with need, she said, "I want . . . I need more, Lou." Taking my hand, she guided me to between her legs. She was wet, really wet.

"Easy, baby. Let's take this slow," I said, sliding easily through her wetness before pulling my hand away. I straddled her again, running my wet fingers over my lips and licking them with my tongue, tasting her nectar. Covering her again, I kissed her, sliding my tongue into her mouth. "Can you taste yourself?" I asked.

"Yes," she said.

"I want to taste you again."

"Yes. Please?"

Yes had become the most beautiful word in the universe to me. The salty tang of her skin was exquisite as I descended. Suckling on her tender earlobe made her body tense beneath me. I kissed and licked my way down her neck to the pulse point at its base and lapped up the small pool of sweat that gathered in the small vee at the base of her throat.

Holding my head between her hands, she pushed me, guiding my journey to her breast. I wrapped my tongue around her swollen nipple, licking and then trapping it between the roof of my mouth and my tongue while sucking hard.

"Oh my God!" she said. "I can feel you everywhere when you do that!"

I chuckled deep in my throat. *I guess I did learn something from those books!* I took her nipple between my teeth and gently pulled it. Elise's hips started bucking in time with my pulls and her body quivered. Her reaction made my passion rise to a fevered pitch. I needed to taste her again . . . soon.

I followed the nicely defined contour of her abs with my lips and tongue. Pulling back momentarily, I could see she was wet, curls glistening. She reached down and opened her cunt for me. I inhaled her scent deeply, then blew gently onto her hardening clit. Her body shuddered again. She cried out, "Lou, please . . . Please, I need you!"

Lowering my head, I licked her like she was an ice cream cone, using long, slow strokes from the base of her cunt to either side of her swollen clit. Her hips lifted at my every stroke, trying to push her clit into my mouth. Instead, I pushed my tongue in as far as I could inside her.

"More, Lou! I . . . please, I need more!"

I thrust two fingers inside of her, and when her hips drove upward, I pressed inside as far as I could. Hot juices covered my fingers as I fucked her. The walls of her vagina gripped my fingers, urging me deeper yet.

Feeling her walls start to clench, I stopped pumping her as I took her clit in my mouth once again. Gently taking her distended clit between my teeth, I suckled her as I thrust my fingers upward.

"Don't stop! Don't stop, Lou, Please don't stop!" she cried out. Her body fluttered, her muscles contracted around my fingers, and then her orgasm radiated through her body. Her back arched, her body convulsed. She cried my name into the night along with her pleasure.

When Elise stopped trembling and relaxed back onto the ground, I rested my head on her stomach. It took me a moment to realize she was crying. I covered her body with my own and looked into her eyes. "Elise? Are you all right? Did I hurt you?"

She smiled that sexy grin at me again and said, "No. You were perfect. I knew you would be. I've wanted you all summer long. I knew you would be different, so very good. I wanted you to be the one, my first lover."

I licked the salty residue of her tears from her face, and then softly kissed her eyelids. Taking my face between her hands, she kissed me so hard my head started to spin. Rolling us over, she straddled my body. She looked confident and sexy. "You said you wanted to go slow," she said, her voice low and seductive.

I was already so excited, I knew it wouldn't take much to make me come. She touched me with featherlight strokes, leaving my skin sensitized and aflame. I could hardly breathe as her mouth ascended the swell of my breast, taking my already painfully erect nipple inside.

The feel of her wet tongue wrapping around my nipple sent an electric current directly between my legs. Parting my thighs, she settled between my legs, never once stopping her relentless assault on my breasts. I thought my heart would burst from my chest it was beating so hard and fast, and that beat echoed in the throbbing between my legs.

My hips surged as she pressed her stomach against my center. My wetness coated her belly, perfuming the air around us with my unique essence.

"You smell so good. I can't wait to taste you," she said.

"Yes. I'm so ready for you, baby. Just one touch and I'll be gone," I whispered in a voice made hoarse with need.

I gasped when she spread my folds to the cool air.

"You're so beautiful, Lou," she whispered. "I had no idea how beautiful you would be." She looked up at me. "I want to be inside you."

I used her words. "Yes. Please."

Her fingers barely pushed into me. I don't know what she did, but my world centered only on what she was doing to my cunt. My whole being focused on my pussy and the sensation she created within me with her fingers. My clit throbbed with all my energy, desire and pent-up need.

Out of control and unable to take more of the sweet torment, I surged against her hand to take her deep inside me. She withdrew, then thrust again, taking me over the edge and into oblivion as the waves of orgasm consumed me.

Just when I started to relax, she pressed deep into me again and curled her fingers inside of me, creating a different kind of pressure. Lowering her head, she sucked my hard clit into her hot, wet mouth. My whole body clenched, tight like the string of a drawn bow. I saw her blond head moving between my legs, and, knowing it was Elise's hot lips encircling me, her fingers inside of me, loving me, caused a release so intense that a cry of exultation tore from my throat as the pleasure coursed through my body again.

As I lay spent, Elise gently withdrew from me, pulling me into her arms while my body still quivered. I don't know where the tears came from, but I couldn't stop them. She didn't question, just nestled me against her, stroking my hair and back while she placed light kisses on my head. How could I know it would be so different with *her*?

When I found my voice, all I could say was, "Wow."

"Yes. Wow is right." She kissed me again and said, "This is the best solo hike I've ever been on."

I had to agree as I melted into her body and kissed her, ready to love her again.

Starry, Starry Night
Aunt Fanny

I lived near Fresno, California in 1997, and was a forty-year-old spinster school teacher. My work life was dreary and predictable. Then I discovered the Internet. I started meeting lots of people, all of them far more fascinating and compelling than anyone I knew in my town.

I got busy exploring a bunch of different Web sites, mostly chat sites. A good half of them were about sex, in all its many varieties. It didn't take me long to find www.gay.com.

I experimented with lesbian cyber sex and liked it. A lot. The idea of a woman in my arms—with her soft skin, warm kisses, beautiful body and mind—intrigued me. I soon learned what pleased my lesbian lovers. I took to covering my computer chair with a towel, because I'd make myself wet with my own stories. My lovers participated, each to her own ability. Some I refused to "see" again, others I met with regularly. One of these was Winifred. She was a slow typist, but what an imagination!

Winifred was originally from Holland but was currently living with Deb in Louisiana. The two women shared a house with Carrie, a butch wanderer who'd taken shelter with them and never left. Carrie had gotten a job in the same factory as Deb, and together they supported Winifred, who kept house for the three of them. Winifred confessed to me that she and Carrie were having a secret affair behind Deb's back. She also confessed that Deb beat her.

I reacted impulsively. It was summer vacation and I was feeling relaxed and easy. "If you don't feel safe, come and stay with me," I typed. Two days later Winifred arrived and moved into my guest bedroom.

She was nothing like I expected from her description on the Internet. She was shaped rather like a bull, with a short fat neck, a chest exactly as wide as her belly, and strong arms she crossed continuously. Her hair was black, thick, and cut very short. Her face was round, and closed. She never looked me in the eye. Still, here she was, a living breathing lesbian right in my own drab house in the foothills of California.

The sexual tension was palpable. We'd cybered with each other for months, but I'd never been with a woman in real life, and Winifred was pining for her lover, Carrie. She expressed her sorrow and frustration in food. "I miss her," she said, sighing heavily over breakfast, lunch and dinner.

"My heart is broken," she cried with her Dutch accent while standing in the kitchen. "I love her so much!" Winifred moaned for the millionth time.

"Call Carrie and bring her out here to visit," I said around a mouthful of apple crepe dripping in lemon sauce.

Three days later Carrie arrived with her own suitcases. She moved into the guest bedroom with Winifred. I gritted my teeth as, through the thin walls, I heard them getting it on that first night. I went online and cybered fiercely. That Carrie was some looker. It was easy to picture her making love.

Carrie also looked much more masculine than me. But where Winifred was squat and bullish, Carrie was tall, broad shouldered and muscular. She was dressed in a button-down shirt and pleated slacks, which were carefully ironed to crisp attention. Her face was long, and her shoulder-length brown hair was gathered in a pony-tail at the nape of her neck. Her eyes were sparkling blue—clear and honest.

"How's tricks?" Carrie greeted me in the morning, handing me a fresh cup of coffee. She winked.

"Fine by me," I answered. "How's by you?" I liked the way her eyes followed me as I walked. My breasts were clearly visible through my thin cotton nightie.

"I hear you're a virgin," she said, laughing when I blushed. She rose and crossed the room, giving me a chance to look her over, before returning with fresh muffins. "I can help you with that if you like?"

I didn't know what to say. I'd focused my lust on Winifred. I'd never even cybered with Carrie. But I had to admit, she was a luscious bit of butch bait. I'd admired women like her for any number of years, and envied their self-assured knowledge of who they were. I felt a much stronger physical attraction to Carrie, than to Winifred, who was sleeping unaware in my guest room.

I rose and left the kitchen in confusion. I knew I wanted to try lesbian sex, but I wasn't at all sure that I wanted to, if you know what I mean. I was afraid of acknowledging my own lesbian tendencies. I'd always liked women much more than men, and found myself admiring beautiful women whenever I saw them. I had a secret crush on Queen Latifah that was definitely sexual. She was a fixture in my masturbatory fantasies. But to be a lesbian in rural California was unheard of, I naively believed. And to be a lesbian school teacher was to kiss your job goodbye. It was a huge cliff I was about to jump off, and it scared me. I wondered if I was game enough.

That night Winifred prepared an exquisite feast. The three of us sat down to dinner. "This is so good," I enthused.

"Yes, it is," agreed Carrie, smiling at Winifred but managing to brush my bare arm as she reached for a piece of French bread from the basket near me.

"I haven't had anyone cook for me, since, well forever," I said, managing to catch Carrie's eye and smile.

"Your husband was a fool." Carrie laughed, leaning in until I could feel her hot breath on my shoulder.

"Yes, he was," said Winifred, enjoying her food.

"In more ways than one," added Carrie, leering at me.

I blushed, and settled for enjoying the fabulous dinner, but Carrie was determined to win my attention. It wasn't long before Winifred began to catch on to the little glances and surreptitious touches that were going on between Carrie and me. I nearly choked on a mouthful of fish when I felt something nudging my knee.

I glanced under the table and found it was Winifred's sock-covered foot. She was tickling my inner thigh. Winifred grinned knowingly at me, then turned and looked triumphantly at Carrie. The competition was on, and I was the prize.

No one had ever wanted me this way before. I blushed, but relished the situation. They became witty and entertaining. I began to reward each one with small touches to her hands. They smiled at each other and doubled their efforts.

After dinner they shooed me from the kitchen and attacked the dishes together. I could hear their easy joking, voices husky and deep. I was excited as I lit candles in the living room, and turned on the CD player. My only Melissa Etheridge disc began playing, and I heard my lesbians laugh in the kitchen.

I knew I was going to get laid that night. The question was, which one? I was every bit as interested in finding out the answer to that as they were. It was fascinating and fun.

They entered the living room and we all leaned back to listen to Melissa, eat cake and drink wine. Electricity crackled in the air.

Carrie kissed me first. It was the texture of her lips that surprised me. Soft, yet firm, they settled on mine as a bee takes a flower. It shot a bolt of electricity straight to my crotch. I felt myself grow wet, and my nipples were tight and clearly visible through my midriff-tied white blouse. My short shorts got shorter.

Winifred sat back grinning until Carrie finished. I caught my breath and drank my entire glass of wine in a few swallows, checking to make sure all the window curtains were pulled.

Then Winifred kissed me. Her big strong hands grabbed my shoulders, pulling me against her chest. I felt her large breasts meet mine. I sighed with shocked delight. She wasn't as skilled as Carrie, but she was every bit as enthusiastic. When she released me, my wine glass had been refilled. I drank it just as fast as the first one. I enjoyed having one woman watch the other kiss and fondle me. I was shocked at myself, and titillated.

I suddenly remembered the hot tub sitting in my backyard. There was a meteor shower expected that night. "Do you want to sit in the hot tub and watch for shooting stars?" I heard myself ask. This moved the competition up a notch. I wanted to see these women's bodies, and have them see mine.

We changed. I put on my green bikini, the one that accented the color of my eyes, the curve of my hips, my flat belly, and voluptuous breasts (hey, that's my story and I'm sticking to it). I turned the lights on in the hot tub, and was the first one in. I was adjusting the jets when my guests came through the sliding glass door. I was struck by the differences between them.

Winifred was overweight, but also very muscular. She carried most of her weight in her upper body, which made her look barrel chested. She wore a white undershirt, her large breasts thrusting before her, and cutoff shorts.

Carrie was in a black T-shirt and bikini bottom that fit her slender form like a second skin. Her breasts were much smaller, but stood high and proud. Her long legs were shaven, and she turned her ass to me as she climbed in the tub. It was fabulous, well rounded and firm. She sat on one side of me, while Winifred took up position on the other.

We drank wine and pretended to scan the skies for meteors.

First Winifred's ham-shaped hand, then Carrie's strong slender one, claimed my knees. I shivered in delight. With the lights on in the hot tub I could see everything they were doing.

First one, then the other initiated a new move. They advanced in their competition quickly. My legs were stroked, my belly tickled, and finally my breasts were claimed. I moaned as each woman manipulated a breast, the sensations so different, and yet combining to drive me wild. One pinched my nipple, while the other one palmed me, squeezing gently. Then one traced a finger inside my bra, while the other tugged at my neck ties. Soon my breasts were bare, floating in the water freely. My nipples were pink raisins of delight.

Carrie dipped her head and sucked one nipple into her mouth, as Winifred circled the other with her thumb, watching. Slowly she too descended, until I had two women suckling me. The sensation of teeth and tongues pulling at me, teasing me into a sensitivity I'd never known before in my life, undid me. I wanted more. I wanted them both. I wanted them here, and now.

I pulled away from them. "Take off your clothes," I said, glancing from one to the other. Lust made my voice husky.

Carrie eagerly complied, peeling her shirt and bikini bottom off quickly. Winifred was shyer, but soon she too was seated in the water, exposed to three sets of eyes. I reminded myself that the two were lovers, and knew each other intimately. I was the stranger here.

I still had my bikini bottom on. Each took a string, and pulled. Flickering light splayed shadows across our skin. Mine burned to be touched. I leaned sideways and raised my feet, effectively spreading myself across their laps. I gave myself over to pleasure.

Carrie cradled me in her arms, but reached over and switched off the underwater lights. She bent her head and kissed me. One hand began massaging my breasts, which were floating on warm water. I opened my eyes and saw a moonless night, filled with shining stars.

Winifred had my bottom in her lap, and was stroking my legs.

Her short, powerful fingers started probing my pussy. "We both make love to you," she said to me with her Dutch accent. With one hand she held me open, while with the other she entered me with first one, and then two fingers.

I saw stars shooting across the sky as it dawned on me that I had not one, but two lesbians giving me my first lesson in Sapphic love. I felt so woman centric in the dark warm world of the hot tub with two women servicing me and a meteor shower over head. I was starved for more. More of what, I didn't know. But I had a hunger I'd never had before. "Look at the stars," I said, motioning up into the heavens.

"I see them in your eyes," said Carrie. She was looking at Winifred. Her hand left my breast to descend under my bottom to Winifred's lap. Her fingers delved into Winifred's pussy, her wrist pushed up against me. As I felt her thrusting into her lover a surge of lust burst within me. I felt my pussy clench tight on Winifred's fingers as Carrie pushed my back up, grabbing my nipple in her mouth. She sucked, hard. I moaned.

The water around us was filled with small waves from the jets: fast, furious bubbles butting against us, urging us to float. Winifred moved easily to one side, turning her legs into Carrie's lap under me. I shifted until I could fasten my own lips on Carrie's small tight nipples. Winifred leaned over me and caught Carrie's lips in a kiss, while her fingers plunged in and out of my pussy, over and over again.

"I love this," I said, ecstatically happy. My two lesbians broke their kiss.

"Me too," said Winifred, looking first at Carrie, and then at me. A huge smile lit her face. She pulled her fingers from inside me, slithered up, and joined me in sucking Carrie's tits. Carrie took one of mine and one of Winifred's in her two hands, and squeezed. I wrapped my legs around Winifred's thighs, and rubbed my pussy against her bottom.

The meteors exploded into the night around us as we shifted positions. I explored their breasts with my hands and mouths. I enjoyed the feeling of Carrie's hand grabbing my bottom, then descending between my cheeks and teasing first my opening, and then my clit. I returned the favor on her lover Winifred. What one did to me, I did to the other. Warm water, hot touches, steaming kisses, I was the volcano at the center of it all, providing the heat which made the night sizzle around us.

At one point Winifred hopped out of the hot tub and disappeared for a moment. When she returned, she held in one hand a large double-headed dildo, and in the other a bottle of lube. She motioned to Carrie, who helped me to my knees on the bench, and bent me over the side of the hot tub. My steaming breasts, back, and bottom were exposed to the night breeze. My pussy was hot and throbbing, even more so now when exposed. I gasped when Winifred drizzled the cool oil down my back.

Carrie's hands smoothed the oil over my hips and bottom, massaging my skin and teasing the folds of my sex, slicking me up. Winifred liberally lubricated both ends of the dildo, then motioned for Carrie to bend over the opposite side of the narrow tub and lubricated her shapely ass and pussy. She pushed the dildo deep into Carrie as I watched over my shoulder. I gasped to see it disappear into the brown curls peeking just above the water level. Winifred pumped it in and out gently, twisting it back and forth until a moan escaped Carrie, who was also staring over her shoulder. She grinned at me as Winifred approached me with the other head of the dildo.

I thought my heart would burst as she spread my pussy lips, and rubbed the dildo up and down my slit. Carrie was watching with eyes filled with lust, pushing in and out with the other end. Together they drove the dildo into me. I pushed back until it filled me deeper than I'd ever been filled before. My ass brushed Carrie's and she began rocking back and forth. I did too, and soon we'd established a fucking rhythm that sent me soaring out of my head.

Winifred's fingers touched my clit, and I saw that she was also under Carrie, stroking her, too. I gripped my own breasts, pulling at the nipples. We fucked each other, a dance of hungry passion.

She moaned, I groaned, she growled. My mind soared into the sky and I screamed out my orgasm into the night. A shooting star burned up before my eyes.

Carrie climaxed immediately after I did, thrusting her bottom against mine as she strained on the dildo, Winifred's fingers moving madly. I helped by bumping and swirling my ass against Carrie's. The water swirled around us as the meteor shower overhead ended. Together we twisted, until the three of us were embracing as one, our arms wrapped around each other. We kissed. Yes, all three together.

They both came to my king-sized bed that night, and we explored every possible combination the three of us could manage. We fell asleep sometime the next afternoon, only to wake and take each other again.

This went on for two wild weeks. Then they bought an RV and drove off into the sunset to find their destiny. I went back to teaching, but came out to my school superintendent at the Christmas party. He fired me three days later. I took up professional storytelling.

I still keep up with Winifred and Carrie through e-mail. They've traveled the country twice in their RV, meeting other lesbians from the Internet. They visited last year. As luck would have it, there was a meteor shower that night.

My Secret
Saundra W. Haggerty

At the time, it mattered to me more than anything else in the world. Of course, deep down I know that there was no way she would ever reciprocate my feelings, but that was beside the point.

I was fifteen and obsessive. I was in the process of realizing that my pathetic attempts to go out with boys didn't excite me half as much as it did for my friends when they had new boyfriends. More to the point, I was more interested in *being* the boyfriend. Now don't get me wrong, I had no desire to be male, but I was starting to realize that dating for me was not as straightforward (no pun intended) as it was for my peers. I would feign interest in this boy band or that male actor, but all I really wanted was a girl—but not any girl.

She was a senior and I couldn't stop looking at her. She was two years ahead of me and unaware of my existence. Yet I was very, very aware of hers. Her name was Alex, and I could not help but to notice her every time I saw her. She had the most gorgeous figure—toned without being skinny—and strawberry red hair. I could have drowned in her green eyes if she ever actually looked at me. She was captain of the debate team, class president and perfect. I obsessed over her my sophomore year, but never once received a hint of acknowledgement. And why should I? I was nobody in her world, even though she took up a huge chunk of mine.

She graduated in the spring of 1980 and headed down south to UCLA, while I remained in high school, and life had to go on. I graduated in 1982 and, having decided to remain close to home, attended San Francisco State University. Alex meanwhile seemed like a distant memory, although occasionally I did stop to wonder about her.

One evening, as I argued a point during a game of pool, I noticed a particular girl come into the club with a few friends and go up to the bar. I hadn't seen her there before—and I was regular enough to know most of the regulars who frequented this gay club—but there was something about her I couldn't put my finger on. She seemed somehow familiar to me. She was well dressed in a fitted shirt that showed off her figure and a miniskirt that accentuated her legs. She had short black hair, and was in a group with three other people. I watched her for a moment, and then it hit me.

"Alex," I said out loud.

"What?" said my friend Rochelle, who was lining up to take another shot.

I stood transfixed, a million things going around in my head. What was she doing here? Was she gay? I'd never had an inkling of her being so when we were in high school. Should I talk to her? Would she remember me? What if I was wrong—what if it wasn't her? No, it was definitely her; I'd held her face in my memory for the last four years.

Rochelle broke my train of thought. "Saundra, are you okay?"

"Yes," I said, spinning around.

"What's up with you?" asked Dee, another one of my posse.

"You see that girl at the bar in blue?" I said to both of them.

"Well I went to high school with her and had the biggest crush on her when I was in the tenth grade."

"Wow," said Rochelle. "I can see why."

"Hands off," I said.

"What are you going to do?" asked Dee. "Are you going to go and talk to her?"

"I can't do that!" I exclaimed. "She didn't even know I existed. Anyway, she's probably taken."

"You won't know unless you try," said Dee. "Just buy her a drink or something."

"Dee," I began lamely, but she cut me off.

"You know I'm right," she said, giving me a little push in Alex's direction.

I nodded and drained my glass of white wine. Rochelle and Dee kept egging me on, so I took a deep breath and went to the bar. My heart was thumping, I was terrified that I was being too hasty—four years was a lot of time and she probably wouldn't remember me.

"Excuse me," I said, tapping her on the shoulder. "But are you Alex?"

She turned to look at me. The moment I saw her face I knew I was right: I could never forget those incredible green eyes and finally, for once, they were focused on me. She looked puzzled and I started to get an awful sinking feeling that I was about to make a huge fool out of myself.

"Yes," she said slowly. "I'm sorry, have we met?"

"You probably don't remember me," I said. "I'm Saundra, we went to high school together. I was two years behind you."

She thought for a moment, then, to my astonishment, remembered. "Did you play basketball?"

"Forward," I answered.

"Yeah, I remember you," she said, smiling. "Wow, how long as it been?"

"Four years, I think," I said. "I'm nineteen now. I guess you've graduated from UCLA."

"I have."

"Can I buy you a drink?"

"Yes, that's sweet of you. Thank you. Tequila, please."

Next thing I knew, we were sitting at a table outside on the patio talking as though we had been friends for years, which I found a little odd seeing as we had never exchanged a word before that evening. I found out that she'd recently moved back to San Francisco, was working and had an apartment near the club. I also discovered that she was single, which set off mad rejoice.

About an hour and a half later, one of the three people she had been with came out and said that one of the other girls was ill (too much gin and juice I figured) and she was taking her home.

"That's my ride," said Alex, looking like she was about to get up and leave.

Without thinking I burst out, "I can give you a ride home."

"No, I can't ask that," said Alex.

"It's no trouble," I said earnestly. "I'll be happy to."

"Well, if you're sure."

"Think nothing of it."

The friend went away, and we stayed until last call. I showed her to my car (not technically mine, but now was not the time to tell her I borrowed my mother's car for the night). Fifteen minutes later, we arrived at her building.

"Come on in if you like," she said.

"I probably should go."

"Oh, come on."

"Someone could take that the wrong way," I replied.

"And what is the wrong way," she said, smiling.

"Er"—I stopped, not sure of how to proceed, then went on— "you should probably know that when we were in high school I had a major crush on you." I knew it was likely to be a silly thing to say, but it slipped out before I had a chance to think about it.

She paused for a second. "What about now?" she asked.

"Nothing's changed," I muttered.

"Well that's just as well then," she replied. "So come in."

My eyes widened when she said this, and the look on her face told me she meant it. She got out of the car and I followed her up the stairs to her apartment. She opened the door to let us in, and switched on the light. The moment the door was closed behind us I pushed her up against the wall and kissed her, deeply and strongly. Much to my delight she clung to me, pulling me closer to her as we plunged our tongues into one another's mouths. The fire emanating from within me was incredible, and it was manifesting itself in a passion so great, I was surprising even myself as I kissed and kissed and kissed her; I felt her wrap one leg around my waist. Seeing this as an invitation (as I was prone to) I lifted my leg, pushing my thigh up against her pussy, which was met with a deep-throated groan from her.

I hurriedly undid the buttons of her shirt and let it fall open, giving me full access to her still bra-covered breasts. I was kissing my way down her body, and though tempted, did not stop to linger at breasts, instead raising her skirt and pushing her lace panties (always pleased to see those) to the floor, exposing her pussy. It was covered with a fine layer of hair and was obviously very wet already. Alex waited, still standing up against the wall as I knelt down between her legs.

I wanted to savor the sight and scent of her for a moment or two but she was having none of it. She grabbed my head and held me right under her pussy, giving me no choice but to lick her. She tasted amazing, and I ran my tongue in a figure eight around her clit. She was already wet, but once I began tasting her I could feel her pussy releasing more of its precious juices. She was grinding herself into my face, and still gripping my head so that I couldn't escape. I slipped my tongue inside her as far as I could, and was greeted by yet more of the wonderful liquid before I slipped two fingers inside her and searched for her G-spot. It took me a short while to find, during which time I ran my tongue all over her pussy and sucked on her clit, but once I did I knew about it. Alex started to thrust onto my face harder and harder, and was getting quite vocal about how good she was feeling. This inspired me to work her harder, both from the outside and the inside and before long she was starting to climax. She was gushing her come all over my face, and I loved it. She was getting louder and louder, and I placed my free hand on her hip and pulled her pussy even closer to my mouth.

Finally, with one last thrust, her orgasm subsided and I felt her body go limp, held up only by me. I extracted my fingers from her pussy and kissed her gently on the navel, my face smeared with her delicious come. Then I looked up and saw her smiling back down at me. I got back onto my feet and held her for a few minutes, trying to comprehend the whole range of emotions I was feeling. The only one that was clear was an undeniable state of bliss.

After a while, and without a word, Alex took me by the hand and led me into her bedroom. She turned on a small lamp in the corner, which provided just the right amount of lighting. Then she stepped over to me and put her hand on the back of my head before drawing my mouth to hers and kissing me once more.

When she pulled away she spoke at last. "What you just did was amazing, I haven't felt so good for a very long time."

"What can I say?" I replied, blushing slightly, "You must have inspired me."

She smiled. Then, without warning, she pushed me, and I lost my balance and found myself on my back on the bed. The next thing I knew, she was above me, kissing me again, and I pulled her down on top of me. We were necking like teenagers (well, I suppose I still was one technically) and rolling about on the bed, I thought my lips would go numb. My tongue was exploring her mouth and I could not get enough. During all of this we were tugging at each other's clothes (I never had got as far as removing her shirt and bra) until we were both totally naked. At that point I pulled back, simply to admire her, as this was the first time I had been able to see her in all her glory. And my God, she was beautiful. Her body was in perfect proportion, she looked athletic without being scarily muscular, and I wanted to devour all of her there and then.

I could also feel the way her eyes were inspecting me, and next to her I was feeling rather self-conscious (I was sure I didn't get as much time to work out as she did). I needn't have worried though, as she moaned "wow" and pulled me back to her again. Her lips blazed a trail from my neck to my breasts, and she began to play with my already hard nipples with her tongue. It felt like heaven, and I could feel myself becoming more and more turned on. When she was done with my breasts I could have sworn both my nipples were twice the size they were when she started.

She leaned over my body and I could feel her hand brushing down my thigh and toward my waiting pussy. My legs opened further, and when I first felt her fingers part my lips and stroke my clit I could have died. However, my initial pleasure was to be short-lived as she quickly brought her hand away, and on its way up I could see that her fingers were coated with my juices. Just the sight of them was hugely arousing, and when she put those fingers in her mouth and sucked them clean, making very appreciative noises, I knew I needed her desperately.

I pushed her onto her back on the bed and straddled her head. The expression on her face said to me that she was eager for what was to come, so I slowly lowered myself down onto her waiting mouth.

The first stroke of her tongue along the whole length of my pussy made me shudder. It was the purest, most unadulterated pleasure I had ever felt, and yet I knew that this was just the beginning. I could feel her tongue running along the valleys between my lips climbing to the mountain of my clit. She clearly had an expert tongue, and I was only too pleased that I was getting to experience it. Her hands were on the back of my hips, and she set in motion a slow rocking rhythm that increased all the sensations I was having. When she started to probe my opening I thought my knees would go. Her tongue was soft and gentle at times, hard and precise at others, and she seemed to know exactly what I enjoyed the most. She was making me feel amazing. When she added her fingers to the mix I wondered how much longer I could hold out. She was licking and sucking my clit as she plunged her fingers in and out of me.

Finally, I could not control myself anymore, and I started to tremble as the first waves of my orgasm hit me. I was screaming out her name as she continued to fuck me. I must have woken all the neighbors, but I didn't care, I was in the midst of the greatest climax of my life.

Eventually, though, I could take no more, and sensing this, she slowed down. I fell onto my side and rolled so I was on my back, panting. I was feeling euphoric and didn't know what to say. She hauled herself up onto one elbow so she was leaning above me. She looked very smug.

"You know you're good," I said eventually, gasping.

Alex smiled tenderly and kissed me gently on the lips. I could taste my come on her mouth. I nuzzled against her breasts and felt her kiss my forehead. Her arm was around me and she was stroking my back. I felt very content.

I glanced over at the clock and saw that it was four o'clock, later than I had thought. Alex must have seen me do this because at that moment she said, "You are going to stay, aren't you?"

"If you'll have me," I said.

"Of course," she said.

In the morning, I was woken by light coming into the room through the curtains. I realized right away that I was alone in the bed and wondered where Alex had gone. I heard sounds from outside the room and, just as I was about to get up and investigate, she came in holding mugs of steaming coffee. She smiled when she saw I was awake, and greeted me with a kiss before handing me one of the mugs.

"You were sleeping so soundly, I didn't want to wake you," she said.

I sipped at my coffee, smiled, and looked at her. She was wearing a long, dark-green silk robe—though that was still one more garment than me.

"Want to take a shower?" I asked.

"I like your thinking," answered Alex, and she took me by the hand and led me to her bathroom. She switched on the shower and let it warm up for a moment before pushing me up against the wall. The tiles were cold and were a shock, but I forgot all about it as soon as she kissed me. It was a kiss like the one we had shared when we arrived there the night before, only this time I was the one pinned against the wall. Then, suddenly, she pulled away, stepped out of her robe and into the shower, beckoning me to follow her. I did and the sensation of the water hit me immediately. It was hot, and that coupled with the feeling of Alex's skin against mine was wonderfully erotic.

I grabbed the bath gel from the stand and squeezed some onto my palm, before rubbing it onto her body. I started at her bush and across her shoulders before turning her around and going down her back to her ass. She did the same to me, and our two bodies slid over each other as we caressed and touched one another. I wanted her so badly, even more than the previous night, and I couldn't stop myself from running my hand between her thighs and touching her pussy once again. Although the environment we were in wasn't exactly a dry one, I could feel that she was wet with arousal and my fingers slid into her easily. I slid as much of my hand as possible into her and rubbed inside of her, feeling once again for her G-spot. This time it was easy to find, having acquainted myself with it the night before. As Alex's thighs thrust forward she began contracting them in readiness for the orgasm that was beginning inside her. Harder and harder I thrust into her, and harder and harder she came, screaming out my name and pushing down onto me. Her wild abandon was amazing and I never wanted it to stop. Of course, it had to in the end, but not before my hand was coated in her juice and she was completely spent.

I held her after that, kissing her and stroking her as she came back down. She put her arms around me, too, and we stood there like that for some time, not saying a word. I knew I was onto a very good thing, and didn't want to leave, ever. It took some time for us to get out of the shower and dressed, as we kept grabbing one another for a kiss or similar. I was having a lot of trouble keeping my hands off her, and she too seemed reluctant to go away from me.

Finally, I made it out the front door. After exchanging numbers, I walked to my car and I heard her call to me. "See you at seven."

"What's happening at seven?" I called back, turning around.

"You're coming back over here again!" she called back.

I grinned. "Of course I am."

Hustler
Heidi Edwards

I was almost certain my mom could see the devious smile lurking behind my emotionless face when she told me to behave myself while she was at work. Every Saturday, I anticipated her departure and craved the beginning of a new month.

Once I saw the tail end of her rose-colored Buick take a right turn out of the driveway, my eager bare feet would slap furiously against the hardwood floors until I reached my destination. The top drawer of mom and dad's dresser would always make an eerie creaking sound as I slowly pried it open. I would push aside the neatly woven together socks, grab it, and run back to my bedroom, slamming the door behind me.

It was against house rules for me to have a locked door, even at 17, so I made my hideaway in the empty right corner of my closet. The doors folded inward and created just enough space for me, my imagination and my *Hustler*.

I never told anyone how the naked bodies on each page excited me, or how the stories dampened my panties with desire. I was almost 18 and still couldn't figure out my fascination with these naked lovelies.

I was glad that Terry, my boyfriend of over a year, chose skateboarding with the boys over me. It gave me time to sink into the pages of my bold curiosities. I had a lot of friends, but no one I could tell about my innate intrigue for pictures of naked girls.

I was a tomboy who spent most of my spare time skateboarding with the "VB Crew," as the group referred to themselves. The only girl in the group, I was appropriately nicknamed "Skate Betty."

I had also been playing soccer for a couple of years, and that was my only social interaction with the same sex. I usually preferred the company of sweaty boys and dirt to fingernail polish and gossip. That was, until the day I met Jenna. She was the newest girlfriend to David, Terry's best friend. A year older than me, she exuded confidence. Jenna's hair naturally corkscrewed itself into darkened fiery twists that cascaded down the side of her face and hung almost to her chin. The sunlight created a rainbow of reddish hues that shimmered with each ray that shone down upon her. Her nose, sharp and tiny, made her puckering lips seem even larger. Her sun-baked skin looked like a cup of coffee tinted with just a splash of milk.

I often wondered how David, a pale prepubescent punk, could have landed a girl like Jenna.

It wasn't long before the four of us were inseparable. The more Terry and David thought they were getting closer to getting into our pants, the more Jenna and I became disinterested and created humorous anecdotes for their testosterone-filled behavior. We would sit on my bed and giggle endlessly at the goofy things the boys would say to try and seduce us. Jenna would cringe as she described the tongue-filled thrusts David called a nightly goodbye kiss. I would laugh as I talked of Terry's hard, bizarre tongue, which seemed to be searching for the lost city of Atlantis inside of my mouth.

I still managed to save plenty of time for my ritualistic

Saturdays of turning the pages of *Hustler* with one hand tucked inside my jeans.

There was one weekend, however, that opened the threshold of my imagination and pushed me farther into the reality of my desires.

Terry and I planned a trip to Busch Gardens and, of course, our cohorts were coming along for a day of roller coasters and upside-down excitement.

Jenna spent the night at my house that Friday. We stayed up late listening to Jane's Addiction and pointing out hot boys in the latest edition of *Thrasher* magazine, the same edition that housed my commentary on how so many girls did not take the sport of skateboarding seriously. That was the first time I thought about those "other" magazines in her presence, and I began to feel compelled to show her. I didn't know why, but I was hoping she would have the same fascination with those tantalizing photos that I did. Maybe so I wouldn't feel like such a deviant. My mom was home that night so I wasn't able to get my hands on them anyway. We laid in my bed that night as usual, only this time the scent on her shirt tickled my nostrils, and when I turned toward her, for just a second, I got a quick flicker of the same feeling that shot through me when I turned the pages of a *Hustler* magazine.

"You smell good. What is that?" I whispered, as we began to doze off to the low, yet pounding sounds of our homemade compilation tape filled with punk rock.

"David bought me perfume for our two-month anniversary. It's called Passion. Do you like it?" she inquired as she put the sleeve of her yellow long john shirt up to my nose. The arousing scent suddenly turned into a repulsive stench after she supplied me with its origin.

"It's okay, I guess," I mumbled as I rolled away from her.

The next morning Terry and David came over just after dawn. It was already scorching hot, and Terry's rusted dark blue Volkswagen van had no air conditioning and only one window that could be rolled down. Not to mention there was something wrong with the carburetor and it would not go over 45 m.p.h. The park was almost an hour away, and by the time we arrived, we were all soaked with perspiration.

The dampening frustrations quickly faded as we exited the mobile sauna and entered the front gates of the park. Terry reached out his arm like a leash and clutched my hand as he pulled me toward The Lochness Monster. The continuous clanking sound of the incline of the coaster always made me shudder with fear. Jenna and David swiftly followed behind us.

We spent half the day running from ride to ride until we ended up in the Alfred Hitchcock interactive theater. It was dark, and we were clustered together with our knees touching. We couldn't see anything in front of us. I suddenly felt a soft hand on my thigh and squinted with uncertainty. It was Jenna. I was aroused and confused. Did she think I was her boyfriend? Or did she purposely send shivers down my spine with her motionless hand? I still don't know the answer to that. Maybe I should stop writing and call her to find out.

That night when Terry dropped me off, I crept to that dresser drawer again and picked my favorite issue, August 1987, and flung myself into my favorite corner of the world. I flipped past the too-familiar cover, almost forgetting about the heaving breasts accented with a sand dollar necklace and yellow suspenders. When I flipped through the pages anticipating those customary butter-flies, I was alarmed that my mind circled back to the day at the amusement park. Jenna consumed my thoughts and I found myself aroused when I imagined her face, her eyes and her skin. I heard my bedroom door open.

My mom yelled for me as she laid a stack of folded clothes on my bed. I stayed still and quiet until she left again.

The next night the four of us decided to sneak some beer from Terry's dad and go down to Haygood Park. I told my mom we were going to the movies. As we all lay on the blanket, I couldn't help but watch Jenna out of the corner of my eye. The unfamiliar bitter taste of jealousy congealed inside of me as I watched Jenna's hand grab at David's crotch. I threw Terry's hand off of me and flicked a lighter toward my wrist.

"We got to go. I'm gonna get in trouble," I said as I picked my bag up off the damp grass and headed to the van.

Terry followed me. "Are you mad at me? Did I do something wrong?"

I shook my head. "No, I just don't want to get in trouble again. My mom already thinks Jen is a bad influence and if we're in late she won't be able to come over anymore." Terry yelled for David and Jenna, who were still intertwined.

When we got to my house I realized Jenna could barely walk. The alcohol had attacked her 80-pound body and she was drunk out of her mind. I practically had to carry her in. Luckily, my mom was already in bed. We barely made it to my bedroom before she darted to the bathroom and just caught the edge of the toilet before spewing all over the place. I grabbed a towel and knelt behind her crouched, moaning body and pulled her hair back away from her face. When the heaving subsided, I pried her off of the bathroom floor, changed her shirt, and put her to bed. I spent the next hour watching her sleep. I remember getting a lump in my throat and almost feeling like I could cry. I didn't know why. The sensation was awkward but filled with elation. The next morning Jenna woke up clutching her head and still reeking of alcohol. She had to get home by noon because David was taking her to meet his family. I didn't want her to go. I was jealous, but I could never tell her that.

"Thank you for taking care of me last night. I love you," she said graciously as she bagged up her vomit-covered clothes and shoved them into a plastic bag.

"That's what friends are for," I responded as I flopped down on my bed.

"I'll be back over later," Jenna said as she quickly walked out the bedroom door.

I laid in a daze for what seemed like an eternity until I ended up dozing off for several hours. I woke up to my mom's annoying voice beckoning me to get my clothes out of the dryer because she was late for work and didn't have time. I knew what that meant. I had time for another encounter in the pages. I kept the closet door open that day and stretched out my legs as I flipped open the cover to the newest edition of *Hustler*. With each turn of the page, my mind kept circling back to Jenna. Thoughts of her naked body kept invading the familiar pages. I was only on page twelve when it happened. I didn't hear a single sound and when I looked up, Jenna was standing over me. I had one hand on my *Hustler* and the other down my pants.

"Eww, what are you doing?" she screamed as she snatched the magazine out of my hands. "You're gross," she yelled as she stormed out of my room, slamming the door behind her.

I sat still imagining what her reaction would have been if she knew I thought about her when I touched myself. I tried calling her all day, but she wouldn't answer. Terry and David came over and I casually asked the question.

"Jen said she doesn't feel good," David said with disinterest.

For the next two days my stomach stayed in knots and the phone remained silent except for Terry calling every ten minutes wondering why I didn't want to see him. I stayed sulking in solitude and away from the magazines. I didn't understand why she was avoiding me. Maybe her adoring smiles and interested looks were only a figment of my imagination. Did she hate me? Why? Was she going to tell everyone?

Another Saturday arrived and I was in my bedroom folding laundry again. My mother was trying to make a woman out of me by making me do my own laundry.

And then my door popped open and Jenna was there. She didn't walk in my room, just stood in the doorway with her hands clutching the door frame. Was she going to call me a dyke and try to hurt me? Was she going to laugh? I didn't have any idea. Her face was bare of expression.

I got up. "I'm sorry if you think I'm gross. I can't help it."

She put her snowy white teeth on her bottom lip and bit down as she smiled. "No, I'm sorry. I wasn't mad that you were looking at naked girls, I was mad because I wanted it to be me."

My stomach twisted and turned in delight; I almost couldn't believe my ears. Jenna pushed herself off of the door frame and came to gently push my hair to behind my left ear and run the back of her fingers over my blushing cheek. I couldn't breath. I stayed motionless when she followed the contour of my neck and shoulders with her hands, and I exhaled loudly when the chills raised the fine hair on my arms. She leaned in—almost in slow motion—and still had the widest, most beautiful smile I had ever seen. Her closed lips met mine and the softness melted us together. She pulled back and stared right into my eyes. I cracked a small lingering smile and almost felt tears swelling behind my eyelids again. I grabbed her petite waist and lunged forward to meet her lips. This time she greeted me with her mouth open so her tongue entered me.

Finally, when we needed to breathe, she pulled back and licked my bottom lip, following it with a gentle kiss. I could smell the familiar watermelon Jolly Ranchers on her breath, and I savored the scent for what seemed like an eternity. She raised my shirt to release my nakedness and I trembled. Before I knew it, I was standing naked in the middle of my bedroom with Jenna just looking at every inch of my body while using one finger to touch every spot she looked at.

I pulled her close to me, and she moaned under her breath. I wasn't quite so delicate as she. I ripped her shirt off and yanked off her tight, ripped jeans. She had what most people would call flawless skin, and her breasts with their tiny nipples seemed to yearn for my touch. I got scared. An interior monologue played in my head. *I don't know what to do. I've never done this. Has she? Do girls have safe sex?* I knew about condoms but had never even thought about them before that moment. Never thought about them after that moment either. She twisted me around and we fell naked onto the bed. We kissed passionately for at least a half an hour, then began exploring each other. I ran my tongue down her neck and began to gently suck on her left breast. She arched her back as I slid my hand down her stomach. I could feel her wetness on the insides of her thighs. My clit immediately began to throb, and I was overwhelmed when I slid a finger inside of her. I looked up at her face. She was breathing heavily, apparently every bit as aroused as I. I wanted to taste her so bad, but I was terrified I wouldn't know what to do or how to do it right. I pulled out of her and moved my fingers around, hoping I could please her. The desire to make her come seemed to drive away my every other thought. Just when her hips began to writhe back and forth, she sat up, pushed my hand away and pulled our chests together. Our precarious position at the end of the bed almost sent us falling off. She laughed nervously and moved to the right, then put her hand where my neck and breastbone meet and guided me back onto the bed.

Our hands intertwined, and she kissed me hard. With each touch, I could feel myself becoming saturated to the point I was a little embarrassed. *Jenna must have done this before*, I thought as her fingers teased my swollen clit. The circular motions became harder—almost too hard—and my leg began to jump uncontrollably. I put my hand on my thigh to try and make it stop, but she slapped it off and smiled. Then she pushed herself down my body and dove in. I couldn't believe it was happening. I wanted to play with her hair and pull her closer, but I was too nervous. She licked all the wetness off of me and plunged two fingers inside me. I jumped back a little and grunted. The pain felt damn good. Five hours must have passed, but neither one of us had an orgasm that day.

The following Saturday was different. No *Hustler* needed for foreplay. I had three orgasms and can only hope she had at least one. We never told anyone about our month-long girl affair. Jenna ended up fucking David and walking out of my life. Now she's married with two beautiful children. We talk once or twice a year, but never about what happened that long-ago summer. As for me, I gave up the *Hustler* magazines for the real thing!

Best Friends
Marie Alexander

I will never forget the first time I met Toni. She'd just started working where I did, and when I walked up to introduce myself I felt a connection, as if we had shared a long history together already. During the course of conversation, I learned she had a husband. I remember feeling very confused about why that particular bit of information hurt me so much.

We became best friends almost immediately. Our birthdays were only a few days apart, so we celebrated my twenty-seventh and her twenty-fourth together. That same year we feared the Y2K disaster and celebrated the turn of the century together, along with her husband and my date. The four of us spent a weekend in a cabin in the middle of a blizzard. Toni and I partied our butts off and hung out for hours talking and laughing. It was the best mini-vacation ever.

Somehow, the subject of gay women kept coming up. On one of our Girls' Nights Out, Toni and I sat at the bar alone, listening to our friends singing karaoke.

"I made out with a girl once," I told her, surprising myself. I hadn't told anyone about that before.

"What?" she said, looking at me wide-eyed, but smiling. "You did? What was it like?"

"It was just like kissing a guy. It was fine. I was really drunk." I didn't dare tell her that the realization of how great that kiss was had rocked my world for a while, and sent me straight into the arms of the nearest available man.

About a year after we met, Toni and her husband started to have problems in their marriage, and she and I drifted apart. It was just too stressful for me to be around two people who were at war all of the time. I tried to be there for her, but she was hostile and moody much of the time, and ended up treating the people around her pretty badly. I missed her, but knew we'd get back together when things settled down.

We hadn't spoken at all in a few weeks when she pulled into my driveway unexpectedly one afternoon. I could not have been more shocked when I answered the door and saw her anguished, tear-stained face.

"He left me," she said, sobbing and falling into my arms.

"What do you mean he left you?" I always thought she would be the one to leave him. I held her and let her cry for a long time. I was shocked she hadn't been the one to end it, but I knew in the end she would recover and see she deserved better.

My heart was broken right along with hers, although I was also just a little bit excited. She had never given me a single reason to believe she was bi or gay, but somehow I sensed it, and had since the first day I met her. I ignored this suspicion most of the time, just as I ignored my suspicions about myself, and never mentioned it.

The two of us renewed our friendship and became closer than ever. After the initial shock wore off, she became a whole new Toni. She was happy and beautiful again; she began to enjoy going out and meeting new people. The more she loved her new life, the more I loved her, and things were good that fall and winter for us.

She started dating casually a bit, and I realized I was not okay with it, but chalked my jealousy up to the fact that I was single and unable to find a decent guy.

Meanwhile, our relationship developed a very flirtatious side, under the guise of just being silly or drunk at the clubs, which made that hidden part inside of me a bit excited again. One night I gave her a spontaneous lap dance at a table in a corner of the bar. She got totally into it, which surprised me and made it even more exciting, even though we were just playing around and all the men in the bar were cheering. Afterward, we joked that we'd drink for free all night, but I had no interest in any of the men there. I spent the night tortured by the heat that dance had generated.

I also noticed she was chatting on the computer a lot, maintaining Internet relationships with several women.

"Hey," she said over the phone one night, "you know that woman I've been chatting with? The one from California?"

"Mhmm," I muttered. I thought her online "friends" were kind of lame. I mean, how could she really get to know someone over the 'Net? Who knew what these people were really like?

"Well, she's taking me on vacation to Las Vegas!"

A part of me wanted to drive to her house and smack her on the head with the phone. I was angry and hurt and confused. I wished I could take her on vacation instead of some mystery Internet woman, but being her best friend and not her lover, I knew I should be happy for her. So I gave her all of the requisite warnings and cautions, and prayed this mystery woman wasn't a psycho. I teased her about getting laid out there, and she insisted the relationship wasn't like that because she wasn't gay, she was just excited about getting away for a week

But I knew better.

The day she came home she called and said she needed to talk to me, and that it was very important, so we decided to go out to dinner that very night. I knew what she was going to say, but she really had absolutely no idea I even suspected. I was laughing to myself as I watched her struggling to say the words.

"Okay, so, remember I told you I had something important to talk to you about?"

"Yeah," I answered.

She flagged down a passing waiter and ordered both of us another margarita. "I don't want you to freak out or anything." She was fidgeting and didn't seem able to make eye contact.

"About what? What do you need to tell me?"

"Um." She was smiling nervously. "Remember when I said I would never be with another woman?"

"Yeah." I wasn't letting her off the hook. I was going to make her actually say it out loud.

"Well, I'm pretty sure I'm gay."

I grabbed my drink and took several gulps. "Really?" I sounded calm, but my insides had turned to jelly. Suddenly, her coming out was making me feel very exposed. I felt as if she was shining a spotlight on all of the little secret fantasies I'd been harboring for her. The ones I had only indulged in when I was almost asleep, when I didn't have to look at them head-on.

"Yeah. I mean, I'm sure." Toni was obviously extremely uncomfortable. As much as I was enjoying watching her struggle to reveal what had been so obvious to me, the reality of her words had left me shaking, a reaction I had not anticipated. I decided to do what had worked best for me so far. I drank more of my margarita and swept my fantasies right back into the land of denial.

"I knew you were going to get laid in Vegas!" I laughed. When the smile reached her eyes and she finally laughed, I began to feel better. This was her night, after all. What the hell did I know about being a lesbian?

We partied hard that night, and I wound up stone cold drunk. She thought it was because of the shock of her news, and in a way it was. I didn't know what I was going to do with my feelings for her. Alone in bed I would go over and over it in my head. What if I was wrong about myself? What if she and I crossed that line, and I wasn't actually attracted to her? What if I was really into her, and she wound up not being interested in me? I didn't even know how to pleasure another woman. What if she wanted me to go down on her? How would I know what to do? What if I got there and changed my mind? She was my best friend. What if I messed it all up?

Then Toni got a girlfriend, and I knew that I should have gone for it, despite all the what-ifs. It wasn't that I didn't like the girlfriend, but I knew from the moment I met her that she and Toni were not right for each other. At least, that's what I told myself. I tried to be a good best friend. I kept my mouth shut and supported her because she was in love and happy, but I tried to avoid hanging out with the two of them.

Her girlfriend started answering the phone every time I called and sleeping over for days at a stretch. I became more and more jealous, but kept it to myself. At least, by then, I had already started seeing signs that the end might not be so far away for them as a couple.

A few weeks later, Toni and I went to a Bon Jovi concert together. I had managed to get tickets a few months before, and by the time the day of the show arrived, we were like two giggling teenagers. We'd spent our teen years in New Jersey in the 80s. Being a die-hard Bon Jovi fan then was as much a prerequisite as sparkly blue eye shadow and teased hair. This was a sold out show at Giants stadium, the last night of the tour. It was a Jersey thing, and it was huge.

I hadn't told Toni the tickets were in the fourth row. Her jaw kept dropping as we walked up the floor of the stadium, nearer and nearer to the stage. She was practically vibrating, she was so excited. To me, it felt like we were on a date that night. I didn't even mind much when she called her girlfriend to tell her Sly Stallone was standing a foot away, and Heather Locklear and her posse had just passed by. I got so caught up in the fun and joy we shared that day that when I dropped her off at her car late that night, I actually gave her a long kiss on the lips when I said goodbyc. I didn't mean to. It just happened. We said goodbye, and she drove off. I sat in my car wondering what the hell I'd done, and if she'd really even noticed. Neither of us ever mentioned it, but I felt closer to her than ever, and it was becoming harder and harder not to make a move.

A week or so later, I agreed to go to a club in New York with her and her girlfriend. They were in the third or fourth phase of their breakup, which was taking longer than the relationship itself had. When I pulled into Toni's driveway, she came out of the house to meet me, and she looked so beautiful I caught my breath. There was something different in how she looked at me, but I couldn't figure out what it was. The three of us went to dinner. Toni and I had such a great time we laughed till our sides hurt, while her girlfriend just sat there. Then we decided to go to a gay club in the Village.

We all had quite a few drinks at the club, and were flirting with each other and everyone else like crazy. Then Toni came up to where I was sitting on a barstool, shoved my legs apart, and started dancing between them She was not smiling and being silly, like during our previous lap dance. She had a serious look on her face, and I was very aware that we were surrounded by lesbians who were not going to be buying us drinks in exchange for a little bump-and-grind show. In my head it finally confirmed what I had hoped for, that she was attracted to me, but I was a little surprised she was being so forward. Something in the way she looked at me let me know we would definitely be crossing a lot of lines that night. She was hot, and the crowd was hot, and I was getting hotter by the minute. I decided to sit back and make her make the move, especially since her girlfriend—with whom she had already broken up with ten times—was with us.

We were on the dance floor a bit later, really letting loose. Toni kept bumping up against me in a playful, flirty way, and I wondered if she knew how intense it was. Then suddenly, she grabbed me by the shoulders, looked into my eyes, and kissed me on the forehead. On the forehead! She headed to the bar for another drink, while I stood there stunned. I knew exactly what had happened. She had wanted to kiss me and had chickened out at the last minute! By the time I joined her at the bar, I had stopped laughing and pretended I hadn't even noticed.

She glanced up at me nervously. "Hey," she said.

"Hey!" I smiled. "Wanna buy me a beer?"

"Already did." She handed me a cold bottle.

"Having fun?" I asked her, smirking to myself.

"Yeah. You?" She still looked a little nervous.

"I'm having a blast!"

We stood at the bar a moment, then someone pulled us back to the dance floor. We were just getting back into the music when Toni pulled me into her arms. Before I could react, her lips were on mine.

It was as if every romance novel I had ever read was real. I saw fireworks and felt the room spin away from us. As our mouths opened and our tongues touched for the first time, it was as if every second of my life had led up to this one kiss. I had been waiting all these years just for this moment and this woman, and the world around us disappeared.

We both knew that life had changed forever, that there was no other certainty in the world other than us. We went to the corner of the room, and this time I initiated the kiss. It was longer and even more perfect, and when it was done we both had tears in our eyes.

"I love you," I whispered.

"I love you, too," she whispered back.

"No, I mean . . ." I stepped back so I could look into her beautiful face. "I *really* love you."

"I know, and I *really* love you, too."

It was the happiest moment of our lives.

We had an uncomfortable car ride home with her girlfriend. The next day, Toni broke it off with her for good, then she called me. Our entire relationship had changed overnight, and we could not get enough of each other. We talked on the phone for hours that night, ending with three a.m. phone sex that blew my mind. I could not wait to get Toni in bed so we could do all the things we'd talked about so boldly.

That weekend, we got together at her apartment for a sleep-over. I thought I'd be nervous, but I wasn't. When I arrived, it was a little awkward at first. It was the first time we'd seen each other since we'd kissed, and we kind of just kept looking at each other and smiling. She had the silliest grin on her face, and seeing her nervous around me made my heart flutter. We kept dodging each other, each afraid to make the first move, like it was a first date and we were just getting to know each other.

We decided to watch a movie. Toni was standing with her back to me, looking through her DVD collection for something good. I walked up behind her, leaned against her, and breathed on her neck. Her head fell back and she moaned, and I was lost. She turned. Our mouths met, and it was just as powerful and over-whelming as it had been the first time. Our arms wrapped tightly around each other, we kissed for what seemed like hours. My body had never responded to a kiss this way before. I could barely stand as I became more and more excited, so I stopped and took Toni's hand and led her to the bed.

"Are you sure?" she whispered as she followed me.

I pulled the comforter down, turned toward her, and slipped out of my T-shirt. I heard Toni's little gasp as she stood looking at me. She reached out to stroke my bare arms and shoulders with her fingertips, making me shudder with anticipation.

"You are so beautiful," she said.

"The way you look at me makes me feel beautiful."

I stepped into her arms again, running my hands up under the back of her shirt, loving the warm smoothness of her bare skin.

"Let's take it slow," she said into my ear. "I want you to be sure."

I reached out and slipped her T-shirt up over her head. The sight of her in her bra and jeans made my knees unsteady. Her breasts looked so beautiful, and suddenly I needed to touch them, to taste them, so I reached around to unclasp her bra. By the time it fell to the floor, I was licking her nipples, hearing her breathing get heavier as I kissed and teased them. All of the pleasure, the reactions of our bodies, the love that was filling me dashed any trace of nerves or hesitation or doubt from me forever. I remember thinking for a split second, *My God, I am a lesbian*, and the knowledge felt comfortable and safe.

Toni pulled me back up to her, and reached around to take off my bra. The cool air caressed my breasts, and when her warm, wet mouth found them it was almost unbearable. I could not stifle my moans as I pulled us onto the bed, straddling her and leaning over her so she could keep sucking and biting at my nipples. Watching her, knowing that it was my Toni, a woman, making me feel this way was the biggest turn on ever. Her hard thigh went between my legs, and she thrust upward, pressing against my throbbing clit through my jeans. I felt myself lose control, grinding down on her thigh frantically, bringing her hands to my breasts, urging her to keep her mouth there as I exploded. I had never come so quickly, so powerfully, or so completely, and Toni held me close for long moments as my body calmed and stopped shaking.

"I've got you, baby," she kept whispering in my ear. "I've got you."

I came back to my senses slowly, and the first thing I was aware of was the feel of her naked breasts pressing against mine. Immediately, I felt desire for her grip me powerfully, and I moved back to tease her nipples with my own.

"Beautiful, are you sure?"

I did not know what to say to her to make her know I was sure. I knew I wanted her to teach me what two women could do together, and I definitely knew I needed her to make me come like that again, but I didn't know what to ask for. So, instead of saying anything, I stood and slid my jeans and panties off, then climbed back on the bed next to her. Her eyes were wide as she stared at me, and I felt myself getting more aroused under her gaze.

I laid back and started to caress my clit with my fingertips, making sure she could see every movement. She looked at me, startled for a second, then looked back at what I was doing.

"What are you doing over there?" she asked, and moved in closer for a better view.

I was a little shocked at myself, but something about her made me want to show off, brought out the exhibitionist in me. I had never felt so sexy before, and I wanted her to know that even though I was a lesbian virgin, she wouldn't be bored.

"I don't know what to do, so I figured I'd start with what works for me." I smiled at her. Masturbation, however, had never felt this good. I'd never let anyone watch before, and now her eyes on my pussy were making me hot and very wet. As I circled my clit, flicking it every so often, teasing the hell out of myself, I felt a warm wetness trickling down my ass. Making sure she never took her eyes off me, I brought my finger to my mouth and slowly licked it, tracing my lips, tasting the salty sweetness. As I licked between my fingers it became harder to control the rest of my body, so I let my other hand rub my clit a little harder and faster. Toni moaned again, and I brought my hand to her mouth. When her tongue caressed the spots where mine had just been, I gasped and spread my legs farther, thrusting my hips against my hand.

All I could think about was having her mouth where my fingers were, but I didn't know how to ask her for that. I didn't have to. She gently moved my hand away, and I felt her warm mouth on my pussy. A jolt ripped through me, and my back arched as I spread even wider for her, needing her mouth on every part of me at once. Her tongue caressed my clit, and then moved down, teased me, and moved back again. Over and over she did this, and each time she brought me closer. My hips rose to meet her mouth. Her hair kept brushing over my thighs, and I reached down to tangle my hands in it, tugging it gently, not wanting to hurt her but wanting to press myself harder against her mouth. Finally, her mouth closed over my clit and stayed there, grinding against me, her tongue thumping relentlessly, and I came hard, bucking wildly, grabbing my breasts and pinching my nipples, wishing I could suck her clit as I came. The thought of tasting her pushed me even farther over the edge, and then Toni held my hips firmly in place and began to thrust her tongue in and out of me. I froze for a second, not knowing what to do, amazed that this was a woman making me feel this way, amazed that I had never known this kind of thing even existed. It felt so amazing that I relaxed and let my body take over. I reached up to hold onto the headboard, thrusting my whole body over and over until I felt a warm rush over my thighs and ass and heard Toni groan.

I stopped moving and sat up, still pulsing from the climax.

"Oh my God, I'm sorry. Are you okay?" I was suddenly scared I had done something wrong, or that she hadn't liked it. She immediately pulled herself up to me, her face still glistening with my wetness.

"No, no, don't be sorry," she smiled. "You tasted incredible."

"Wow, I never gushed like that before." I was a little embarrassed.

She leaned in close to me and smiled a sexy, mischievous smile. "That's 'cause you've never been with me before," she said, laughing. "You were wonderful. Amazing. Wow."

The look on her face made me believe it, and I kissed her, long and deep, our tongues caressing each other's, probing and exploring. I tasted myself on her mouth, and felt a familiar throbbing start.

"My God, how can you do that?"

"What?"

"Make me want you again," I whispered into her ear.

When I could move again, I brought myself to my hands and knees to move up next to her on the pillow. Toni had other ideas. Pulling herself up, she growled. "Oh my God, stay just like that." She came around behind me and gently reached between my legs, caressing my thighs and pussy from behind.

"What are you doing?" I asked her, between gasps.

"Ssssh." She bent over and whispered in my ear. "Tell me if I hurt you."

"What?"

I turned my head to ask what the hell she was talking about when she slipped a finger inside me. For a second I was a little taken by surprise, but as she slowly moved in and out of me, my body responded and I stopped thinking. She caressed my ass as she teased me, and I started moving with her, my back arching. I felt her fill me even more, and I loved the way it felt, loved that I could feel her breasts pressing into my back as she reached around me to rub my clit. Her movements were slow and perfect, and she was driving me crazy. It felt so incredible. I tried to wait, tried to see just how much teasing I could take, but I was quickly losing control. By the time she moved her fingers from my clit and brought them to her mouth, I was ready to beg.

"Please," I whispered, thrusting my hips back, needing more.

"Please what?"

She was toying with me, and I was so swept up in what she was doing to me, I didn't know what I was going to say until I heard it come out of my mouth.

"God, fuck me!" I almost yelled. I felt her free hand move to hold my shoulder as she started to move her other hand faster, deeper.

I turned and looked at her over my shoulder, straight into her eyes.

"You need to fuck me, and fuck me hard."

It was beautiful and savage and loving, and I trusted her completely. I let go and let her guide me, and in the end we both were overwhelmed and spent as we lay naked next to each other, panting and smiling.

I was in complete awe of her, and could not look at or touch her enough. She kept me at bay, promising more nights and plenty of time for exploration and learning everything about each other. I fell asleep in her arms, and four years later we still share that same bed, along with a life together and a beautiful little boy. I am still in awe of her, especially when she's naked, and every day I feel as if I've come home at last.

About Me
Teresa Wymore

Beth stared at me, her expressive eyes recognizing my bind as I struggled with some of the reasons I should leave. Her husband would be home from work soon, and I was skipping a calculus final that might put me short of graduating. Beth's elegant mouth curled into a charming smile, and a casual finger wagged at me as if to say she found me amusing in a pathetic, naïve sort of way. She didn't worry too much about sexual ethics, despite the classes she taught.

When she came closer, I stepped back, but I couldn't leave. All I could do was stare in fascination, shaken with awe because I was alone in a bedroom with Beth Shaulis, chair of the women's studies department at the University of South Florida.

Her brunette hair was rather coarse with streaks of gray, and fine wrinkles covered her hands and face. Her neck, attenuated by smooth tendons, emphasized her lean, vegetarian lifestyle. She was stunningly androgynous, a feminized boy with narrow hips and features like the drama of a graphic novel—all black-and-white angles. Her urban sophistication was both daunting and appealing to a small-town girl like me.

As I stood, incapacitated by the struggle between lust and a lifetime of conventional morality, I realized this was what coveting felt like.

Her smile grew until her white teeth showed brilliant against magenta lips. She had a delicate, bird-like jaw and pointed chin. "He won't be home for hours," she offered, guessing at my sudden reluctance. Her hand reached for mine.

"I don't care about that."

Her touch had been tentative, but now she curled a confident hand around my limp fingers.

My heart thudded and missed a beat, the pressure like a tug on my chest. "This is so—"

"Wrong?" One sharp black eyebrow rose to mock me. It wasn't the first time. We had spent an hour after class once, arguing whether honesty and openness are the same thing. We attributed our different opinions to our different childhoods. She had grown up in New York's trendy East Village when it was just the Lower East Side, the daughter of two lawyers. As adept as her successful parents at tweezing shades of meaning from common words, she convinced me she wasn't playing a semantic game when she portrayed herself as honest, despite the many times she failed to tell her husband about her women. However, the Sisters of Mercy convent had enlightened my young conscience to the many ways I had sinned, not the least of which was by omission.

Of course this was wrong, but to say so would be to show how unsophisticated I was. I was supposed to believe that whatever two consenting adults did was acceptable. I was supposed to believe craving physical intimacy with another woman was not immoral. I was supposed to believe her gay husband had agreed to a marriage of convenience.

Afraid she would mock me further, I tried to laugh derisively and succeeded only in coughing.

She leaned toward me and pressed her lips to mine. Her breath warmed my face. The soft brush coaxed me forward, and my body began to ache. I rested my fidgeting hands on her shoulders and let her kiss me. I let her. That was all I could do.

Her hands drew me closer, and her pliant breasts pressed against me, a sensation as startling as the gentleness of her small mouth. "No," she scolded as she drew away. Her hazel eyes narrowed with an insight that left me feeling foolish. "Kiss me."

With weak hands, I drew her into a hug and rested my weight on her shoulders. My heart was racing. "I can't believe this is happening."

She eased me toward her broad bed. The support slats creaked as I sat on the tan comforter. I began to relax until I realized I was about to make love to a woman. As I leapt to my feet, light-headedness made me sway, and her amiable concern vanished. She grabbed hold of my arm, steadying me.

When the pleasure I had imagined for years and a woman I had adored for months intersected, I possessed neither the focus nor the fear to worry about pride. So she might humiliate me. So she might break my heart. As I stood inflamed with an exquisite longing, I knew the pain of loss wasn't the worst thing that could happen to me. Nevertheless, I backed from the room, and when I was in the hallway, I rushed from her house.

The following Thursday after class, Beth pulled up in her car alongside mine in the remote Sundome lot. After obediently getting in her Jeep, I rode with her for ten minutes before I asked where we were going. She winked.

We arrived at The Lighted Tree, a lesbian bar on Pass-A-Grille beach near St. Petersburg. It was nearly eight o'clock. An orange sun seemed to ignite the low clouds over the bay, and the easterly breeze carried the dense sea air inland. Seagulls screeched above us, almost hovering like hummingbirds in the strong wind. Along the sandstone wall that bordered the walkway, palm-sized anole lizards, with their jittery scamper, hunted insects as the noisy gulls hunted them.

Beth led me into the bar. Although The Tree was an open-air

beach bar, few patrons wore bikinis like those I saw in the straight bars. Tattooed butches in boots and T-shirts mingled with tank-topped femmes. A few university students lit up the bar with their fresh, straight-girl looks—all cosmetics and easy-access skirts, like billboards advertising sex. They were the kind of women who said they did anything but usually proved to be merely passive. Their long nails gave them away.

One woman, who made eye contact and let her hand slip across my hip, wore an open brown blouse over a black leather bra, and her piercing eyes alarmed me with their interest. Beth handed me a cold bottle that beaded with condensation. I flung the water from my fingers, took a long drink and relaxed.

My blonde hair stuck to my neck and my pink satin shell clung to my small breasts in the sweltering evening made hotter by the bodies and the spotlights. Shielded from the wind, mosquitoes took opportunities where they found them, and I spent much of the evening swiping at something whining near my ear.

The pungent hops from my beer faded behind the enticing coconut-scented oils that oozed from the shiny skin all around me. It had rained that afternoon, and the pavement around the stage smelled musty from evaporation. Palm trees arched over us, block-ing much of the blue sky, and their spear-like leaves hung with fat drops of moisture.

The Tree was a wind-down bar for those spending time on the beach or at one of the hotels. Few came to dance, so Beth and I were among a handful of couples swaying in front of the acoustic, all-woman band.

"Feeling good?" she asked into my ear.

I hated being the center of attention. "Do we have to dance?"

"I want everyone to see you," she said sweetly.

I leaned away to look into her face. "Why?"

"You're beautiful."

She was lying. I knew I was only pretty. "Do you bring all your students here?"

"Just the hot ones," she replied with a wink.

Resting my head on her shoulder, I dangled the bottle of beer from my fingers and wrapped my arms around her waist. She wore a black-and-white checkered blouse and black jeans.

After dancing for a time, Beth left to get me another beer. When she returned, I was dancing with a muscular woman in a softball jersey, whose jasmine-patchouli scent of Giorgio for Men had me wet with lust. Beth charmed the taut-skinned dyke with a few questions about her team's season and then drew me away.

After I finished my second beer, Beth ushered me from the bar, and we drove for a half-hour before arriving in downtown Tampa. Hulking buildings blocked off two sides of the parking lot, and couples walked some distance away on a broken sidewalk. Beth leaned over and buried her face in my neck. I giggled and asked where we were.

"You're already feeling the beer," she said. She sat back, and after a short appraisal, she shrugged. "Whatever it takes, darling."

Thursday was "alternative night" at Tracks and brought in pretentious university students with their fashionable bandana color codes, along with the kind of women who owned boxes of surgical gloves, soldered chains to their bed frames, and lived their fetish for more than an evening.

The pounding trance music was too loud to talk, so we found a tall, fiberglass table and climbed up onto its blue padded stools. Already scores of women were dancing, but I found myself watching the gay men, some flamboyantly effeminate, others almost caricatures of masculinity, their jocks stuffed with dildoes—unless the mounds of flesh I tried to imagine were real.

A gay couple came to the table. They touched fists to Beth's in greeting. She leaned toward me and shouted in my ear, "This is Teddy and Dom."

Teddy was a redhead with curls and a ruffled blue shirt. He seemed to be an obvious bottom, wearing wrist restraints without the chains. Dom was a swarthy Cuban with piles of chest hair spilling out of his sleeveless red T-shirt. Large pores coarsened his olive skin, and his red nose suggested a man never far from a bottle. Dom took a handful of sealed single-use syringes from his cargo pocket and slapped them on the table in front of Beth. Her small eyes widened with delight as she scooped them up and shoved them into her sock.

Teddy drew Beth to the dance floor. Dom gestured to me, but I shook my head. After finishing my beer in several gulps, I shouted at him, "What are the needles for?"

He smiled, his yellow teeth showing briefly before he pulled an ampule filled with crimson liquid from his canvas pants. "Blood."

I didn't ask why, because I didn't want the answer. I didn't want anything to do with the fetishes I saw around me. I had been living a fantasy for too many years to sacrifice a single evening of reality for new illusions. Besides, rules and codes were what I was breaking.

The driving rhythm of Black Box hip-hop rushed through me like a euphoric drug, the pulsing sounds seizing my senses, magnifying hedonistic desires, and giving every wild thought an erotic life of its own. Slipping from my stool, I paused to watch Beth as she turned to a woman behind her. Their hips joined in motion, the stranger drenched in blue and Beth in black.

Beth drew the length of the woman against her and slid her arms under and around the other woman's arms, spreading them high with her own so that the two women merged as if in flight, and then they moved as one, their bodies joining, separating and locking in a sensual rhythm that swayed to the electronic beat. The hair on my neck stiffened.

When more men and women spilled onto the crowded floor, Beth disappeared. The music's bass tones rumbled through my feet, and chills shivered through me, loosening what reservations I had left. I was a terrible dancer, but I found myself on the dance floor, grinding with Beth. She laughed at me, and I laughed at myself.

When I couldn't ignore my full bladder any longer, I noticed I was dancing alone, or rather, I was dancing with people I didn't know, and Beth was gone.

A thick, leather harness hung from the ceiling in front of the main bar, and I found her whipping a man who hung face-up and splayed out in the harness. Several people had short whips, their ends frayed like cat o' nine tails without the metal tips. The man wore a full head mask that buckled around his throat, and a studded thong belted around a black pouch that sacked his well-packed crotch. The smooth white globes of his ass chafed pink where the more earnest whips had left their marks.

When Beth saw me, she handed me a whip and shouted, "Teddy."

I shouted back that I had to use the restroom, so she took my hand and led me through the crowd until we stood in a short queue. On the opposite wall of the narrow corridor, two women clung together, a redhead heaving her blonde partner against the wall. The redhead had her hands down the back of a blonde woman's purple slacks, and after a moment, I realized the redhead was working something into her partner's ass. The blonde was grinding against the wall, like a cat in heat humping a doorstop.

Beth pushed me into a stainless steel stall. The great relief of emptying my bladder distracted me from noticing that she had stayed in the stall with me. She used the toilet, and as we left the restroom, I looked around at the stainless steel doors and sinks and the utterly foreign object I knew to be a urinal.

Beth noticed my surprise and shouted, "Gender doesn't matter here. Except transvestites always use the women's." She laughed.

I was saturated with arousal, and even focusing on walking took effort. My panties stuck to me like a second skin and tugged on my clitoris, sending jolts of pleasure through me as I walked. Time became a series of snapshots as everything sped by in a flow of drunken indistinctness. We danced for a while more before Beth dragged me from the club, and we ended up in a hotel room on the beach.

Before she closed the door to the room, Beth was kissing me, her hot mouth coming at mine in nipping bites. Her hands grasped my thighs, squeezed and held me. Her hands burrowed under my clothes and squeezed my ass. She kicked the door shut, and with great relief, I peeled off my soaking shell and tumbled onto the bed under the cold stream blowing from the air conditioner. She removed her jeans but not her shirt. The wrinkled tails of checkered cotton covered her to mid-thigh.

She finished undressing me and stared at my naked body. Her chest rose and fell, but I couldn't hear her sighs. The club music was still in my memory and my ears throbbed in the silence. I wondered what she saw. I wondered how desire could grow without mystery, without difference. What could be exciting about another woman's body when she saw hers every day?

Over the years, I had imagined sex with a woman would be comforting or even comfortable, but when she shoved me about, as if I were a device examined for what it could do, raw lust wet my thighs. I realized then why Beth kept her shirt on, and I pulled it off; I wasn't the only fascinating object in the room.

She fell on top of me. When I pulled the clasp loose on the back of her bra, her breasts toppled onto my face. They were soft and heavy. I squeezed one in each hand—substantial, resilient, like bread dough. As I massaged them, I muttered, "God, Beth. You're so beautiful."

As I kneaded her breasts, pleasure sparked across skin that had seemed insensate all my life. The feel of her lit every part of me with a sexual fire. Every nerve cried out in a carnal chorus that overwhelmed the voices of conscience and fear still whispering to me.

One of her nut-brown nipples brushed across my face until it slipped into my mouth. The tight bud had a rough texture that stimulated my tongue. She pressed her chest against me and rubbed her hips against mine. Her hot breath sent chills along my spine when she began to suck my neck. Drawing my leg between her thighs, she spread me and slid her groping fingers around my slippery labia with the abandon of a child finger painting. She gave me her tongue to suck, and I held her face with shaky hands.

Her finger penetrated easily. Cushioned by the creamy

response to relentless arousal, my slick pussy felt only a vague pressure, but then she flexed her finger, stretching my tight walls. Thrilling convulsions shuddered through me. My body churned, trying to draw her probing finger deeper, and she eagerly dug into me. When a stray finger brushed my anus, I lost my already shallow breath in a single, violent sigh.

"Hmm," she murmured into my ear. "I see." She rolled me onto my stomach. I tightened against her exploration until her persistent finger lured me into submission. I eased my muscles, and when she wiggled her nimble finger into my ass, my mind seemed to explode.

Although the pleasure was all wrong for orgasm, my body wanted more, just more. The pleasure grew painful because it found no resolution. She jabbed her expert finger in-and-out, and her rhythmic finger-punching so unstrung my strength that I drooled and whined.

She talked gently, but I understood only her soothing tone— compassionate affirmation, as if she were managing a mentally ill patient. I tore at the pillow and wondered how long I could stand such wanton intensity. Any sense of caution, any sense of time, any sense at all, vanished until what remained in all the world was the finger inside me. I fainted.

I awoke to a tight grip on my thigh and realized Beth lay beside me masturbating. I reached down and joined her hand. She startled but didn't stop rubbing herself. "That feels good," she said, her voice cracking. "Do you like it when I touch myself?"

Desire rushed like a river between my legs, and my attention riveted on her shapely mouth. My voice was hesitant, imploring as I asked, "Do you like to fuck yourself?"

"I love it."

"You like to fuck yourself," I said, as a correction, a request. I wanted to hear the word.

She smiled and said distinctly, "I love to fuck myself."

As her mouth formed the word—such a scandalous word, such a defiant word, such a powerful word—I slid down and clamped my hungry mouth onto her velvet pussy. I had always wondered how another woman tasted. She was salty and musky, and breathing her in was like immersing myself in the fertile, humid air of the tropics.

My greedy tongue rooted for her clitoris, so easy to find as it plumped in response. She smiled down at me and her fingers alternately stroked my tongue and her clitoris. With steady pressure, I flicked her tender clitoris over my teeth. She grew still as she concentrated. I maintained my rhythm, and she began to rock gently and finally came with a long cry.

Resting my weight on my knees, I straddled her waist. The sticky sound of slapping skin syncopated with her breathing as I furiously fingered myself. She scooted down, curled her arms around my thighs, and as she tickled my anus with her tongue, I came in waves that radiated to my toes. When the paroxysms subsided, I rolled to my back, physically satisfied but emotionally unleashed.

When I was in bed with Beth, I wasn't self-conscious or preoccupied; as she had shown me, sex was not just about her. It was also about me. Sex was about my pleasure and my power to give pleasure. Trespassing boundaries I had obeyed all my life, I discovered a secret, a man's secret. Desire wasn't a weakness; it was a strength. It was a simple idea, but one not so obvious to someone taught that a woman's love was only a reaction and followed rules made by other people.

In those few months of beachside escapes, I came to understand how sex could be a transcendent experience and why people show up crying drunk at someone's door at three in the morning.

Beth enlarged the beauty of my life because she enlarged me. Although she hadn't transformed my life, she had changed my path, and the challenge for my future would be to live the honesty of volatile and often transitory desires, while accepting no one's definitions of their significance but my own.

One Wild Night at Mills Creek
Rae Kimball

It was the summer after I graduated from high school, 1997. I was working in a small-town grocery store at the time, but in two short weeks I would be leaving for college. I couldn't have been happier—nervous about leaving home but excited about the new possibilities (and women) that awaited me in a more liberal atmosphere. But all that seemed years away as I spent the last, muggy dog days of summer stocking shelves over the late shift.

This week it was a double special on bottled water and jumbo Gatorade. I spent the better part of my shift loading and unloading carts and didn't finish up until the store closed. It was hard work but I didn't mind: I was in the best shape of my life. I paused for a moment to consider my reflection in a nearby window. *Not bad*, I thought inwardly. A summer of vigorous recreational soccer had left my 5'6" frame tanned and buff; my black store-issue pants were a little baggy but my crisp white polo went well with my deep tan. I bent down to tie my shoe and catch my breath for a second.

"You cut your hair." I felt soft fingers glide through my newly shorn hair and come to rest on the back of my neck. I didn't need to look up to see who it was. Sarah. My heart was pounding. She was close enough that I could smell her perfume. I stood up but couldn't meet her eyes: I was embarrassed. During a moment of insanity I had let my sister cut my shoulder-length brown hair. It was now just a few inches long, trimmed neatly around my collar. The guys in the back room had been teasing me all evening.

"I know, it's terrible," I admitted, barely making eye contact.

"No, I like it. It suits you," she said appraisingly as she reached up to stroke the hair behind my left ear. I felt as though we were frozen in time—I could hear my heart pounding in my ears. The store lights dimming brought us out of this trance. She took a step back and ran a hand through her own hair. "They're closing up," she said, exhaustion in her voice. She looked tired . . . and beautiful.

Sarah had only been working as a cashier at the store for a few months—I noticed her from the very start. Very petite, with waist-length brown hair, fair skin and beautiful green eyes, she was quiet, like me, but not as shy. If the store got busy and I was called up to bag groceries, I would make a beeline for her register. She was kind and seemed very innocent. I always felt a little ashamed that our encounters were so titillating to me. Every time she smiled at me my heart would pound; if our hands brushed against each other, my stomach would clench. I always assumed her kindness was platonic, but sometimes I had to wonder: was she flirting with me? Once she came around a customer's cart and brushed against me in the narrow aisle.

"Sorry," she had whispered, looking up at me through long eye-lashes.

"No trouble," I had mumbled, hoping no one could see the blush traveling across my face.

"We should go," she repeated. *What?* My mind shifted back to the present. I noticed the tired look on her face.

"You look tired," I said, stupidly, and immediately regretted my choice of words. "I mean . . ."

She cut me off, laughing and pulled her hair back into a loose bun, exposing the delicate ivory skin of her neck. I'm sure my swallow was audible. "You're quite the charmer, aren't you?"

I didn't know what to say—she was looking at me with a glint in her eye and I was looking at her with my mouth hanging open.

"You wanna get out of here?" she asked, a hint of challenge in her voice.

"With you?" I asked, confused.

"Yeah," she answered, smiling.

"Absolutely" was at last my response. It was the first intelligent thing I'd said in our entire conversation.

I didn't have a car and usually caught a ride home with someone from work; I assumed Sarah was, at least, offering me a ride home. I walked us out to her car, a beat-up '82 Dodge Omni. Why is it that quiet, petite women always drive like bats out of hell? As we hurtled along the country road to my house, which was only a few miles away, I had a chance to look through the cassette tapes scattered about in Sarah's car: the Indigo Girls, Melissa Etheridge, kd lang. It was almost too good to be true—literally: I liked Sarah a lot, and Lord knew I'd fantasized about her a thousand times since we met, but I had never dreamed I'd actually be in such close quarters with a real live lesbian who might have designs on me. I had no idea what was about to happen, but I knew it would be life-changing. I paused to consider the fact that I had been staring down Sarah's opened blouse the entire ride home and that a hot moisture was beginning to pool between my legs. Maybe I did know what was about to happen.

She pulled into my driveway and we sat across from each other in silence for a few minutes. The tension was palpable.

"I don't want to go home," she said and I soon began to realize why she often looked so sad. She explained how she had graduated from high school the previous year and couldn't afford to go to college. She was living at home and not getting along with her parents. Sarah was in the process of saving enough money to move to Seattle to start a new life; she had a cousin she could stay with there until she got on her feet.

I nodded, empathizing with her. I was closeted and my parents had no idea—I was too afraid to tell them. Although I loved them very much, I was anxious to be "out" on my own.

"You know I'm gay, right?" I surprised myself by asking. I knew one of us had to say it, otherwise we would have sat in that car for another ten years. She laughed again—she had a beautiful laugh.

"It was very brave of you to say that," she said. But I didn't feel brave—it seemed like the most natural thing in the world to say.

And then she attacked me. In a fraction of second, Sarah crossed the distance between us, grabbed my face in her hands, and placed a scorching kiss on my lips. She was ravenous—I felt like she was devouring me. After an initial moment of shock, I quickly reciprocated, wrapping my arms around her, leaning in close. She pulled away from me for a second.

"Is this okay?" she asked, panting.

"Absolutely."

Grinning, Sarah quickly released her seat belt, climbed over the gear shift and straddled me. She took my face in her hands and began kissing me as ferociously as before. I was still in shock, but that didn't keep my hands from quickly trailing to her waist. Her shirt was raised slightly and my fingers found soft, white flesh. I let out a groan. This seemed to further excite her. She ran her hands through my hair, kissing my neck, my cheeks, and back to my mouth again. Sarah pressed her body close against me and we began to develop a steady rhythm. Her tongue was soon thrusting in and out of my ear and I heard myself moaning. The last thing I wanted to do was stop.

"Sarah . . ." I tried to slow her thrusting. "Sarah . . ." I was not succeeding. "Oh God . . ."

"Rae . . ." she said, pulling away slightly as her hands reached up and under my shirt, cupping my breasts through the sheer fabric of my bra. My nipples were erect.

"Oh Jesus . . ." My eyes rolled back in my head before I snapped back into the moment. I managed to grab her wrists and pull them away from my breasts, but she continued to ride me, staring lustfully into my eyes. I was soaking wet and I'm sure she could tell.

"We can't do this here." I said before I completely lost control of the situation. I may have been surprised when Sarah attacked me, but that didn't mean I didn't like it. Maybe we didn't know each other that well, but as an eighteen-year-old virgin I was well past due for some sexual exploration—I just didn't want to do it in my parents' driveway. And I was far too excited. "I think I'm going to c . . ."

She continued to thrust against me slowly. "Shhhh . . ." she said, placing a finger against my lips. "I know a place we can go . . . if you want." She drew her finger down the front of my shirt to my pants. "I really need to be with you now . . ." she panted, cupping my mound in her hand, " . . . and I think you need to be with me."

Moments later we were hurtling down another country road. It was dark out and I should have been frightened by the way she was driving, but I was otherwise occupied. Somehow during our previous embrace Sarah's shirt had become unbuttoned. Fascinated, I reached between us and slid my hand onto her breast. Her nipple became instantly hard and she let out a short moan, but kept her hands on the wheel and her eyes on the road. I squeezed her nipple gently through the thin fabric of her bra. Nothing had ever felt so good. I reached my hand into her bra and cupped her breast roughly. She was panting heavily now, hips grinding into her seat, but she continued to drive. I was seized with a hunger I had never experienced before. I pulled her breast toward me and took it into my mouth, sucking hard. Sarah let out a shriek of what I hoped was ecstasy and pulled off into a rough-hewn parking area. Luckily, we had arrived at our destination: Mills Creek, an isolated recreational area on the edge of town. It wasn't the Ritz Carlton, but it would do.

Sarah kept her hands on the steering wheel and I continued to feast upon her perfect, round breast. When I stopped to look up at her, our faces were very close and I suddenly felt shy.

"Hi," she said, a nervous but hungry smile on her face.

"Hi." I didn't know what else to say.

"It's okay," she said. "Is this your first time?"

I nodded, keeping my eyes down. I hoped that my inexperience wasn't obvious.

She lifted my chin and looked into my eyes, "Well, I couldn't tell—you're doing great."

I smiled, elated that I had pleased her.

"Do you want to do this?" she asked sincerely.

Do what? I thought for a moment and realized that the answer would be "yes" to whatever she was asking. My clit was still throbbing from our previous embrace.

I took her face in my hands this time and gave her a long, piercing kiss, and slowly began to thrust my tongue in and out of her mouth. We were both breathing hard when I broke away. "Does that answer your question?" I asked, my voice rough with desire.

Sarah smiled and quickly exited the car, running around to my side. She opened my door, took my hand, and led me across the parking lot and down a hill to the recreational area on the edge of the lake. There was a large playground and a small stretch of beach. It was after hours and we were the only people there, but there was an element of danger in the air. A park ranger, or anyone else, could have stumbled upon us at any moment. For some reason, I didn't care.

We took off our socks and shoes and stood in the sand, staring out over the moonlit lake.

"I've been thinking about you since the first moment we met." Although she wasn't looking at me, she must have sensed my surprise. "Haven't you noticed how we always work the same shift? It's no coincidence."

Finally, she turned and walked up to me, placing her palms against my chest. "I watch you all the time—so strong . . ." She ran her hands up and down my arms before cupping my butt roughly in her hands, "I especially like it when you bend over."

I may have been overwhelmed by the events of the evening but that didn't stop me from taking her into my arms. I wanted to show her my strength so I lifted her up and she wrapped her legs around my waist. We kissed passionately, her hands in my hair, my hands gliding up under her shirt.

I knelt and laid her back in the sand. Our hands were all over each other. She tried to pull my shirt off and I did it for her. She had her hands on my waist, trying to remove my belt while I fumbled with her blouse.

"Rip it," she groaned into my ear. I tore off her blouse and she, mercifully, removed her own bra. She was so beautiful, lying there in the moonlight, eyes hooded with desire. I began to panic a little because although I had imagined these moments a hundred times before, when it came down to it I wasn't sure I knew what to do.

I didn't have to worry long. Strong for such a small girl, Sarah quickly flipped me onto my back. It was then that I was sure this wasn't Sarah's first time, but I didn't care.

She removed my bra, whispering "You are so beautiful." I'm sure I was blushing. She began to blaze a trail with her mouth from my collarbone to my left breast kissing and stroking it with her tongue, before moving over to my right breast. This contact, along with her now thrusting hips, had me on the verge of orgasm.

"Oh God . . . I need to . . ."

"I'm going to take care of you right now," she said.

Sarah quickly removed my belt, unbuttoned my pants and slid them off. I was wearing boy-cut briefs and this seemed to be the right decision. Sarah let out a growl when she saw them, grabbing the waistband between her teeth. As she tugged them down my hips, the fabric dragged against my already throbbing clit. I did my best not to cry.

She seemed to sense I was close, removed my briefs, and quickly laid back down between my legs. A second later my clit was in her mouth and I was on fire, coming harder than I had ever done before. She continued to lap at me, soaking up everything I had to give. I exploded in another orgasm.

She stopped short and looked up at me. "Did you just . . . ?"

I was a little embarrassed. "Yeah."

"Can you always?"

"Usually. Quite a few anyway." I thought everyone could.

She paused and considered me thoughtfully before dipping her head down to run her tongue along the length of my clitoris. I let out a moan.

"How many is few?" she asked. "I mean, what's the most you've ever had?"

I thought for a moment. She didn't seem bothered by the fact that I could have multiple orgasms, so I decided honesty would be the best policy.

"I think the most I've ever had in one sitting was nine," I tried to say casually.

It was Sarah's turn to moan this time. "Girl, am I going to have fun with you."

I almost came again when she said the words.

Sarah feasted on me for the next twenty minutes and I came more times than I can remember. Sometimes my heels were thrust into the sand and my hands in her hair, urging her deeper. Other times my legs were over her shoulders or spread wide by her insistent hands, my hands tearing at my own breasts.

By the time she was done, I lay in the sand a quivering mess. I thought I may have been dead. "Thank you," was all I could say.

She crawled up to lay on top of me. "You tasted so good," she said, kissing me on the lips. I was relieved to know that although it hadn't occurred to me at the time. With Sarah kissing my face and pressing her thigh between mine, it didn't take me long to come back to life.

"Show me what to do," I said, kissing her.

She grinned and stood up before me. I was completely naked, but she was still wearing pants. She slowly undid them and lowered them to the ground. I remember the wind blowing through her long hair and the way the moonlight illuminated her pale skin. I sat up and reached for the waistband of her panties, pulling them slowly down her legs. I could smell her and see the moisture glimmering on the insides of her thighs: my clit began the throb again.

She pushed me gently back onto the sand and laid on top of me, straddling my thigh. The contact was exquisite. She began to rub herself along the length of my body. I could feel her wetness. She placed her arms in the sand above my shoulders and I took her breasts in both hands and into my mouth. She began to moan loudly as we developed a steady rhythm.

Again, she surprised me by quickly flipping us over so that I was on top of her. We maintained our rhythm and she took my hands in hers and placed them over her head. I understood what she meant for me to do and, with light pressure, held her hands back with mine.

"Oh yes . . ." she said. "Use your fingers . . ."

I continued to hold Sarah's wrists over her head with my left hand as I brought my right hand down between us. Although I had never touched another woman in this way before, I had touched myself and instinctively knew what to do.

Sarah was very wet and I was glad to know I had such an effect on her. I slid my fingers lightly up and down the shaft of her clitoris. I loved the feel of her wetness gliding between my fingers. She was moaning, almost crying it seemed, and her eyes were shut tight. For a moment, I thought she was in pain.

"More . . . faster . . ." she said. I increased my pace as Sarah began to thrash about in the sand. I did my best to keep her wrists held down. My fingers drifted tentatively to her center and I looked into her eyes. "Yes . . . now . . ." she said, begging.

I entered her easily with two fingers while maintaining the thrusting of my hips. Sarah's entire body began to buck and she was soon screaming—it seemed to go on forever. As soon as her body stilled, I slipped out of her and quickly climbed up to lay beside her.

"Are you okay?"

"I'm great, thanks." She was smiling.

"Anything else I can do for you?" I asked, hopefully.

"I'd love to but I think we both need to get home."

I wanted to do more, but I realized that my parents would already be furious that I was so late and didn't call. I also didn't relish the idea of getting Sarah in trouble with her own parents.

We managed to locate our clothes, dress and wipe off as much of the sand as we could. Sarah found a spare shirt in her car to replace the one I'd torn. We were silent most of the way home, but we held hands. Sarah drove at a reasonable speed and I was reluctant to leave her.

I didn't know at the time that night would be the first and last time I'd ever make love to Sarah. We talked about it the next day, sitting next to each other in my parents' driveway after our shift. She knew I was leaving for college upstate in two weeks, and I knew that she had plans to move across the country in the near future.

I was drawn to her even then, and had to resist the temptation to reach over and kiss her; I could tell that she was struggling too. In the end, we decided to remain friends, but not see each other anymore, not wanting to risk the temptation of further, more emotional contact.

I kissed her goodbye, thanking her for the experience. I ended up leaving early for school: I never saw her again, but I will always be grateful for the night we had together.

Joining The Mile High Club
Rachel Kramer Bussel

Two days before our trip to Los Angeles, I tell my girlfriend she's not allowed to masturbate until we arrive in the city of angels. I've never given her an order like this, and I'm not sure how she'll react. Two days may not seem like a lot, but I know what she's had planned for those lonely hours between the end of *Friends* and the sleep she needs but tries to put off as long as she can. I'm pleased that even though she is usually a once-a-day masturbator, she not only follows my command but delightedly tells her friends about it. The power of having her instantly not only doing my bidding, but thrilled with the challenge, surges through me, a rush more powerful than any endorphin high. I feel my lips humming, trembling with more orders, more opportunities to put our unspoken power dynamic to the test.

After her parents drop us off at the airport, I pull her into an extra-large stall in the airport bathroom and make her close her eyes before fastening a glistening new magenta collar around her neck, another surprise that will make her think of me every time it so much as touches her skin, every time she catches it winking at her in the mirror. It's not the kind of toy that passes for anything but 100-percent kinky, a complement to her cascades of California blonde hair and endless blue eyes. It fits her perfectly, as I'd hoped it would, and once it's there I can't imagine her without it. We exit and both admire the blazingly bright choker, our eyes drawn to this simple addition that in a moment seems to drastically change our relationship, securing all the unspoken promises into one shiny, attention-getting band.

We board the JetBlue flight, not caring so much about the multiple cable stations as the chance to get it on while in the air. She has the aisle seat and I have the middle. I know she's scared of flying, but I intend to make sure she doesn't have time to worry about disaster befalling us. After we're seated, I start playing with the collar, my hand automatically reaching for the metal loop in back. It looks so good on her, so natural, and I can't help but look up at it and smile every few minutes. We've been inching toward playing like this—me ordering her around, spanking her, assigning her special outfits—but the collar has raised the bar for our play together. Since she likes to be choked, likes the way my hand feels pressing lightly, and sometimes firmly, against her neck, whether sprawled in bed or out on the town, I know that every time I tug on the collar and the band digs into her tender skin, she gets excited, and I use this knowledge to my strategic advantage, already anticipating its magical ability to make her instantly wet.

We settle into our seats, claiming dominion over the three-row aisle with our assortment of pop culture goodies. I have a surprise planned for her and she is trying to guess, but clearly has no idea. She's an impatient sort, but also doesn't want me to give it away too early. Besides, for this surprise, I have a co-conspirator in the form of our stewardess, though she hardly knows it. We have piled huge stacks of books and magazines in front of us, all the ones I've been meaning to read but haven't had a chance to. The flight attendants keep stopping to examine our towering media piles, picking up Ellen DeGeneres's book and saying "oh, she's so funny!" before heading on their way. When the drink cart arrives, I ask for a water and a tomato juice, and some ice. When they ask my girl if she wants ice, I nudge her and she says yes. I'm delighted when our drinks arrive with not one but two cups of ice each—perfect! She still doesn't know my plan, and is pestering me with questions, so I finally whisper her mission to her.

"There's an 'iced T-shirt' contest coming up at a local dyke play party next month. Like a wet T-shirt contest, but with ice, and you'll have to slide your chest across a huge block of ice for as long as you can stand it."

She gives me a big grin and says: "You're fun," agreeing immediately, as if this were an everyday request, like wearing a miniskirt or going to my favorite restaurant, even though I know she's never done anything of the sort.

As quickly as possible, before she's really figured out what she's gotten herself into, I start prepping my contestant. I grab a piece of ice and slide it into her bra, hoping that no one around us has noticed. I do the same for the other nipple, leaving them clinging to the space between her tight top and her rapidly hardening nipple, and watch as a stain quickly spreads across the fabric. I don't linger and rub them into her nipples for fear of getting caught, but can tell by the way she squirms that the ice is having its intended effect, chilling her tender buds but warming her down below. She giggles silently and whispers to me, giving me a rundown as freezing droplets fall onto her stomach, as the cubes become ovals, chilled puddles as they absorb her body heat and she accepts their arousing offering. Without her cooperation, the game wouldn't be any fun, wouldn't be a game at all, but as she looks at me with those bewitching eyes while I assess every inch of her, getting used to covertly copping feels as the ice melts against her skin, I know that we're both playing to win. Though we're each half-aware of the chance of getting caught, like every time I'm with her, everyone else has faded into semi-oblivion; I only have eyes for this blonde minx with the devilish smile that's focused on me.

Every fifteen minutes or so I slide more ice into her shirt, and we try to cover our giggles. Even once it melts, her nipples are prominently visible through her shirt, the wetness giving her a look at odds with the rest of her put-together appearance. Her breasts are small and can easily fit in my hands, but what they lack in size, they make up for in sensitivity. I know the swollen cold stiffness as they press against her clingy shirt will have her panties soaked, her body straining for more, wishing there were ice in her mouth, in her pussy, on the back of her neck—in places she could never have imagined until this moment. I am content to just watch her try to figure out my next move, her body and mind eager for the next step, the next leg of the challenge I've issued.

After I've had my fill of watching, I need to touch, to prove my suspicions correct. We spread most of the magazines strategically across her lap, so when I slide my hand under her skirt nobody will notice. The guy sitting by the window is preoccupied with his computer and the other passengers are watching their TV sets, so I have time to slide her panties aside and slip two fingers inside of her, while trying to move my arm as little as possible. The magazines teeter but stay in place, and I hope that I'm the only one who can hear the way her breathing has changed as she gets wetter. I arch inside her, my fingers still cold from the ice, but her body is warm, and when we meet, it's the frosty heat of pleasure I've come to expect as she grasps me tight, keeping me there, both of us doing our best to pretend the latest round of gossip is what has captured our attention, rather than this affair more sordid than any celebrity's.

I bend my wrist as best I can from my seat, not able to enter her as deeply as I'd like, but teasing her nonetheless, stroking the entrance to her pussy and playing with her clit. I tease her, taking her to the brink, then pausing whenever the lumbering cart rolls by or a booming announcement makes me pause. My still fingers promise more to come, promise endless hours of seeking and stroking, of hot and cold, stop and go, pushing her to the brink and then keeping her there for as long as we both can stand it. I slide them out and feel her body beg me to stay, beg me for one more thrust, one more slam of my now-omnipotent fingers before I ease back. I give her exactly what she's asked for, push my way between her tight, clinging walls, so hot and wet it's all I can do not to unstrap myself and nestle right there on the floor in front of her, my head buried under the blaring headlines, the pages flopping against my hair as I see us through to the end of our mission. I finally stop after only a few minutes, the kind that feel like hours, as the captain announces our descent. I knowing that this is only a warmup, and we'll both be ready for lots more action later. The flight has gone surprisingly quickly, as if all it took to get from one coast to the other was the space of an almost-orgasm.

As we exit the plane, after gathering all of our stuff into our multiple bags, one of the flight attendants gives us a knowing look and says, "Be good, girls," a twinge in her voice letting us know that she has a clue that we haven't been exactly "good" up to this point. We smile and exit. The plane ride is only the start of our public sex, but she doesn't need to know that . . . yet.

Brownout
Brigit Futrelle

I don't sleep much.

Sleep is one of those necessary evils, y'know? You lay there—prone or supine, take your pick—dead to the world, motionless. Sometimes, the dreams are good, but most nights it's just wasted time. I've got shit to do, after all—plenty to keep me occupied as soon as I get home from work. Tunes to listen to, beer to drink, books to read, pots to throw.

Yeah, that's right, I do pottery. Got a wheel and everything, sitting in the den of my apartment. Let me tell you, there's *nothing* in the world like the feeling of centering a lump of clay on a spinning wheel. The wet clay will fight with you to deform every which way, but if you lock your elbows tight and hold it steady for long enough, in *just* the right place: bingo. You gotta center it, see, before you start working on it—before you dip your fingers in and down, slowly creating the open space that will eventually be filled by . . . something. Anything. Hot cocoa, if it ends up a mug, or mashed potatoes if it turns into a serving bowl. Or floating candles if it's especially pretty. But they all start the same—a perfectly centered lump of clay, my thumbs pressing down oh-so-gently into the center. I love it.

So no, I don't sleep much—but when I do finally fall into bed, I'm generally exhausted and often buzzed, and I'm always looking forward to drifting off right away. For the past three nights, though, that's been impossible, thanks to one of my next-door neighbors.

This neighbor, Sarah, has had a boyfriend for a while. Brian. He's a nice enough guy—good looking, I suppose, if you're into lean, dark-haired men. Me? I'm into brunette girls, and Sarah just so happens to be one of those. Her hair is thick and just a little curly, falling to her shoulders in these beautiful waves that make the tips of my fingers itch—even though she's straight. Anyway, like I said, they've been dating for a while, but she and Brian Boy just (finally!) started fucking three nights ago. For some reason, they insist on doing it between two or three in the morning, and since the wall of their bedroom is the wall of my bedroom—well, I hear them. Hear *her*.

Now don't get me wrong, I love the sound of a woman coming. Hell, I love it all—sight, smell, taste, touch and *oh* yeah, those breathy little moans. But I've got two issues with overhearing Sarah and her boy: first off, *I'm* not the one rockin' her world, and secondly, neither is he.

How do I know, you ask? Well, when a girl's on the very edge, she's usually pretty wild. Things aren't in control out there, y'know? It's all sensation, all body, totally and completely selfish, no rhythm or rhyme. But Sarah's gaspy little cries start out three seconds apart (I'm serious—I timed her, just last night) and they stay that way. Consistently. To me, that spells two words: *high* and *dry*.

Now, in my opinion, a woman should never have to fake it. Not with a dude, not with anyone. If it's not working for you, slow your partner down, dammit, and try something else until it does. Sure, I can understand that Sarah wants to make her man feel good about himself, seeing as they just took their relationship to the next level or whatever. But if she doesn't teach him soon, they'll be over within the month. Cross my heart.

I'm not exactly thinking any of this when the power shuts down, early one evening. I'm on the wheel, see, and I don't think about much of anything while I'm working on a project. My stereo is blaring heavy metal just loud enough to drown out most of the treble strains of "Memory,"—that song from the *Cats* sound-track—from the apartment of my *other* neighbor. Not Sarah—she listens to old school U2 and Guns 'n' Roses and shit like that. She's cool. But "Memory" is Annoying Annie's favorite piece of music, so she plays it over and over and over and . . . you get the idea. If I ever have a mental break, that song will be the trigger.

So yeah, I'm sitting there with my elbows jammed between my knees, and since this is a pretty big lump of clay, I can feel the tension in those little muscles in my forearms as I work to get it all centered up, and I'm almost there . . . when *snap*, the power goes out. The wheel shuts off, of course. As does my sound system. As do the lights, and the fridge, and—thank God for small favors—Annie's stereo.

It's dark. I grab a few candles from my bedroom, arrange them on the coffee table, and light them. Annie starts singing "Memory" from, well, memory. Off-pitch. I'm just about ready to go over there and throttle her when there's a knock at my door. Huh.

When I open it, there's Sarah. I'm really glad that my eyes have adjusted to the dim twilight, because I can tell that she looks really cute in these tight gray sweats that show off her shapely legs (she does aerobics every day—Denise Austin—I can hear it) and a paint-spattered T-shirt. Definitely not wearing a bra. Her hair is down and somehow it looks curlier than usual—but maybe that's just the shadows. Have I mentioned that I'm a sucker for curls?

"Hi, BJ," she says.

"Hey," I answer, leaning against the doorjamb and sticking one thumb in the back pocket of my jeans. "Bummer about the power, huh?"

"Yeah," she replies. "Hey, do you have any matches? I found one candle, but I've got nothing to light it with."

"Sure, yeah," I say, shifting my body so it's not blocking the doorway. "C'mon in." As I lead her down the short hallway, my brain manages to think up a way to get her to stay for a while. Good job, brain. "I have a bunch of candles, actually," I tell her. When we turn into the den, she can see the small mass of light for herself. "Want to just hang out here—have a beer or something—until they turn the power back on?"

"Okay," she answers, smiling at me. "That's sounds great."

When I get back with the drinks, she's staring at the mass of mud on my wheel with a curious expression. "You do . . . pottery?"

I lift one shoulder in a shrug. "Yeah. Saw that movie *Ghost* when I was twelve . . . it made me want to be Patrick Swayze. Ever since then—pottery."

Sarah laughs—one of those *I think you're funny but I don't quite know how to reply* laughs. She's sweet—it's easy to tell even though we're not much more than acquaintances. A sweet, nice girl who has probably never had a decent orgasm in all her life. Crying fucking shame. I hand her the beer and sit down on the futon, and she follows suit.

"So," she asks after taking a swallow. "What were you making?"

I turn to look at her. The candlelight flickers off the pale skin of her neck and somehow makes her hair seem darker. Jeez, she's attractive. "I don't know," I answer, before tipping my bottle back and swallowing twice. "I never really know what's going to happen until it does." I raise my eyebrows at her. "But I take requests if you need anything. New mug? Bowl? Watering can?"

"Watering can?" She sounds impressed.

"Sure, yeah, no problem." Watering cans are fun, and they're also a challenge because it's not like you can make them entirely on the wheel, see, because you have to—

But just as I'm getting ready to explain the finer points of ceramic watering can construction, Annoying Annie decides to go for a stunning and completely off-pitch crescendo at the end of her a cappella rendition of "Memory." She sounds like a *dying* cat, frankly—I mean, it's just awful. I nearly snort beer through my nose, and when I finally calm myself down, there's Sarah laughing helplessly next to me on the futon. In fact, she's even leaning against me, a little.

"Oh, that's terrible," she gasps into my shoulder. "Does she do that all the time?"

"Well," I say, careful to not move a muscle, "usually, the sound-track backs her up and mostly drowns her out."

She laughs for a few more seconds before finally sitting up straight and reaching for her bottle. "There's nothing on the other side of my apartment, and you're pretty quiet," she says. "I had no idea the walls were so thin."

I can't even *begin* to help myself—I have to smirk at her. "It's like you're practically in the same room," I drawl, feeling very abruptly like I've been transported into a twisted version of *Bound*. But that would make me Jennifer Tilly, and I do *not* sound that annoying, nor do I wear dresses, nuh-uh, no way, and even in the dim light, Sarah's blush is unmistakable.

"Oh dear," she says in a small voice.

I drain the rest of my beer, because dammit, suddenly I realize what I'm going to do. I'm not just going to change the subject— I'm gonna call her out. Right. Now.

"I probably shouldn't mention this," I say as I lean forward into her personal space, "but I think you should let Brian know that he's not exactly doing it for you."

Her frown is sharp and her eyes glitter. Angry. That's good—I'd rather have her angry than unsatisfied. "What are you talking about?" she demands.

I smile, just a little. "He can't make you come. And he'll never learn unless you show him what to do."

Now here, I figure, she has two options. One is to get up and walk away and never speak to me again. The other is to stay right where she is and hear me out. And . . . well, okay, I guess there's a third—because she could always stay right where she is and let me *show* her. I silently but enthusiastically vote for number three.

"I don't see how that's any of your business," she snaps. But she doesn't move.

"I guess it's not, technically," I reply. "Except that it's damn hard for me to go to sleep when I know there's a needy woman in the next room over."

Her mouth clicks shut and her eyes get really, really big. I watch her jaw work for a few moments, wondering whether she's going to chew me out or keep arguing. "What am I supposed to do?" she asks finally, her voice shriller than normal in frustration. "I can't just tell him he's doing it wrong!"

I raise my eyebrows at her. "Why not?" When she just sits there in a sort of shocked silence, I shrug. "Look, if I were the one f—, uh, making love to you, I'd want you to tell me if it didn't feel right." I shake my head a little. "It doesn't have to be that hard—just show him how you touch yourself, y'know?"

The rest, as Shakespeare said, is silence. Now Sarah isn't looking at me anymore, but down at the carpet, and her fingers are picking at nonexistent lint on my futon. Huh. Is this for real? She doesn't know how to touch herself? I mean, yeah, sure, it takes some folks longer than others, but . . .

"Hey," I say softly, brushing one hunched shoulder with a few fingertips. "Sorry, I didn't mean to make you feel bad or anything." I lean back to stretch a little as she looks over at me, and I flash her a charming grin. I know it's charming, 'cuz an ex told me that, once. Many exes, actually. And it does exactly the same thing to Sarah as it did to them; her eyes widen and her breaths come a little faster and she sort of melts into the embrace of the futon. Excellent. It's go time.

"I could always . . . help you out." I'm proud of my voice—deep and melodious, soothing yet exciting. Or, well, I hope that's how it sounds to her.

She blinks at me, but even as I watch, her pupils get huge. Oh, yeah—at least part of her wants this. Wants me. Wants to feel good. I scoot a little closer and put one hand on her knee.

"What are you doing?" she whispers. Half-scared, half-curious—the anger is suddenly gone. Progress.

"Seeing if you'll let me touch you," I reply evenly, massaging the muscles just above her joint. "I'd really like to show you what you're missing," I continue, unable to resist a smirk. "I bet you'll like it, too."

"I"—she licks her lips and swallows audibly—"Um, I—" Still not pulling away. Good.

"What do you think?" I ask as I run my hand up her thigh to lightly squeeze her waist.

She shivers under my touch, but doesn't pull away. "I'm not going to kiss you," I continue, tracing the contours of her rib cage with three fingertips. "And I won't go inside unless you want me to." I stare into her deep, dark eyes as my fingers get closer and closer to her breasts. Her heart is going a mile a minute, and she's breathing hard, too. And still not pulling away.

"I'm just going to touch you. Here"—I run one finger over an already hard nipple and feel it stiffen further beneath my touch— "and here." Slowly, I move back down the center of her body, down over the slight curve of her belly, down between the vee of her legs. Her hips lift, and a little sigh escapes from between her lips. The material of her sweats is thin, and it's easy to find the slight ridge of her clit, to pluck at it with gentle fingertips. She gasps.

"Yes, oh—"

"Take off your shirt," I order. When she doesn't hesitate, I know she wants this just as much as I thought she did. I straddle her legs smoothly, my abs straining as I hold myself apart from her skin. Her pale breasts glow whitely in the candlelight. I cup them with my hands, massaging tenderly. Another little sigh.

"That feel good?"

"Mmm." Eyes closed, Sarah hums. Frankly, I bet Brian's never touched her like this. Men can't understand it—how good it feels to have someone else bear your weight in their palms, just for a little while. How relaxing. And Sarah is much more relaxed, now—her breaths are steady and her head is lolling against the back of the futon—so I bring both thumbs up to slide simultaneously across her nipples.

Her head jerks up and her eyes fly open. "Oh, god—"

I do it again. She shivers. I let my palms fall away so I can take her between my fingers—rolling, pinching, twisting. Her hips shift under me and her hands grab at the futon cover and her perfect teeth worry the red ribbon of her lower lip.

"How 'bout this?" I ask, daring to squeeze just the slightest bit harder. "Good?"

"Ye-es," Sarah whispers harshly. "So good . . ."

I lift my hands away. She groans. "Shhh, don't worry," I say, leaning against one railing of the futon and urging her to sit between my legs. "It's about to get a lot better." I pull her close, my chin on her shoulder, my hands resting lightly on her hipbones. Experimentally, I trail two fingers down between her legs, testing out my reach. A low whimper. Perfect.

"Take your pants off for me. And your underwear." I caress her breasts as she complies, and settles back against me—completely naked, now. "Sit like this," I whisper hotly into her ear, drawing my knees up. Her bare legs slide against the soft fabric of my jeans, and for a moment, I wish I could feel her against my skin. But then I slide both hands down to rest on the soft skin of her abdomen, just above her dark, curly hair, and her cheek slides against mine as she half-whispers, half-groans my name.

"Pay attention, now." I slide one finger down—slowly, so slowly—down along her clitoris before tracing the soft skin of her swollen lips. Down into the waiting moisture—and she is so beautifully wet—down to circle her opening before looping back up and around. I pause and lean to one side enough to see her face. Eyes squeezed shut, mouth slightly open to admit her panting breaths—she's exquisite and she's loving this. I grin triumphantly.

"Give me your hand."

"What?"

I don't ask again. Instead, I take her right hand and hold it under my own, aligning our fingers. "Like this," I murmur, retracing my path, teaching her the feel of her sex before slowly guiding her inside her own body.

"Oh," she says breathlessly as I curl our fingers up, stroking against the grooves of her. "BJ—"

"Other hand," I urge as I draw her left arm down, my fingers teaching her to tease herself. The slow, curling slide, the fast and furious circles against her clit, hips surging erratically and those cries, those breathy groans hitching in the back of her throat only to blossom on the air . . . and our hands, our hands, molding her passion, forming it, shaping it, her cunt like wet clay on my wheel—so perfect, *too* perfect, collapsing under its own beauty, collapsing into ecstasy . . .

I lean forward to shield her body with my own, feeling her tremble in my embrace—and the power comes back on as *she* comes—the flick of the lights and the whirr of my stereo and the low buzz of my refrigerator, all celebrating her passion.

She presses back against me, gasping. I withdraw my fingers and wrap my arms around her waist in a light hug. She turns to look at me, eyes wide and hazy, and I grin. "Now that," I tell her, "was a neat trick."

Sarah laughs breathlessly and buries her face into my biceps, and I snuggle her close for a few more seconds. She smells good, and I'm proud of myself.

"I'd better go," she says finally, as I knew she would. So I release her, and she gets up and pulls on her shirt and pants without looking at me. I blow out the candles.

She runs her fingers through her hair as I stand up. "Um," she says shyly. Her cheeks are pink. "Uh . . . thanks . . . for the beer."

"Glad I could be of service," I reply, grinning. I reach out to touch her arm, and I'm glad when she doesn't pull away. I wink. "Give Brian my message, 'kay?"

She laughs nervously, but at least she's laughing. I show her to the door and watch her walk slowly, dreamily, back to her own apartment. Smiling to myself, I nod and return to my wheel—but when I sit down, I realize that I've lost the urge to throw. Maybe because I've already created art today. I can feel my smile get bigger as I look down at my hands. Her scent, her feel, clings to them.

I wrestle the lump of clay off the wheel and return it to the cupboard, snagging another bottle from the fridge on my way back to the futon. Maybe I'll hunker down with the novel I'm reading—or maybe I'll pop in a movie. Hell, maybe I'll just surf the 'net for old reruns of SNL. The possibilities are endless—life is never boring.

It's late, of course, by the time I crawl into bed. As I tug the blankets up under my chin, Brian's distinctive low groan of pleasure trickles through the wall. I grin into the dark. Right on cue.

Only this time, I can hear Sarah talking to him. Her voice is too soft to make out the words, but . . . well, let's just say that her little moans start out three seconds apart as usual, but they sure don't stay that way for long. I think I even hear her say "fuck" once, which *really* makes me proud!

Sighing contentedly, I roll over onto my side and tuck my legs in close to my body. Mission accomplished. Tonight? I'm gonna sleep like a baby.

It Never Happened
Anne Bonney

I never touched her. I never wanted her. I never wrapped my legs around her hips and never, under any circumstances did I come twenty-three times in a single night.

If I say I'm a habitual liar, you won't know what to trust, will you? So, yeah, this is all a lie and you shouldn't believe a word of it.

It was a night that wasn't supposed to happen. Life threw one of those curves and there we were, unchaperoned, just me and her. She sat down on the daybed in her studio, where I was never supposed to end up alone with her.

There was a choice of seating for me: her desk chair or next to her on the bed. I thought about it for maybe thirty seconds. In those thirty seconds I relived every flirtatious conversation we'd had, every frank discussion about sex, the years we'd been sharing strengths and flaws, triumphs and hurts. Finally, I let myself feel again the furtive, stolen kisses that we'd agreed would never happen.

No kisses, we had promised. But we had kissed the last time we'd had a moment of privacy. Long, hot, panting, deep, aware kisses. Tingling, wet, pulse-pounding kisses. I thought I knew how to kiss, but she taught me all over again.

The kisses weren't supposed to happen, and neither was my choked confession that I'd fallen in love with her. She was tender with my heart. I hope I was with hers. It wasn't like either of us was going to do anything about our feelings, we agreed. Neither of us had room for this complication. We would kiss and go back to being friends.

We had kissed like lovers, at least it felt like that. Her hands, on my back, my hips, my shoulders, cupping my face, were sensuous and warm. She even knew, when I started to shudder in her arms, that we had to stop. She pushed me away, gently, and reminded me that even though we were doing things we never said we'd do, we weren't going to do *that*.

Lots of things weren't supposed to happen. A mutual friend wasn't supposed to die, and I wasn't supposed to be away from home for the funeral. Tomorrow I went back to my life. Tonight it seemed as if we'd fallen out of time.

Her desk chair or the bed?

On the unexpected flight across the country, I'd thought about the minor surgery gone awry that had claimed our friend, about plane crashes and errant buses, and accidents that ended lives early, accidents so commonplace they don't even make the news. I thought about being in love, about wanting someone and having to turn my back on it because of a single promise made before I'd even known her, or even dreamed of feeling as I did about her. I thought about her eyes and that when I was with her I felt like the woman I'd always wanted to be. I thought about our friend, who had been alive one moment, and gone the next. What kept circling through my brain was that if the plane I was on crashed I'd curse heaven that I'd wasted love.

I chose the bed.

We were both sad from the funeral, and I think—for like a half of a heartbeat—I intended just to hug her. Then I was kissing away the tears. We held each other. The kisses deepened.

Finally, I was able to say, "Life can end at any moment, and I don't want to die not having loved you, been with you. It would be a stupid waste."

We both had moral lines that loomed large, but she asked me if I was sure. Denial had us both in pain, and I couldn't stand to see her hurting. I wasn't supposed to ask her to love me. She wasn't supposed to let me into her bed.

"I'm sure. Yes, I'm sure."

I should have felt shy, but I didn't. We slipped out of our clothes and into a close, naked embrace that felt safe and real. She asked me again if I was sure.

"I'm sure. Yes, I'm sure."

My mind is filled with snapshots, images that never happened and couldn't happen again. Like the shivering awe on her face when her fingertips brushed my soaked labia for the first time.

I think she meant to tease me a little, but after years of unconscious and conscious foreplay, she didn't. Her sure fingers opened me. She slipped inside. We kissed and cried while she loved me, soft like that. My first climax was so quiet and quick that it surprised us both.

Her fingers began to play and, without words, I knew she was thinking of my many confessions about what made me crazy in bed. I felt like liquid fire inside, dripping heat around her fingers.

"Heaven above," she whispered, "you're so responsive."

A brush of a fingertip brought a deep shudder, and I stiffened into another climax, stronger this time, shivering a little cry out of me. The awe in her eyes gave way to a smile of delighted pleasure.

"You can do that again, can't you?" She licked my mouth as she twisted her fingers inside me.

My body said yes, I could do that again, and I did.

I was in love with her, and we might never have another night like this. I wasn't going to be less than I could be. For the rest of my life I would look back and treasure these memories. Treasure all the time I was ever given with her because we weren't supposed to have any.

Her deliberate, slow touches began to hasten. We panted against each other's mouths. At some point we were beyond what I would have called making love, and she was fucking me, fiercely and possessively, claiming my body for herself, for now. For these hours we were lovers, bound by passion and honesty.

I was more responsive, more passionate, more needy and more vocal than I had ever been in my life. She enjoyed me that way, adored the sounds I made, the way I came for her, and came for her, and couldn't stop.

She left the bed for a moment and returned with a bottle of lube in one hand.

I had no air to speak. No breath to even moan. I knew . . . I knew what that meant and my heart was pounding louder than the driving need I felt for her touch.

She carefully slicked the back of her hand, her palm, her fingers, then, with a look at me that seared my skin, she smeared her wrist and forearm.

She asked me if I was sure.

"I'm sure. Yes, I'm sure."

She straddled my leg and drew my hand down to grind herself on my fingertips and thigh. She was as soaked as I was and her moan matched mine as she moved away from my fingers and watched me as I rubbed her silk onto my nipples. Her slippery hand, cool from the lube, cupped my swollen lips. Two fingers, then four. I trusted her absolutely. I said so. Then I begged her to please, please take me.

The awe was back in her eyes as she pushed and I rose and with almost no pressure at all she was inside me, all the way.

Her gaze met mine and she exhaled with a groan as her hand curled and she made a fist. She pushed in gently, and rolled her hand from side to side, a sensation I'd never felt before.

I was moaning, it might have been her name, I'm not sure, but

I felt filled, not just my cunt but all of me, my heart, my mind, my soul. I was filled completely with her love and passion and this moment would never be lost.

She said, a rasp in her voice, "My wrist is inside you."

Believing and not believing at the same time, I reached down to feel her forearm. She was very deep in me, and I pulled her deeper. She groaned again and then it felt like she reached up, from inside me, to love my heart with her hand. Caressing and stroking, learning me as I bucked wildly on the bed, sobbing. She stayed with me, pleasuring me through one climax after another, and another and another.

She only stopped because I needed water and air. She soothed me, made me drink, held me, dried my tears.

Then she kissed me, pushed me back down on the bed and fucked me again. And again.

We slept, finally, woke, loved, dozed, woke again, held each other. With breathless whispers of desire and love, she touched me. And every time I came for her. I had given myself, for this wild, endless night, and there was nothing I didn't want her to have. What was the point of holding anything back?

When I tasted her, for the first time, I came again and laughed. Her puzzled look became a grin of pleasure when I told her, and then I went back to drinking all the excitement that my abandonment had wrought. Her hands touched my face while I licked and enjoyed her and when she asked me to go inside, I did. It felt as much my fingers fucking her cunt as it did her cunt fucking my fingers. Rich and easy, when she came I felt like a goddess. The gift of her love was a kind of treasure I'd not understood before.

I wished then, and I still wish now, that every woman could have that moment, when making another woman feel pure ecstasy is an all-consuming celebration of trust and love. I was born with all the pieces of me, from my G-spot to my brain, and I used them all that night, and experienced myself as a complete woman for the first time in my life.

None of it was supposed to happen, and I'm making it all up

anyway. The fine line between true and wish-it-were-true seems pointless when it comes to love. I wanted her to kiss me. I wanted her to love me. I was born to love and be loved by women, and celebrating it *is* supposed to happen. But whether I do it for real, or in my head, or on this page is my secret and maybe your fantasy.

The truth among the lies, however, is that if I'd chosen the desk chair, then this story would have not been worth reading.

The Voyeur
Therese Szymanski

It's always seemed to me that the attraction for "True Story" anthologies lies in the voyeuristic appeal of such . . .

The night was quiet around me as I crept up to the glass door, carefully inching forward so as to not be seen or heard by those within. They had again left the drapes open just enough for me to peer through. The darkness of the night gave me all the further cover I required.

Keri and Alicia were again in the basement, Keri bringing the clean laundry out from the utility room to fold it on the couch, a scene I had watched many times before. Alicia stood up as if to help her, which she sometimes did, but instead this time she wrapped her arms around the curvy brunette from behind, gently kissing her neck until she started to squirm under the attention.

Keri has long, curly brown hair, a slender, yet well-curved body, and full breasts. Alicia is slightly taller, with short, thick, blonde hair, broad shoulders, and a grin that could brighten the country under a total eclipse. Even from this distance I could see the mischievous twinkle in her eye.

Slowly Alicia began pulling Keri's nightshirt up and over her head. Keri resisted at first, but ended up dropping the laundry on the floor when Alicia persisted. When Keri reached for a blanket from the couch to cover her nakedness, Alicia let her do it. But then she pulled Keri into her arms, running her hands over Keri's pale rear end, caressing it lightly. As Alicia caressed Keri, she also slowly coerced the blanket off of her body, unveiling her to the chilly night air.

Woodhouse, their tiger-striped cat, wound around their ankles, slipping between them to rub against both of them at the same time. Meanwhile, Taylor, a gray-and-white tabby who was still almost a kitten, climbed through the soft, warm laundry on the floor, burying herself in it.

Alicia fondled Keri's breasts, cupping them in her hands while she kissed Keri. She then roughly squeezed Keri's nipples, causing Keri to shiver in delight. Alicia pressed and squeezed the hardened buds, slowly bringing her mouth down to take one into her mouth while her other hand continued to pinch the other nipple. Keri began to slowly writhe under her lover's touch, wrapping her arms around Alicia to steady herself.

I chanced a closer look, carefully inching up even closer to the door, wanting to see them better, know them better. I practically had my nose pressed up against the glass.

Alicia backed Keri up through the laundry, sending Taylor running, so the couch pressed against the backs of her knees and caused her to fall back into its welcoming softness. Alicia lay on top of Keri, pressing into her and molding their bodies together. Keri arched up into her lover, urging her onward by opening her legs up and wrapping them around Alicia's waist.

I could see the warm, soft expanse of her skin, and I could

almost feel the passion between them as they melded into one on the couch with their kitties around them—Taylor lay along the back of the couch, and Woodhouse curled at their feet.

Alicia inched her way down Keri's body, spreading open her legs to look down at her lover's body in all its revealed splendor. She knelt between those very long legs and reached down, between them.

Keri enjoyed it. She was in heat and wanted it bad. She wanted to feel Alicia inside of her; it was obvious with each of her movements. She urged Alicia on, raising her pelvis so Alicia could touch, caress and taste her.

Alicia leaned down, wanting to taste with her mouth and tongue what her fingers had just felt.

I knew that Alicia would continue this for a while before she would put her fingers inside of Keri. She enjoyed teasing the woman and making her squirm and ask for it before she would give her the fulfillment she wanted so badly.

If you watch people long enough you learn a lot about them.

What I knew most of all was that I wanted to be a part of all they had.

The next night Keri pulled into her assigned parking spot and laid her head down on the steering wheel. She was exhausted. It had been one fiendishly long day at work and she was just glad to be home. She smiled briefly: She couldn't wait to be in Alicia's ever-loving arms. She grabbed her purse and got out of the car, hitting the alarm as she walked away . . .

And then she felt it—someone watching her. She glanced about nervously in the dimming twilight, but didn't see anything out of the ordinary.

It had been a long day; she must be imagining things. No one would blame her for being a bit on edge, perhaps even a bit paranoid, after a day like today—a day when everything about her job was being questioned. She strode boldly forward, her purse swinging against her leg, with her keys jangling in her hand.

A bush off to her side moved as if someone was jostling it, and Keri jumped toward it.

"There you are!" Mrs. Padgett called, rushing toward her as fast as she could with her walker. "Have you noticed anything strange lately?"

"Well, uh," Keri said, glancing toward the bush that had now stopped moving, "now that you mention it, I've felt . . ."

"Yes dear?"

"I've felt as if someone's been watching me lately."

Mrs. Padgett smirked. "Now you're just making fun of an old lady," she scoffed. "You know perfectly well what I'm talking about; the raccoons have not been coming to get the little treats we put out for them. The Chinese take-out you put out for them Saturday has been there ever since, and now it's Tuesday!"

"I . . . I hadn't noticed."

"I know I put out their very favorite last night—tuna noodle casserole—and they haven't touched a bite of it!"

Keri glanced nervously about, not quite sure if she could still feel the eyes on her. The one thing she was sure about was that the shrubbery was no longer making any strange movements.

"They've studied how much cyanide *we* can have in *our* water, but what about the poor little raccoons? How much can they take? Or do you suppose they did it on purpose? Planning on killing off all the dear little animals?"

Keri knew that once the old woman got on a roll—especially about any sort of a conspiracy theory—there was simply no stopping her. "Um, Mrs. Padgett, I hate to leave you like this, but I simply must go shampoo the goldfish and vacuum the cats," she said, pulling herself away from the now bright-eyed and bristling woman and rushing toward the door.

"You vacuum your cats?" Mrs. Padgett yelled after her. "Is that effective against fleas?"

♥

Keri closed and locked the door firmly behind herself before calling out, "Honey, I'm home!"

"Hey baby," Alicia said, walking over from the kitchen and wrapping her arms around her. "Tough day at work?" she asked, leaving Keri to pull off her shoes and drop her purse while she returned to making dinner.

"The worst. And then I get home and Mrs. Padgett launched herself at me—coming up with some sort of a conspiracy theory about—you're never gonna believe this one . . ."

"What is it this time? Aliens, Elvis, the President or . . . ?"

"Raccoons."

"What?"

"Raccoons. She's convinced someone's done something about them. Done something to get rid of them." Keri walked into the kitchen and wrapped her arms around her lover. "What's cooking? It smells good."

"Veggie tacos," Alicia replied, stirring the mixture in the saucepan just a bit more before shutting off the gas and going to the counter. "And now they're done."

Keri walked out the back door onto the balcony, looking around briefly.

"Hon? Didn't you hear me? Dinner's ready."

Keri studied the woods behind their balcony, looking for anything out of the ordinary. "Did you say something?"

"Yes, dear, I did. Dinner's ready," Alicia said, joining Keri, who was still scanning the woods. "Are you looking for the 'coons?"

"No, I'm . . ." Keri shook her head. "Never mind. Let's eat."

"Keri, I'm serious. What is it?" Alicia stopped Keri by grabbing her arms.

"It's silly. I'm just overworked, underpaid and stressed out." Alicia stared at her. "Seriously."

"What is it?"

"I've felt kinda like someone's been watching me, us, lately. I got out of my car tonight and thought I felt it again. And then I saw some bushes move, or at least thought I did."

"Was there anything there?"

"I don't know—Mrs. Padgett came up and then it was gone. Or it was never there to begin with."

Alicia stood looking at her for a moment, her hands not releasing Keri's forearms.

"What is it babe?"

Alicia turned from her, to look out over the woods herself. "I've felt the same thing. Like last night, when we were downstairs . . . doing you know what . . . I could've sworn someone was watching us."

"Why didn't you say anything?"

"We were kinda busy at the time, and we had the curtains closed."

"No, they weren't quite closed. I wanted to close them, but thought you'd think I was a freak for it."

I had almost been caught. I couldn't let that happen again. I mean, it was just luck that Mrs. Padgett distracted Keri while I made my way stealthily through the bushes and escaped around their neighbor's neat little townhouse.

But still I was drawn back to their place. It was just that I had been so bold as to try to watch during the daylight, but now I had the cover of night to conceal me.

I went down to the patio, hoping for a repeat of last night's events. Alas, it was not to be: The basement was dark. I glanced up through the deck and didn't see any light emanating from the cheerful kitchen, which was almost a lucky thing because that was one of the areas of the house I didn't have access to.

I went into the backyard and looked up at the back of the house. The lights in the upper rooms on that side were also dark, which was another lucky thing—so Alicia and Keri were either in the bedroom or the living room. I went to the front of the house and peered into the darkened living room.

They had gone to bed for the night. I looked at the large tree in the front of the house with its wonderfully long and strong branches.

I couldn't lose them for the night, not yet. Just one more glimpse was all I needed.

I climbed the tree and carefully inched my way out on the limb as far as I dared. I didn't need to worry them anymore, but I had to see them.

Keri was sitting in bed reading with her glasses on. Alicia was sitting more upright, writing in a book. Woodhouse was on Keri's pillow, nestled against her head. Taylor came into sight, jumping onto the bed. Keri began absentmindedly stroking her while she wound between the two women, enjoying the attention she was getting from both.

Alicia leaned over the kitty and kissed Keri before rolling back onto her side of the bed and turning out the light. Keri took off her glasses and turned off her light as well.

My last vision was of Keri lifting the covers and letting Taylor curl down under them at her feet.

I wanted it all.

"Oh, go home," Keri said to the little orange tabby circling her ankles as she walked from her car on her way home from work. "You're not Sydney, baby." She was still missing Sydney, the cat who had taken off a few weeks ago, abandoning Keri and Alicia to a life with just two kitties.

Seeing the kitty, whom Keri had seen previously, actually on and off for several months, reminded her of her own lost one, of dear sweet Sydney. She wanted to pull the little baby into her arms, keep her warm and tight against her bosom.

Was this an omen? Woodhouse and Taylor were still there,

trying desperately to fill the teeny footprints and loud jumps of Sydney, trying to fill two hearts with enough kitty love to make up for three kitties. But they, too, were lonely, and Keri didn't want them to become accustomed to being by themselves. They needed a third, someone to intervene in their arguments, someone to play with, someone to help keep them happy.

The next night on her way home from work, Keri again saw the little kitty, who was begging for attention. She was obviously not a feral kitty. She once had a home, but now had none. Or else her people didn't take adequate care of her. Everyone knew kitties couldn't be allowed out so much or else they'd become Killer Kitties, ones that killed and could never be really happy inside all the time.

But Keri wanted her Sydney back. She was still hoping her little baby would show up. Besides, this kitty, although a bit dirty and lean, looked well-taken care of enough that she couldn't be a total stray. "Go on home, baby," Keri told the little tabby. "Go on, shoo."

The kitty looked up at her expectantly, pausing just a moment before trotting purposefully away.

"Probably just looking for a handout," Keri said to herself as she propped open her front door so she could carry in the groceries. "She'll just go home and eat there."

Later that night after dinner, Keri and Alicia were in the basement watching "Never Been Kissed."

"Would you like a massage, baby?" Alicia asked.

"You know I never turn down a massage."

Alicia pulled out the bottle of oil, and while Keri lay on the couch, underneath a light blanket, Alicia began rubbing first one foot, caressing it gently, then kneading her heel, arch and the base of her toes. She ran her hands over it, rubbing just hard enough to not tickle, but lightly enough to relax it. Then she continued the process on the other foot.

Her loving hands continued on up Keri's body, lovingly massaging first one calf, then the other; then moving up to work on one thigh, then the other, slowly pushing higher and higher the blanket that hid her lover's body from her gaze, thus revealing more and more of its lusciousness.

But before she became too tempted to go for the apex, to reach for it all, she poured more massage oil into her hand and took one of Keri's delightfully long-fingered hands in her own, intertwining their fingers and gently pulling through Keri's, relaxing every bit of her digits. She then began rubbing the oil into the rest of the beautifully crafted hand.

She continued her attentions, finishing the one hand and moving to the other; then she proceeded to Keri's incredible arms.

"Roll over," she whispered through the darkness to Keri. Keri rolled onto her stomach, and Alicia pulled the blanket slowly down so that it now only covered Keri's gorgeous ass. But, she thought, patience is a virtue, and so continued her leisurely pace to work first on Keri's back, then her nicely rounded butt.

She finished by giving her long strokes across her entire body.

"Roll over, baby," she again instructed.

Keri shyly obeyed, pulling the blanket back up to cover herself.

"Oh, now baby, why do you want to do that?" Alicia asked, urging the blanket lower so she could kiss Keri's neck and collarbone while her hands went further up Keri's incredibly long legs. Everything about Keri was long and elegant.

Her fingers brushed the triangle of hair nestled between Keri's thighs, and she gently nibbled at the soft skin of Keri's neck. She cupped the nest of hair, slowly working her fingers between the swollen lips, and dipping into the dampness within.

"Oh God," Keri said, opening her legs further and arching up toward Alicia's talented fingers, urging her inside.

Alicia pulled the blanket off, and worked her way down Keri's body with her lips and teeth, nibbling and biting her skin, pulling a hardened nipple into her mouth and running her tongue over it. She ran her fingers up and down Keri's slickness, teasing and toying with her before entering her and giving her what she wanted.

"Please, Al, don't tease me!"

Alicia slowly dipped her fingers inside her lover, causing her to arch and buck further. Then she went down to taste the woman as well, running her tongue where her fingers had just been, lapping up the sweet juices while her fingers plunged into and out of her.

They were lying together, cuddling and finishing watching the movie, which they had rewound so they could see the parts they missed.

Taylor and Woodhouse, seeing that things had calmed down, came over and joined them on the couch, where they curled up on each of the arms.

Suddenly, another kitty, the orange one Keri had seen earlier, timidly came over to the couch, looking for its own spot with a questioning, "Meow?"

"Hello? Who are you?" Alicia asked, sitting up slightly, so the blanket fell forward onto Keri. Her hand continued to rest on Keri's hip.

"Oh, that's the kitty that came up to me when I got home from work."

"Isn't she the one the Johnsons had?"

"Mrowr?" the kitty asked again. It finally seemed to decide to take matters into its own paws as it jumped up onto the couch to curl up with Keri and Alicia.

"They moved a month ago!" Keri said.

"I've tried to catch her, but she always ran away when I got near," Alicia said, stroking the kitty, who purred like a motor car.

"Poor dear, she must've gotten in when I had the door open to bring in the groceries."

Alicia rolled onto her back and held the kitty up in the air above her. It purred and butted heads with Keri, who was sitting up now.

"What a little lover, I think she'll be Valmont!"

❤

Keri climbed into bed, and Woodhouse nestled against her head on Keri's pillow. Taylor was curled down under the blanket at their feet at the foot of the bed.

I cuddled on the pillow with Woodhouse, who moved slightly to share her pillow with me.

"Aren't they cute?" Alicia said, kissing Keri goodnight and turning off the light.

It's nice to get just what you want.

About the Authors

Marie Alexander: I live in northern New Jersey (think black bears, not toxic waste) with Toni, who has been my beloved partner for five years, and our son. My life is brimming with soccer games and laundry, and we are proud to fight for equality by demonstrating every day that lesbian families can be as boring and dysfunctional as everyone else. My professional career in retail not only funds my suburban existence, but also provides an exquisite source of characters and storylines for my writing. This is my first published work, and I am currently finishing the last chapter of my first novel.

Lynn Ames is the best-selling author of *The Price of Fame* (which was short-listed for the first annual Golden Crown Literary Society award in the category of lesbian romance), *The Cost of Commitment*, *The Value of Valor* and *The Flip Side of Desire*. She is also a contributing author to *Infinite Pleasures: An Anthology of Lesbian Erotica*, *Telltale Kisses, Stolen Moments: Erotic Interludes 2, Romance for Life*, and *Call of the Dark: Erotic Lesbian Tales of the Supernatural*.

Ms. Ames is a former press secretary to the New York state Senate Minority Leader. For more than half a decade, she was also an award-winning broadcast journalist. These days she is a nationally recognized speaker and public relations professional with a particular expertise in image, crisis communications planning and crisis management.

Ms. Ames resides in the southwestern U.S. with her favorite guys (relax, they're dogs): a golden retriever named Alex, who bears a remarkable resemblance to a character in her books, and Parker, another golden and the newest addition to the family.

For additional information, short stories, etc., please visit her Web site at www.lynnames.com, or e-mail her at authorlynnames@cox.net.

Becky Arbogast was born and raised just south of the Mason-Dixon Line. When she was thirty years old, she wandered to Florida and found her true calling when she went to work for Naiad Press. Becky spends much of her time working and reading . . . and any spare moments are spent with her three dogs. Becky credits any praise she receives for her writing to the special authors she is lucky enough to be surrounded by.

Aunt Fanny has published stories in Bold Strokes Books' Lammy winner *Stolen Moments*, and their upcoming *Extreme Passions*. Her stories also appear in *Ultimate Lesbian Erotica 2006* by Alyson Books, Cleis Press' *Best Lesbian Romance 2007* and Bella Books' *Wild Nights: True Lesbian Sex Stories*. Aunt Fanny claims she was born during a flying carpet ride, a bumpy start at best. She currently lives quite happily in America's Heartland with her rainbow family and friends, fighting the good fight against discrimination. Professional inquiries for Aunt Fanny can be addressed to: auntfannystories@yahoo.com.

Born in Hawaii, *Bliss* was raised on the eastern seaboard and now hangs her hat in the mountains east of Albuquerque, New Mexico. She enjoys any outdoor activity, reading, renovating her house and of course, writing. An animal lover, she currently shares her home with three FeLions.

Anne Bonney has never published anything before and may be too shy to ever publish anything again.

Victoria A. Brownworth is a syndicated columnist and author and editor of more than twenty books including the award-winning *Too Queer: Essays from a Radical Life* and *Coming Out of Cancer: Writings from the Lesbian Cancer Epidemic*. Her fiction has appeared in numerous anthologies as well as her own collections, including the award-winning *Night Bites*. Her lesbian erotica has appeared in magazines, online and in anthologies. Her most recent collection, *Bed: New Lesbian Erotica*, was published by Haworth Press, Alice Street Editions. She teaches writing and film at the University of the Arts in Philadelphia where she lives with her many cats and shares her life with the painter, Maddy Gold.

Rachel Kramer Bussel (www.rachelkramerbussel.com) is Senior Editor at Penthouse Variations and writes the Lusty Lady column for The Village Voice. Her books include the Lambda Literary Award finalist *Up All Night: Adventures in Lesbian Sex, First-Timers: True Stories of Lesbian Awakening, Glamour Girls: Femme/Femme Erotica, Ultimate Undies, Sexiest Soles, Secret Slaves, Caught Looking: Erotic Tales of Voyeurs and Exhibitionists* and *Naughty Spanking Stories from A to Z 1 and 2*. Her erotica has been published in more than 60 anthologies, including *Best American Erotica 2004 and 2006*, and *Best Lesbian Erotica 2001, 2004, and 2005*. She has written for AVN, BUST, Cleansheets.com, Curve, Diva, Girlfriends, Rockrgrl, The San Francisco Chronicle, Velvetpark, and Zink, and posed nude for On Our Backs. She blogs incessantly at lustylady.blogspot.com and cupcakestakethecake.blogspot.com.

Jean Byrnell: I did go to theater school in New York and I worked in the theater before I married and had four children. Eighteen years ago I met my beautiful partner and knew I needed to spend the rest of my life with her. We now have six grown children between us. We live in a small B.C. town where I write and raise Australian Labradoodles while my partner takes care of everything that breaks.

Heidi Edwards is a freelance writer from Virginia Beach who has just finished her first erotic romance novel, *Firefly*. She gave up snowboarding for a living in Colorado to become a Disease Intervention Specialist by day and an erotica writer by night.

Amie M. Evans is a widely published creative nonfiction and literary erotica writer, experienced workshop provider and a retired burlesque and high-femme drag performer. Her short stories and essays have appeared most recently in the *Ultimate Lesbian Erotica 2006* (Alyson) and *Show and Tell* (Alyson), *Call of the Dark* (Bella 2005); 2006 Lambda Literary Award nominated *Rode Hard and Put Away Wet* (Suspect Thoughts Press 2005); *Best of The Best of Lesbian Erotica* (Cleis Press); and *Ultimate Lesbian Erotica 2005* (Alyson Publications). She also writes gay male erotica under a pen name. Evans is on the board of directors for the Saints and Sinners GLBT literary festival. She graduated magna cum laude from the University of Pittsburgh with a BA in Literature and is currently working on her MLA at Harvard. She is currently co-editing an anthology on Drag Kings for Suspect Thoughts Press with Rakelle Valencia and co-editing an anthology with Trebor Healey for Haworth Press on Being Queer and Catholic. Evans is the author of Two Girls Kissing, a column on writing lesbian erotica which can be found at www.erotic-readers.com and co-author of a writing tips column, unsolicited advice, with Toni Amato which can be found on www.sasfest.org. She can be reached at pussywhipped-productions@hotmail.com.

Brigit Futrelle was named for the Celtic deity Brigid, the goddess of fire and the patroness of poets. Speaking of poets, her favorite is Dylan Thomas. Her favorite knight of the Round Table is Lancelot du Lac. Her favorite food is mashed potatoes (molded into a volcano, filled with a pool of butter, and salted and peppered). If you'd like to ask Brigit about some of her other favorite things, she can be contacted at brigit.futrelle@gmail.com.

Saundra W. Haggerty has wandered around the world trying to find her true calling. Many have stated that she is like the wind . . . you never know what direction she's coming from or where she is going, but you always know that she has been there. Saundra began writing at an early age, and published several articles, poems and short stories in college. Her passion is poetry, but the idea of writing about sex has always interested her because she believes good writing comes from passion and good sex is all about passion. A native of San Francisco, she currently lives in Victoria, Texas. You can visit her Web site at www.myspace.com/G5361.

Karin Kallmaker is best known for more than a dozen lesbian romance novels, from *In Every Port* to *All the Wrong Places*. In addition, she has a half-dozen science fiction, fantasy and supernatural lesbian novels under the pen name Laura Adams. Karin and her partner will celebrate their twenty-ninth anniversary in 2006, and are Mom and Moogie to two children.

Rae Kimball is a big nerd who enjoys reading, good movies and long, thoughtful pauses. When she is not writing dirty stories for her own amusement she can usually be found taking a nap on the nearest available couch or advising college students at the prestigious southern university where she is employed. This is her FIRST published work.

Joy Parks doesn't change her clothes in subway bathrooms anymore, but she still feels oddly dressed at most lesbian functions. She's traded in her Revlon Wine with Everything for Aveda's

Color Concentrate in Cerise—far less chemical, far more kissable! But she still likes women in desert boots, still refuses to submit to the will of the group, and still loves women with the courage to be exactly who—and how—they want to be.

Radclyffe is the author of over twenty lesbian romances including the 2005 Lambda Literary Award winners *Erotic Interludes 2: Stolen Moments* edited with Stacia Seaman and the romance, *Distant Shores, Silent Thunder*. She has selections in multiple anthologies including *Call of the Dark* and *The Perfect Valentine* (Bella Books), *Best Lesbian Erotica 2006* and *After Midnight* (Cleis), *First-Timers* and *Ultimate Undies: Erotic Stories About Lingerie and Underwear* (Alyson) and *Naughty Spanking Stories 2* (Pretty Things Press). She is the recipient of the 2003 and 2004 Alice B. Readers' award, a 2005 Golden Crown Literary Society Award winner in both the romance category (*Fated Love*) and the mystery/intrigue/action category (*Justice in the Shadows*) and a 2006 GCLS finalist in the romance and mystery categories. She is also the president of Bold Strokes Books, a lesbian publishing company.

Nell Stark lives in Madison, WI with her partner and two cats. Her first novel, *Running With the Wind*, will be published by Bold Strokes Books in the spring of 2007. When not writing or working as a graduate student of medieval English literature, she enjoys reading, sailing, soccer, cooking and Dance Dance Revolution. She would like to thank her partner, Lisa, for her continued love, support, and superb editing skills, and her beta-readers JD and Ruta for their essential feedback and encouragement. Nell can be reached at nell.stark@gmail.com, or feel free to visit her Web site: www.nellstark.com.

Born in Chicago, *Kate Sweeney* is the author of the Kate Ryan Mysteries. The first in the series, *She Waits*, was released through Intaglio Publications in May of 2006. Kate also has a collection of short stories, other novels and novellas. Her sense of humor is evident throughout her writing, which runs the gamut from funny to sad, erotic to romantic, and everything else in between. Please visit her website www.katesweeneyonline.com and drop a line at mks@kateryanmysteries.com. Kate currently resides in Villa Park, Illinois.

Therese Szymanski is an award-winning playwright. She's also been short-listed for a couple of Lammys (mystery and erotica), a Goldie and a Spectrum, as well as having made the Publishing Triangle's list of Notable Lesbian Books with her first anthology.

Wild Nights is the fourth anthology she's edited for Bella Books (*Back to Basics: A Butch/Femme Anthology*, *Call of the Dark: Erotic Lesbian Tales of the Supernatural* and *The Perfect Valentine* (with Barbara Johnson) are the others).

She's written seven books in the Lammy-finalist Brett Higgins Motor City Thrillers series (in order: *When the Dancing Stops*, *When the Dead Speak*, *When Some Body Disappears*, *When Evil Changes Face*, *When Good Girls Go Bad*, *When the Corpse Lies* and *When First We Practice* (*When It's All Relative* is due out in 2007)).

She's part of the foursome—with Karin Kallmaker, Julia Watts and Barbara Johnson—who created (and write) the bestselling/Lammy-finalist Bella After Dark (BAD) *New Exploits* series, which include *Once Upon a Dyke: New Exploits of Fairy Tale Lesbians*, *Bell, Book and Dyke: New Exploits of Magical Lesbians* and *Stake Through the Heart: New Exploits of Twilight Lesbians*.

She also has a few dozen short works published in a wide variety of books, including one short story about, well, her shorts.

Oh, and yes, she really did wear her brother's uniform to security guard a bachelor party once, but, for the record, she's never been a cat, nor owned one.

You can e-mail Reese at tsszymanski@worldnet.att.net.

Tanya Turner often finds herself getting into trouble unexpectedly. She frequently writes about her exploits, but changes names to protect the innocent. She can often be found playing pinball or video games at her local dive bar. Her erotica has been published in *Ultimate Undies*, *Secret Slaves* and *Ultimate Lesbian Erotica 2005*, among other anthologies.

Kristina Wright is a full-time writer and part-time graduate student working toward an M.A. in Humanities. Her short fiction has been published in over thirty anthologies, including *Best Women's Erotica 2000*; four editions of the Lambda-award winning series *Best Lesbian Erotica; The Perfect Valentine; Call of the Dark: Erotic Lesbian Tales of the Supernatural; Amazons: Sexy Tales of Strong Women; the Mammoth Book of Best New Erotica, Volume 5*; and *Ultimate Undies: Erotic Stories About Lingerie and Underwear.* Her writing has also been featured in the nonfiction guide *The Many Joys of Sex Toys* and in e-zines such as Clean Sheets, Scarlet Letters and Good Vibes Magazine. For more information about Kristina's life, writing and academic pursuits, visit her Web site www.kristinawright.com.

Teresa Wymore: After graduating summa cum laude from the University of South Florida, Teresa lapsed into chronic unemployment, so she mooched free drinks at a local tavern and joined in barroom debates. When these raucous discussions turned revolutionary, she was placed on a national "persons of interest" list, although her name was removed when it was discovered that she was not interesting at all. One day, having finally achieved the status of an economic unit, she moved to the Midwest, where she now cohabitates with various significant others and writes erotic fiction. You can find out more at her Web site: www.teresawymore.com.